KT-501-295

Praise for

A Mother's War

'Mollie Walton captures your attention from
the very first page, and doesn't let go, even on the last
– leaving you longing to know what happens next!'
Diney Costeloe

'Immersive and atmospheric . . . pulls you right into
the story. I can't wait for the next instalment.'
Judy Summers

'A tender tale of love and strength in the midst of war.'
Val Wood

'All the characters are finely drawn, engage your affection
and stay with you long after you have finished reading.'
Margaret Dickinson

'Mollie Walton is such a skilled and natural storyteller.
A Mother's War really zings with the warmth of her
characters and the vividness of the period.'
Sarah Sykes

'Vivid, compulsive, and heart-rending.
Had me hooked from page one.'
Louisa Treger

C334788065

ALSO BY MOLLIE WALTON

The Ironbridge Saga

The Daughters of Ironbridge
The Secrets of Ironbridge
The Orphan of Ironbridge

Mollie Walton

A Mother's War

Book One of the Raven Hall Saga

WELBECK

First published in 2022 by Welbeck Fiction Limited,
part of Welbeck Publishing Group
based in London and Sydney
This paperback edition first published in 2022 by
Welbeck Publishing Group based in London and Sydney
www.welbeckpublishing.com

Copyright © Mollie Walton, 2022

The moral right of Mollie Walton to be identified as the author of this Work has been
asserted by her in accordance with the Copyright, Designs & Patents Act 1988

The newspaper extract on page 189 is taken from *The Courier,*
31ˢᵗ May 1940

All characters and events in this publication, other than those clearly in the
public domain, are fictitious and any resemblance to real persons,
living or dead, is purely coincidental.

All rights reserved. No part of this publication may be reproduced, stored
in a retrieval system, or transmitted in any form or by any means,
electronically, mechanical, photocopying, recording or otherwise, without
the prior permission of the copyright owners and the publishers.

A CIP catalogue record for this book is available from the British Library

Paperback ISBN: 978-1-78739-941-9
E-book ISBN: 978-1-78739-939-6

Printed and bound by CPI Group (UK) Ltd., Croydon, CR0 4YY

10 9 8 7 6 5 4 3 2 1

This story is dedicated to Patricia Owtram, whose work as a wireless telegraphist Wren in World War Two played a crucial role in saving lives and protecting our country. To Pat and all the secret listeners like her, my eternal respect and gratitude.

Prologue

September 1939

The house stood at the edge of nowhere. It was perched on the cliff above the endless sea, surrounded by grounds peppered with hiding places. When the fog rolled in, it became a seat in the kingdom of the clouds. When the sun was out, it was a throne to the best view in the world: the sweep of the bay, bordered by cultivated fields and wild moorland tumbling steeply down to the beaches. Beyond it stood Robin Hood's Bay; from here one could spy just a hint of its intricate network of alleys and lanes crowded with fisherman's cottages. To the north lay Whitby, to the south, Scarborough. And here, above the village of Ravenscar, the gulls chattered and swooped beyond the walls of the grounds of Raven Hall, mocking the generations that had made their home there, hemmed in by walls, feeling safe against encroaching nature: the bracken and nettles bristling against the stone, the sea below crashing against the rocks ceaselessly, the salty wind assaulting the planted trees by the border walls causing them to bend over like women picking strawberries, the lowering sky frowning down upon the house and its ordered grounds. The battlements that were built upon the walls acted as though the house imagined itself a fortress against nature, but everywhere nature encroached, the rock walls mottled with lichen and creeping ivy. The gardens of Raven Hall were tamed and orderly: box hedges, fuchsias and roses. Domesticated, yet surrounded by wildness, the sound of the constant, distant roar of the sea below a reminder of the abandon beyond these safe walls. The undercliff below the house was replete with thick foliage, sweeping down to the rocks below. The lush plants looked soft, as if they'd cushion a fall, but of course the ravine was steep, jagged and deadly.

Rosina stood on the path, inhaling the sharp smoke of her cigarette, gazing out towards the bay, watching the tiny waves break harmlessly on the shingle below. The sea fret was patchy that day, rolling in like playful clouds, revealing a perfect patch of blue sky or a swathe of many-hued green fields, replaced by white fog in an instant. She could hear the sheep bleating in the fields that surrounded her home, the gulls calling and the little brown birds twittering in the trees and she watched the swifts dip down for insects on the wing. The sky was vast, the sea looked endless, a glimpse of the horizon revealing it misty and mysterious. The fog rolled in, silent and stealthy. Rosina shuddered, slightly from the chill held in the mist, yet partly too from the feeling that unseen forces were moving over the sea towards her home, just as the fret trespassed on her land beyond her control. She glanced back at the house and exhaled a puff of smoke that obscured the view as one of her daughters appeared at a window then disappeared again. All five of them were home for the announcement. All of the servants were assembling in the servants' hall too. Rosina needed to get back inside soon. But she wanted these last few moments of peace to herself. Peace from the busy household and all its demands, but peace too from the historic moment that was about to be played out on the wireless. For the family and servants were all gathered for one reason only: to hear the Prime Minister announce what they had all feared for months.

Rosina finished her cigarette and stubbed it out on the stone wall. She didn't wish to litter the rose bed so took it in with her and dropped it in the ashtray on the hall table that was emptied periodically. She could hear the girls inhabit the house. They weren't making much noise yet their presence was as obvious as sound to their mother. For mothers are always on duty when their children are around, even if they're not doing much, even if they're asleep, even if they're grown up. Rosina was happy to have her brood all back under one roof. It didn't happen much these days, what with Grace down at Oxford and Evelyn over in France until recently, whilst Constance and the twins Daisy and Dora were mostly away at school. She'd need to walk the house over to summon all five of them, or send one or two to find the others. She found Grace at the writing desk in the window of the study. A quick look over her shoulder confirmed that her eldest daughter was working on her modern rewrite of the Greek myths. She'd just finished her degree in Classics and her head was still buried in that ancient world.

'It's nearly time, darling,' Rosina said.

Grace looked up, her grey-blue eyes concerned, her long, straight russet-brown hair draped in a curtain across her back. 'All right, Mummy,' she said and nodded, placing the lid carefully on her ink pen. She looked younger than her twenty-one years and seemed younger too, Rosina thought. Three years at Oxford had seemed to have had little impact on her experience of life. She was still the reserved, modest girl she'd been when she'd left school.

Rosina walked back out into the hallway and along the corridor to the stairs, past the lounge through whose windows the sun now streamed in defiance of the sea fret. She took the steps up to the small landing, standing beneath the stained-glass window there, the coat of arms of her family name Lazenby emblazoned in rich coloured panes.

'Evvy?' she called

'All right, Mummy,' came her second daughter's strident voice from the room on the first floor that had once been the playroom and had now become the art studio when Evelyn was at home.

'Is Connie with you?' Rosina called.

'Yes, driving me mad with her incessant ball throwing against this wall.'

'I am not driving you mad!' Rosina heard Constance's throaty voice exclaim. 'You said the rhythm helps you concentrate, you big, fat liar!'

'Oh, do shut up, Connie!' snapped Evelyn.

Always at each other's throats, those two, yet when it came to boys, they were thick as thieves and knew all of each other's secrets. Rosina walked upstairs and stood in the doorway, noting the floor strewn with paint tubes, brushes, canvas and paper.

Evelyn looked up at her mother and said, 'We're coming! Don't fuss!'

She was a messy genius, that one. Nineteen going on twenty-nine, with strawberry-blonde hair and a freckled, peachy complexion, a lipstick-wearing, cigarette-smoking, adventure-seeking beauty. Rosina smiled and shook her head, glad in a way that Evelyn had been in France for a year, beyond her mother's reach, where she had little knowledge of what scrapes her daughter had got herself into and thus could only worry vaguely from a distance.

Constance started up her ball throwing again and the ball hit the wall hard, straight and true. The girl had an excellent aim. At sixteen, she was captain of the lacrosse and hockey teams, as well as a keen shot-putter. Stocky and strong, she had none of Grace's tall gangly frame or Evelyn's curves. Her straw-coloured hair in a perpetual bob since she was eight, she despised preening or make-up of any kind. Still striking in her way, her skin creamy-pale and freckled, she would be the perfect model for a government poster about rude health. Rosina chuckled at the thought.

'Come on then, you two. And clear up that mess on the floor later, Evvy. The last thing we need is paint stains on the carpet.'

She went back down the stairs and turned right to walk along the passageway to the games room. There she found her twins, Daisy and Dora, identical in appearance with their mid-blue eyes and long, wavy fair hair, yet alike as two snowflakes in character: same design, different details. Now fifteen years old, they had come as a surprise so soon after Constance. This meant that the three of them grew up inseparable, especially Connie and Dora. Daisy was the odd one out of the whole family in some ways, more similar to her eldest sister Grace than anyone, both pianists, both a little awkward in company. Daisy was playing at the upright piano, a little piece by Bach that had her fingers in a twist. She kept on at the same phrase, over and over, forcing her muscle memory to learn it. Rosina smiled at how much better a pianist her daughter was than she herself. *That should be the way of things, that your children outshine you*, she thought. She glanced over at Dora, who was making notes on her latest natural experiment: this time, an ant farm in a glass case. Dora loved living, breathing things and studied them, sometimes killing them to study them further. A scientist's cold eye had that one and an analytical brain, yet when it came to matters of the heart, she was as hopelessly romantic as Connie. How different all her girls were and yet how much they overlapped and echoed each other, as well as having aspects of herself and, of course, their father, dead three years now.

The thought of George Calvert made Rosina shudder. Though she missed virtually nothing about him, his death being a blessed release from an ill-conceived and poorly executed marriage, she realised that his absence now gave her a slight feeling of panic as she felt more alone than ever. Usually, this sustained her because she valued her independence above everything, but now that history was moving its shadowy purpose towards her own door, as it was to every house in Britain that morning, she suddenly felt wholly alone – the matriarch, in charge of these five girls, this vast house and grounds and all the servants and farmers and tenants who made it work. After three years of widowhood and years before that of orphanhood, Rosina thought she'd be used to this by now. And so she was, in peacetime. But change was coming and fear gripped her. She swallowed it down and tapped on the door to alert the twins.

'It's time, girls,' she said, and they stopped what they were doing and turned their heads in the same way, with the same slight tilt to the right.

Rosina turned and walked back along the passage towards the lounge. On the way, she heard footsteps behind her and turned to see a housemaid, head down, clutching a dustpan and brush. The girl stopped dead at her mistress's notice and dropped her gaze to her feet.

'Hardcastle, hurry back to the servants' hall,' said Rosina.

'Yes, ma'am. Sorry, ma'am,' said the maid, bobbing a curtsey, eyes still down, too shy to look at her mistress.

'It's only that you'll miss the Prime Minister's broadcast if you're not careful. And it's important that you hear this. Everyone should hear this.'

'Yes ma'am. Sorry, ma'am,' the girl said again. Only fifteen years old, Rosina recalled, younger than Constance.

Rosina reached the lounge and found Grace about to switch on the wireless. Evelyn and Constance came in, still bickering, the twins arriving quietly behind. They were all gathered together and found seats around the fireplace to sit on and wait. Rosina hoped that at the other side of the house, the housekeeper and butler had managed to gather all the servants together around the kitchen wireless, as families all over the country must be doing at that very moment. A nation acting as one – how rare that was. How admirable. And how terrifying.

The Home Service announced its star speaker, the Prime Minister. The girls' slight restlessness was stilled and every head in the room was bowed slightly, eyes intent, ears pricked. *They'll remember this moment for the rest of their lives*, thought Rosina.

'I am speaking to you from the Cabinet Room at 10, Downing Street. This morning the British Ambassador in Berlin handed the German Government a final note stating that unless we heard from them by eleven o'clock that they were prepared at once to withdraw their troops from Poland a state of war would exist between us. I have to tell you now that no such undertaking has been received, and that consequently this country is at war with Germany.'

There it was. They all knew it was coming but it was truly shocking to hear it spoken aloud by Chamberlain himself.

'Oh, good lord,' muttered Grace and Evelyn hissed, 'Ssh!', as Chamberlain went on about assurances and settlements and Hitler and the Poles and France, about God and the Empire, about evil and force and injustice.

'And against them I am certain that the right will prevail,' he said and then there was a pause. He had come to the end of his speech. They listened to the announcer say important details would follow, then they heard the bells ring out of the wireless, tinny and eerie in the lounge. There followed a list of directions for the foreseeable future, about places of entertainment being closed until further notice and that people should not crowd together for any reason. It went on about air-raid warnings and how they would sound; about shelters and what people should do in a gas attack; sirens, rattles and handbells would be used. Schools would be closed for a week but thereafter open again. Many children would be evacuated. Everyone must carry gas masks. There were other things they could have listened to after this, but Rosina stepped over and turned off the wireless to silence it. She did not wish to hear any more at the moment. The fact of war was enough, that morning. Glancing outside at the gardens she saw how the sun was now completely free to shine down on their house, all morning mists having dissolved away into the warmth of a balmy September late morning. It seemed to mock the sombre mood of the room, of the country, of Europe and beyond.

'What does it all mean, Mummy?' asked Dora, always questioning, always wanting to know more.

'It means the end of every bloody thing,' said Evelyn in a grump. Selfish as ever, she thought only of her art studies in France coming to an end.

'Evvy, language,' chided her mother, though gently.

'Oh, who cares about words now!' cried Evvy, dramatic as ever.

'Come on, girls,' said Grace, sitting upright and forcing a smile. 'Now is not the time for strife, but for togetherness. Mummy needs us to help her. And so does our country.'

'Thank you, Grace,' said Rosina, at which Evelyn huffed and folded her arms. Rosina went to Evelyn and gave her long, red-blonde hair a single, affectionate stroke, which soothed her a little. 'Grace is right, girls. Now is the time to think not of ourselves, but of others. Of what we can do to help, to support, to provide and to manage without. It won't be easy. Remember that I have lived through a war before and never thought to see it again in my lifetime.' She shuddered inwardly at the thought of it, the horror of the Great War burned into the memory of her late teens and early twenties. Her mother had died the year before the war started and Rosina could chart the downward spiral of her life, and indeed the world's it seemed, from that moment. 'But here it is. And here we are. And we must make the best of it.'

'Will we have to fight?' asked Daisy, her face unreadable. Rosina couldn't tell if she liked the idea or not.

'I'll fight 'em!' cried Constance.

'I was going to say that!' added Dora.

'Nobody will be doing any fighting,' said Rosina. 'Now—' But she was talked over by another daughter.

'I'll be off to London,' said Evvy. 'They'll need artists there, I'm sure of it. To design posters telling us all to do our duty.'

'I'm not sure that London—' Rosina began and was interrupted again.

'I'll join the Air Force then,' announced Constance, 'and fly planes and gun down Germans floating on parachutes into the sea and a watery grave.'

'Don't be a dunce,' scoffed Evvy. 'You're far too young.'

'Am not!' cried Constance, her cheeks colouring, eyes blazing.

Rosina noticed that Grace had been sitting quietly and staring at the fireplace, pensive.

'Are you all right, darling?' Rosina asked her eldest daughter. 'I know it's a lot to take in.'

Grace turned round and surprised her mother by giving her a bright smile. 'Actually, Mummy, I've been thinking a lot about this over the past few months, since we knew that war was inevitable. And I've come to a decision: I want to join the Wrens.'

'Really?' said Rosina, quite shocked. 'I'm not sure the Navy would be right for you.'

Evvy added, 'It's rough and ready in the Navy, Gracie. Sure you're up to it?'

This is what Rosina feared too. Grace was so ... unworldly. Evelyn often said the thing that Rosina herself was thinking, but didn't have the nerve or did have the tact to keep it quiet.

'I'm not sure I'll ever be up to it,' said Grace thoughtfully. 'But I'd like to do my duty. And duty is never easy. It's not meant to be easy, I think. They say the Wren uniform will be the nicest, with a smashing hat! But seriously, I feel it's about time I saw a bit of the real world, don't you, Mummy? And when I was a girl, living on the edge of a cliff, I always loved the idea of running away to sea.'

'Ooh, can I come?' piped up Constance.

'Oh, Connie, do put a sock in it,' said Evvy, with a toss of her hair.

'Will school be closed forever?' added Daisy, hopefully. Her twin adored school but Daisy had never found boarding school easy. All those people in close quarters ... She was the kind of person who found small talk horrifying and sharing her space utterly draining.

'No, dear,' said Rosina. 'Only for a week or so while they sort all the evacuees. But your school is deep in the countryside and will be safe, so you will go back there. Life must go on, you know, the things that matter must prevail. Grace and Evelyn, we will discuss your plans later. Connie and twins, you will study at home this week. I'll see to it you will have plenty to keep your mind occupied. Now, girls, I must go and see the staff for there will be things to discuss. I'll see you all at luncheon in an hour and we'll talk everything through then. Try not to fret too much; some things will change, but many will stay the same, school being one of them! Take comfort in that, my darlings.'

As Rosina left the room, she heard Constance tut and Daisy sigh, probably at the thought of school going on as normal. She knew she ought to stay with the girls and let them bombard her with their inevitable questions, but the truth was that she felt as clueless as them. She even wondered if Grace knew more about the state of affairs than she did. Rosina read *The Times* each day, but she did not pay such close attention to worldly matters as Grace did. Evelyn was worldly in a different way, had more knowledge of the streets than herself or her other daughters had. The others were young and foolish, except Daisy, who had a kind of otherworldly peace about her. She'd be stoic, Grace would be sensible and the other three would probably go wild, falling in love with soldiers and sailors and airmen.

Rosina sighed as she walked down the passageway that led towards the ballroom and, further on, to the servants' hall, kitchen, scullery and outhouses. Again, she felt very alone walking down that long corridor that stretched the depth of the house, facing away from the sea beyond. She saw, through the ballroom's glass-panelled doors, the trees of the driveway stretching away in parallel lines and thought of the horses she and the girls had ridden on, ambling down that driveway on to the moorland they would gallop across for fun. She'd probably have to sell some of the horses, if all the grooms were called up. She thought then of her two gleaming motor cars parked in the garage, of petrol and food, of how both would probably be in short supply. The land and the farmers surrounding her estate – how crucial they would be! How could she be crucial too? What could she do to help her nation?

As she approached the servants' hall, Rosina could hear the hubbub of her staff discussing the news. She knew her entrance would hush them all and, for a moment, she had a strange desire to be one of them, amidst colleagues and friends, talking about their families, their futures, relying on each other for advice and hearsay. As she arrived at the door to the servants' hall, in the moment before her appearance was noted, she saw a kitchen maid – Nancy, her name was, Nancy Bird – stand up from the table and announce something to the room.

'I'll be joining t'Wrens!' she said and beamed a beautiful smile.

She was scolded by Cook, Mrs Bairstow, who told Nancy to think on, that she'd be beaten with a rolling pin before she left them all in the lurch like that. But as the servants near the door noticed Rosina's presence and the customary hush fell, Rosina realised that while Nancy might be the first to announce her role in the new world of wartime, many other servants would also leave – the young first, of course, but if the war dragged on past Christmas, as the last war had, then perhaps this room bustling now with staff would dwindle and empty, leaving only the middle-aged to keep the big house and estate from grinding to a halt. That would be her task, to keep all this going, with little to no help. She'd have no time to be noble and aid the nation. She'd drown in the responsibility of Raven Hall and all its hungry needs. The thought both energised and exhausted her.

'Now then, everyone,' she said brightly and smiled. But nobody else was smiling, except the kitchen maid, who looked extremely pleased with herself. *My Grace will join the Navy with Nancy Bird*, thought Rosina and in this one bare fact, she saw how the world would be changed forever by this war, bringing some together, separating others. And she felt as if the room would tip, that she'd lose her footing and slide down into nothingness. But it didn't and she didn't. She heard herself talking to her staff calmly, reassuringly. Whatever changes came, she knew that through all the years of loneliness since she'd lost her beloved mother, she had built an iron spine for herself to see her through the hardest of times. War would be no exception. Whatever the world threw at Raven Hall, would dare to aim at Rosina Calvert-Lazenby, she would face it. And prevail.

Chapter 1

January 1940

Grace was glad she had found a seat by the window. As the bus heaved its way up inclines and raced down dips, wending its bulky way through the country lanes of Hampshire, she stared across the fields and tried to swallow her nerves. She was surprised she was anxious because she had already faced her worst fear – the weeks of initial training she'd completed down in Devon from October to Christmas. Leaving her digs in Oxford and then the comforts of home and arriving in Plymouth at a Women's Royal Naval Service barracks had been pure terror and she'd spent the first evening on and off the loo due to a worried belly. Full of zeal four months before in September when signing up to the WRNS – known as the Wrens – she had closed her mind to the reality of bunking down with dozens of other women and living with them for weeks in very close quarters. She had detested this at school, had enjoyed far more the civilised rooms she had had at Somerville College in Oxford. But she had put a brave face on that, as well as the other strange and sometimes awful rigours of initial training as a Wren, such as endless marching and scrubbing floors.

The marching had been her greatest trial and she had found it so hard she'd nearly given up. She'd always felt like a clumsy person, feeling too tall and too awkward, her legs too long, her feet too big. And marching in step eluded her to begin with and so she was shouted at a lot. Mortified, feeling that she was letting the side down, she had practised in the toilets when alone, marching on the spot and often lying awake in bed at night, going over the marching drills in her mind to force herself to keep time. And it had worked; before long she got the knack of it and fell into rhythm with the others. Her first victory! Everything felt easier after that. She had survived and even made a bunch of friends in the process.

Her initial training had been done at Devonport and she'd adored being so close to the sea. The drills and constant chilblains from wintry marches and other privations of those early days were not much fun, but she enjoyed meeting a wide range of girls from different backgrounds. They were mostly young women in their early twenties, some as young as eighteen, some in their late twenties – these older women often nicknamed Mother or Ma – or even one at twenty-nine that everyone called Gran! They had all become fast friends very swiftly, in the way people often do when thrown haphazardly into an unexpected and difficult situation together. It was a kind of trench camaraderie, as people compared it to the last war. Once she'd completed her initial training and gained her smart blue Wren uniform, she was informed that she was being drafted to the village of Bramshott in rural Hampshire, where she was to begin training as a wireless telegraphist. All she knew of this mysterious occupation was that it involved listening to wireless communications through headphones and that you needed to know the Morse code, which she'd heard of but knew little about.

And now here she was, on the bus to her new temporary home. She had been given a week's leave at Raven Hall and had travelled down that day from Whitby to London on the train, then taken one bus to Basingstoke and now this second bus to her destination. She was exhausted, cold and worried. She knew that only two of her Devonport colleagues were being sent to the same place as her and they were very pally and not that close with her so she knew she'd have to make new friends quickly and she was dreading it. Having only known them a few weeks, she missed her Plymouth friends desperately already, having surprised herself at bonding swiftly with them, despite finding it hard in her younger life to make new friends. Now she was having to start all over again. She hoped there would be at least one nice girl there who liked reading and talking as much as she did, who she could pair up with and not bother anyone.

As she tried to picture this person, she saw a young woman stand up at the front of the bus clutching a bag and holding on to the pole to steady herself. Immediately Grace realised two things: this girl must be going to the same place as her because she was dressed in the Wren uniform of navy-blue serge jacket and skirt, white shirt, collar and tie, black stockings and the smart hat worn at an angle. The second thing Grace realised was that not only had she not noticed this girl when she got on the bus, but that she vaguely recognised her face. Was this the girl who'd been a maid in her own home, the girl from Raven Hall? She recalled her mother saying, back in September, that one of the kitchen maids was also joining the Wrens but, as they must have been sent to different training establishments, she'd thought no more of her, couldn't even remember her name. This bus had been full of different people in uniform when she boarded it at Basingstoke and so the girl must have been hidden from Grace's view until now. She wanted to call out to her but was too shy to do so and, anyway, the girl seemed to know something she didn't as the bus was starting to slow as it drove past the outlying cottages of a village or hamlet.

Before long, the bus pulled up in front of a large house which was surrounded by fields, with chicken coops and other sheds in its grounds. This must be it, her training establishment and Wrennery, the place where she would spend the next few months in specialist training. The other Wren got off and Grace followed her, stepping down on to the road and glancing at the bus as it went on its way. She almost wanted to jump back on it, but she knew that was daft. She really must develop more courage, she scolded herself, especially in a time of war.

'Hello,' Grace said, smiling at the girl and trying to sound cheerful, though she actually felt sick.

'Ma'am,' the girl replied and nodded.

'Oh gosh, please don't call me that. We're all equals here.'

'All right, then,' she said. ''Ow do?'

Well, there was a Yorkshire voice if ever she heard one. Was this the maid?

'You stood up first on the bus, as if you knew where to get off. That's awfully clever of you.'

'Ah no, I were just chatting with a local woman on t'bus and she told me what t'village were like and what to look out for. It's hard to know when all the road signs've been ferreted away to confuse German spies!'

'It is! Oh, well done! I didn't have the nerve to talk to anyone. I'm still a bit shy with total strangers, if truth be told.'

21

'That's all right. I can talk enough for t'both of us. And we're not exactly total strangers, but 'appen tha don't know that . . . ?' The girl looked at Grace with a twinkle in her eye. It was then that Grace noticed the name of her training establishment – H.M.S. *Raleigh* – on her Wren's hat. Though not actually trained on a ship, instead in mostly ordinary buildings, all Wren training establishments were named after ships and each Wren proudly wore the name of their ship on the ribbon on their hat.

'My goodness, you were in Plymouth too!' said Grace. 'Look,' she added, pointing to her own hat ribbon: 'I'm H.M.S. *Drake*. Did we meet at a dance or something?'

'Nay, it were closer to home than that. But tha'd not be expected to notice t'likes of me.' She said it good-naturedly, with a wry smile and Grace liked her already.

Grace said, 'Actually, I *did* recognise your face. I think you might be a maid at Raven Hall.'

'Aye, I were! I were a kitchen maid there for three year. I'm Nancy Bird. And tha's Miss Grace, eldest of t'Calvert lasses. Sorry, that's what folk call thee; I should've said, Calvert-Lazenby girls.'

'Oh, don't be sorry! *I'm* sorry I wasn't sure who you were at first. It's only because I've been away at Oxford for three years and when I'm home I don't go down to the kitchen much. Would you accept my apology for my utter gaucheness?'

22

'If I knew what it were, I would. But I dun't need no apologies. You've not done nowt wrong, Miss Grace.'

'You're too kind, Nancy. And for heaven's sake, please don't ever call me Miss Grace or ma'am again. We are the same now. We are Wrens, after all.'

'That we are,' smiled Nancy. 'Shall we go in?'

'Yes, we shall.'

And that was how Grace walked into her second phase of Wren training, with a new friend beside her, bolstering her confidence to such an extent that as they arrived in the room where they were to sleep, filled with bunk beds with perfectly smart blue-and-white counterpanes, Grace realised she didn't feel sick any more, just excited. The room was filled with young women, all around their age, all chattering away, bags on their beds, belongings already splayed across bedside tabletops. Nancy wended her way through them and found them two unclaimed beds beside each other, their top decks also empty. Grace noticed that some of the women had Wren uniforms on but quite a few were wearing civilian clothes. They must have come 'straight from shore', as the Naval slang had it. They were new recruits. But they did not seem nervous. None of them did. Not for the first time in her life, Grace felt that everyone was part of clique to which she had missed the invitation. Again, she felt desperately glad that Nancy was there with her. They dropped their bags on the beds and sat down,

23

taking a few items out and negotiating which drawers they would have to themselves and which they'd share in the bedside cabinet.

'Why did tha choose t'Wrens then, Grace?' said Nancy.

'Oh, I've been fascinated by the sea for as long as I can remember. I harboured delusions of running away to sea, or being kidnapped by pirates or such nonsense. Then, when I was a bit older, I learnt about the polar explorers and became quite obsessed with them, as well as reading the Greek myths. I wanted to be Odysseus and . . . ' She paused. 'You may not have heard of Odysseus, sorry.'

'Is it that story, *The Odyssey*? We were doing that at school before I had to leave. It were a grand tale.'

'Yes! That's him. Wonderful story.' Grace wondered why Nancy 'had to leave' school, but felt it was too personal to ask. 'So, why the Wrens for you?'

'Well, I signed up as cook, but I made it known that I had ambitions to better missen. I wanted to use my brain. So, I argued and argued that they should let me change to t'writer side of things, which eventually they did, when I got my father to send some of my old schoolwork from four year ago and they saw I wasn't a dullard. And here I am.'

Grace was impressed, hugely so. Such determination! Her own reasons for joining seemed pathetically childish in comparison. 'That's extraordinary. What strength it must

24

have taken to fight your way here on your own merit. I'm full of admiration. Well done, Nancy!' she said. She wanted to say more, but a voice behind her interrupted them.

'And who in the world might you two be?' Grace looked round to see a pretty blonde Wren standing beside her bed, her hand draped loosely over the top bunk as she primped her perfectly curled fringe.

'How do you do?' said Grace and nearly bashed her head on the bunk above, before remembering it was there and shooting her head forward at a crazy angle, which made the blonde girl giggle. Not for the first time in her life, Grace felt graceless. At five feet nine inches, she always felt too tall. She gathered herself and stood up straight. 'I'm Grace Calvert-Lazenby.'

'Jolly good name,' said the blonde. 'I'm Lucinda Pryce-Masterson, of the Norfolk Mastersons. Are you the Dorset Lazenbys or the Kent?'

'The North Yorkshire ones, actually,' said Grace. 'And this is Nancy Bird.'

Nancy stood up and said, 'Of t'Robin Hood's Bay Birds. Me and my father, that is. And t'two bairns, my brothers. And my cousins. 'Appen there are more Birds about than Pryce-Mastersons, I'd wager.'

Grace watched as Lucinda's face turned from a simpering smile to a clouded look of disgust, replaced finally with a smirk.

'Ah . . . ' Lucinda said. 'A *local*.' She spoke the word as if she were pronouncing the name of some kind of vermin. Grace glanced swiftly at Nancy, who was beaming at Lucinda and didn't seem to be fazed in the slightest.

'That's right,' Nancy said. 'And proud of it. Now, if tha'll excuse me, I need to answer a call of nature. Nowt like a long bus ride to make tha need to piss like a shire horse, eh?' And with that, Nancy walked confidently across the room, watched in shock by others around who had heard her extraordinary utterance.

Lucinda turned to Grace and said, 'However did you end up with *that*? I would have thought better of the Navy letting rubbish like that into telegraphy training. Best change your bunk now, dear.'

Grace wanted to tell this Lucinda person to get knotted, in no uncertain terms. She wanted to defend Nancy. And she wanted to say something devilishly cutting and put this awful snob in her place. Instead, she muttered, 'Well, my things are all unpacked now, so . . . ' letting her utterance trail off, accompanied by a vague hand gesture.

'All the same, think about moving. And never fear, we'll look after you.'

Oh, I do hope not, thought Grace, resolving next time to be braver and to stand up for her new friend, although she could see that Nancy could absolutely stand up for herself; Grace felt a pang of envy that the younger girl had so much confidence, a quality she lacked herself.

Lucinda introduced Grace to a few of the others nearby. From their accents and demeanour, Grace could easily tell that all the girls had been born with silver spoons in their mouths. This was so different from her time in Plymouth, where she had delighted in the mixture of classes and types, which though it was unsettling, at first, she had soon realised it had given her a sense of *everyone* clubbing together to face their foe. She felt it was the way of things these days, that all differences must be put aside in favour of unity. Grace realised that there must have been a very particular type of selection taking place here by the powers that be, to bring these well-to-do women together in Hampshire. Yet, somehow, Nancy Bird had sailed above this snobbery and earnt her place here beside these posh girls. She was indeed a local girl with a local accent and local dialect, with no attempt to hide it or fit in, and Grace liked her all the more for it.

Chapter 2

There was little time to settle in, as classes began the very next day at 9 a.m. sharp. The first class was a gas lecture. Grace had heard these before and sighed to think she'd have to sit through it all again. It was a local Air Raid Precautions man who gave them this lecture and he had a face like thunder as he warned them all of the dangers of gas. He told them that if they got a whiff of gas before they managed to get their masks on, they might end up vomiting inside their mask and so, to ensure they didn't suffocate, they must immediately eat the vomit. This was met with great hilarity by the Wrens, who were scolded. Grace thought of their old family cat Pickle who she and her sisters once saw in the courtyard gobbling up its own vomit and how they'd all shrieked with disgust. And now she was being asked to do the same! But despite the Wrens' laughter, they all knew that gas was a deadly threat and could arrive at any time.

It was now early 1940 and the war had been going on for a few months, with little sign that the Germans were about to invade immediately, but the constant fear was there and it was thought by many that gas would be the first thing to come, drifting over in deadly clouds, so Grace pulled herself together and listened carefully to the ARP man, though his red face made her smirk at Nancy, who was also trying not to giggle.

Next, they went into their first Morse code class, taught by a Chief Wren telegraphist, an impressive woman with a perfectly pressed uniform, marvellous coiffed hair and a wedding ring: all things Grace wanted one day and feared she'd never attain given that she'd always felt clumsy and ungainly.

Dit dah. Dah dit dit dit. Dah dit dah dit.

And so on. Those were the letters A, B and C in Morse code. All twenty-six needed to be memorised, of course, as well as numbers and a few other symbols. So began their education in a brand-new language. That evening, back in the 'cabin' on their 'bunks' (as Wrens called their dormitory and beds), Grace and Nancy tested each other on Morse.

'Let's do t'easy ones first,' said Nancy. 'What's dit dah?'

'A,' said Grace, emphatically.

'Correct. What's dit?'

'E.' So Nancy was going through the vowels. That would

30

be simple.

'Right. Now then . . . dah dah dit dit.'

'I. No, it isn't. Uh . . . oh, I don't know that one. I thought you were going through the vowels! What is it?'

'It's Z. I'm not going to make it too easy for thee, lass,' chuckled Nancy.

'Oh, you rotter! All right then, it's my turn.' She grabbed her own Morse book they'd been issued and said, 'What's . . . dit dit dit dah, then, clever clogs?'

'Easy. That's V.'

'You're too good at this, Nancy Bird!'

Some of the other girls nearby saw them practising and wanted to join in.

'Sounds awfully dull to me,' said Lucinda. 'Morse code is just a lot of gobbledygook. I'm waiting for them to give us something important to do, not these childish games.' Lucinda was sitting on her bunk with her shapely legs stretched out, looking as if she were reclining on a chaise longue in the ancestral home.

But the others ignored her and soon a great quiz was underway, with most guessing incorrectly, except Nancy, who rarely put a foot wrong. After that they went to dinner, which was served in the ballroom of the house, now adapted to become a dining room. The food was cooked by Wren cooks, as Nancy used to be, and served by Wren stewards, another job Nancy said had been suggested to her, but she'd

31

refused. It was good, hearty food – lots of stodge served with gravy for the main course and more stodge with custard for the pudding. Afterwards, they went back to the bunk and chatted.

'You're so good at Morse already, Nancy. What's your secret?'

Nancy was sitting on her bed, her legs crossed, one of her civilian dresses on her lap as she sewed up a hole under the shoulder. Grace had been delighted to discover that Wrens were the only women in uniform who were permitted to wear their civilian clothes when not on duty and thus dresses for dances were in great demand. Nancy stopped sewing for a moment, tapped her nose and winked.

'Oh, don't be so mysterious. How do you manage it?'

Nancy leant towards Grace, who moved forward to be closer. Nancy whispered, 'I learnt it on t'railway journey down. I copied it down from a library book.'

'Oh, I wish I'd thought to do that! I just stared out of the window.'

Nancy smiled and went back to her sewing. 'Girls like me need a bag of tricks to get ahead, Grace.'

'I suppose so,' said Grace thoughtfully.

'I *know* so,' said Nancy, turning to her sewing bag and pulling out a very pretty piece of lace. She began to pin it to the rather plain lapels of the dress.

'What do we have here?' said a sneering voice, which

Grace immediately recognised as Lucinda's; she was now standing right next to their bunks. 'The poor little seamstress girl sewing her poor little collar on her poor little ragged dress?'

Nancy carried on pinning, a little smile on her face, acting for all the world as if Lucinda had never spoken.

'Didn't you hear me, *local*?' said Lucinda, annoyed she was being ignored.

Nancy put her last pin in and looked up at Grace, then said, 'Can you hear owt? Sounds like a fly caught in a trap, buzzing away. Wish someone'd swat it.'

'Oh, you think you're so clever, don't you, *local*? Well, someone needs to teach you a lesson. You can't swan around here, thinking you fit in. You should at least show a little bit of humility that they've let the likes of you in.'

'We'll see how the likes of me and thee fare when we get our first Morse code test. Tha was hopeless in today's class. Tha dun't even remember what a vowel is. Sounds like all that money thi parents spent on thi education were a waste. Will tha be so sure of thissen when we sit our exams, eh, Lady Muck?'

Lucinda looked utterly floored by this comment and Grace saw that Nancy had accurately pinpointed a sore spot. Lucinda had been awfully dismissive of learning Morse and Grace had thought it meant the snobbish girl knew something they didn't. But perhaps it was a lack of

33

confidence and Nancy had had the insight to spot it.

'I'll beat you easily, local. You'll see.' Lucinda stomped back to her bunk and Nancy carried on sewing, that same little smile on her face. Oh, to be like Nancy. But Grace feared she'd never have such aplomb, such inner strength.

That night, once the lights were out, Grace found the day's experiences were swimming around in her mind, as well as the incessant tap-tap-tap of the Morse code she heard in the pipes above her bed. She lay curled up on her side and listened to the sounds of snoring, sighing Wrens around her, glancing across at Nancy, who was fast asleep on her back with her mouth open. Grace smiled and remembered Nancy's little victory over injustice. The look on Lucinda's face was something she'd not forget in a hurry. It must be marvellous to stand up to such a bully. Grace closed her eyes and snuggled down beneath her rather scratchy blanket and felt a huge determination to stand up to Lucinda's – or anyone else's – bullying in future.

Over the next few weeks, their Morse classes continued apace. Hearing these sounds over and over and over again, Grace soon realised that her brain was moving from seeing these as dots and dashes on a page to an instantaneous connection between what she heard and what she wrote down. It was like learning to read music: instead of seeing a crotchet, she heard a beat. Now she would hear the dit dah and immediately see an A, instead of thinking of its constituent parts.

Grace, Nancy and the others spent so many hours each day listening to the strange music of Morse that they began to hear it in everything: dripping taps, birdsong, a tapping foot, the creak of tree branches, rain on a windowpane. It all began to become a code in their Morse-addled minds. One of the girls said it was a kind of madness and called it going 'dit happy'. It was a strange, new world for most of them, but Grace found it comforting; she had spent so much of her education buried in the antique worlds of Latin and Ancient Greek or in playing the piano, that thinking in different languages was nothing new for her. Nancy, too, had a great knack for it. She had not had Grace's linguistic experience, but she had such a quick mind that she picked things up swiftly, without ever needing repetition.

During this first month, their speed at listening and transcribing got quicker and quicker, from five words per minute to begin with, to eight to ten to twelve and, after a few weeks, some were up at fifteen or even nineteen. Their aim was twenty-six wpm and Grace felt sure that she and Nancy would definitely get there one day. Lucinda, however, was lagging behind at twelve wpm, which gave Grace a secret satisfaction.

New responsibilities also beckoned, and alongside their

classes was a new role of fire-watching. This meant staying up half the night on shifts, in pairs, watching out for incendiary bombs dropped by the Germans. Mostly, this involved patrolling all the decks (as Wrens called floors) and around the perimeter of the building, as well as quite a bit of chatting and even some reading. There had been no bombing raids in this deeply rural part of England and none were expected anytime soon, but fire-watching was a duty that everyone took seriously, because one never knew. Grace had not yet done the night shift and, when her time came, she was delighted to hear she'd been paired with Nancy. It was the first time they'd been alone together since that first day and it was nice to be able to talk freely, without Lucinda's sour face in the background or the ears of other Wrens.

As they walked sedately along one of the long corridors of the Wrennery that night, Grace asked, 'Do you miss home, being here?'

'Aye, I miss my father. He's a fisherman at Robin Hood's Bay. I don't miss my two cheeky brothers as much! Just because they're rowdy. Not that I don't love 'em with all my heart, o'course.'

'Of course! So, it's just you and your father and brothers?' Grace wanted to know more about Nancy but felt it was impolite to pry too much.

'Aye, my mam died four year ago. She had a weak heart.

Just went in her sleep one night. She were thirty-eight year old.'

'Oh Nancy, I'm so sorry.'

'Thanks. And I know tha's in t'same boat. I were working at Raven Hall when thi father . . . tha know . . . I'm sorry about that too.'

'Well, yes. Thank you. It was a dreadful shock.'

'I imagine it were. We always knew our mam were poorly, as she'd get out of breath and need a nap. But an accident, like thi father's? Well, that's a right terrible fright out of t'blue and no mistake.'

'Yes, I suppose I never thought of it like that. Do you know, though, it's peculiar, but it really didn't make that much difference in our lives. That might sound rather callous, but it's true. We'd all been sent away to boarding school aged seven and so we spent far more time there than at home. And when we *were* at home, Daddy was hardly ever there. Off gallivanting, as I heard your former boss, Mrs Bairstow, say once! He spent an awful amount of time on the continent, sailing or playing polo or skiing. It was an avalanche, they say. He didn't stand a chance.'

'Horrible thing, that,' said Nancy, softly.

'Yes, yes it must be. I do hope he didn't suffer. He was a jolly chap, even though we barely knew him, and always cheery with us. Mummy is the one who had to be serious. I often felt sorry for her because she would have to deal with all the problems and discipline, then Daddy would sail in with gifts and smiles and we'd all laud him. Poor Mummy got all the trouble and he got all the fun. Doesn't seem fair, somehow. I think it's made Mummy a bit serious.'

'We all like thi mother, very much,' said Nancy. 'If tha don't mind me saying.'

'Oh no, I don't mind at all. I'm glad to hear it. Thank you for telling me that.'

'She's always kind and fair. That goes a long way with servants.'

'Yes, I can see that and it's very nice to know. She's a darling and I truly don't know what I'd do without her.'

'Tha miss her, then? Miss home?'

'I miss Mummy, yes. But not home, or Oxford – or anywhere, really. I think, for the first time in a long time, I feel I'm exactly where I need to be.'

'That's how I feel too. Don't get me wrong, I do miss Father and t'sea and t'streets of Robin Hood's Bay. It's t'happiest place in t'world to me. But I don't miss working as a kitchen maid at Raven Hall, no offence.'

'Oh, none taken! I think you're far too good for that job.' Then Grace wondered if that was an insult and she stopped walking, adding, 'Oh dear, have I just put my rather large foot in it?'

Nancy laughed and said, 'Probably, but I don't care. I know what tha meant and it was meant kindly. And I agree. This training is t'first time since school that I've really used my brain properly, as it should be used. I had to leave school, you see, after Mam died, to help at home with the bairns and Father, then get a job to help make ends meet.' *Ah*, thought Grace. *That's why such a clever girl left school as soon as she could.* 'And I missed learning summat terrible. I'd get books from t'library but there weren't many and I'd read them all before long and had to start at t'beginning again.'

'If only I'd known, you could have used our library at the Hall.'

'Oh, I wun't dream of that!' exclaimed Nancy.

'Well, you should. Daddy was never a reader and Mummy has read most of them so you'd be very welcome. They're getting dusty from lack of use, you know, so whenever you're home, even if you never work at Raven Hall again, I want you to borrow books as you need. If you want to, that is.'

'Thanks. Tha's kind, like thi mother.'

'Oh, I don't know about that!'

'Oh, I do,' said Nancy and linked arms with Grace, which felt lovely. 'Fancy a cuppa?'

'I'd love one, but how?'

'Come with me.'

'Where are we going?' Grace whispered nervously.

'Galley.' (The name Wrens used for the kitchen).

'Are we allowed?'

'Oh, aye. I'm friendly with t'cook and had a little word and she said we could pop in for a brew on night shifts.'

'Oh, jolly good!' said Grace, the thought of a hot cup of tea warming her already on the chilly night. As they walked along the corridors of the ground floor towards the kitchen area, Grace grimaced at the lingering smell that always seemed to hang about the lower floors of the place, something like an old, damp washcloth mixed with wet dog or similar. 'What is that smell anyway?' she said to Nancy, who pushed the kitchen door open and reached around to switch on the light.

In that moment the light came on and illuminated the night-time galley, a sudden movement revealed thousands of tiny, moving objects migrating from the walls, tables and floors. They were insects and they were everywhere.

'Cockroaches!' gasped Nancy and they both watched in horror as the little devils disappeared under every surface within seconds.

'Oh, gosh, they're disgusting!' cried Grace.

'I've seen nobbut a few before in a kitchen, never this many,' said Nancy. 'Come on, let's get t'kettle on.'

'You still want a cup of tea after that?'

''Course I do. Come on, scaredy-cat!'

Grace watched Nancy stride across the kitchen, catching the odd bug under her shoes that made a revolting crunching noise. Now Grace knew what that grim smell was that hung about the house some days: it was cockroaches and it was absolutely revolting. Nancy was at the range making the tea and Grace was charged with keeping a lookout, glancing about constantly, waiting for interlopers who thankfully never came. They got their cups of tea as quickly as they could and left swiftly.

'We're never doing that again at night,' said Grace.

'We are! I'm not letting those little rascals stop me from getting a brew,' said Nancy, laughing.

'Well, I suppose as long as there's two of us, one to make the tea and one to watch, we managed all right.'

'Aye, we did,' said Nancy. 'Life's always easier in twos.'

Grace thought of how impossible she had found it at school and at university to make special friendships with individual girls. She'd always had plenty of people about to talk to, but never found that one person she could call a best friend. She wouldn't presume to call Nancy that now, as Nancy was popular amongst the Wrens and was often to be found chattering away with the others, while Grace retired to her bunk to read a book or write letters home. But Grace thought how extraordinary it was that two such different women found it so easy to get on and she truly valued their time together. And secretly, though it seemed terribly wrong to think it, she was glad the war had thrown her out of her cloistered college life and into the rough and tumble of the Navy. Of course, she wasn't glad there was a war on – nobody could think such a terrible thing – but she had to admit, so far she was enjoying her war immensely.

WRNS Training Depot,
Bramshott,
Hampshire
Friday evening, 3 February, 1940

My own dear darling Mummy,

So here comes another letter from the eldest of the Calvert lasses – this, apparently, is what we're called at home by the servants. I know I've already written to you about Nancy but let me just add that I feel we are becoming firm friends now and she really is the nicest person. So sharp and bright too. We really must make sure she never has to be anything like a kitchen maid again, if we can help it.

The other day Nancy and I got the bus to Chichester in order to see the cathedral, which was very fine indeed. It was good to get away from the Wrennery, even though the weather was bitter and we spent most of the day hiding in tea shops and churches to get out of the biting wind! On the way home, we stupidly missed our bus and so we had to hitch a lift. As you probably know, this is very common these days and one often sees men and women in uniform cadging lifts. But due to the horrid weather, nobody was about and we had walked the long road out of Chichester for at least a couple of miles and were freezing cold before somebody stopped. It just so happened it was a real-life Polish pilot! And very dashing he was too! I've never met a Pole before and his English wasn't very good, so we helped him by giving him a few English expressions he might find useful. Rather, I gave him some useful English idioms such as How do you do? *and* hair of the dog *– I thought he might really need this latter one, as he told us how much he likes a drink or two or three! But Nancy did tease him so, telling him all these curious Yorkshire sayings like* There's nowt so queer as folk *and* nobbut middling *and so forth, which confused the poor chap dreadfully! I'd like to hear him use those in a Hampshire pub and see what response he gets – ha ha! She's a naughty one, that Nancy! But oh, such a fun girl and so easy to talk to. We haven't found a local dance to go to yet, but hope there will be one nearby soon, so we can wear our dresses. Nancy is a great seamstress and adapts our clothes with pretty extras she has in her marvellous sewing bag which is better than Aladdin's cave. Thank heavens for her.*

The others are nice, except for that horrid Lucinda I've already told you about. Nasty piece of work. She still has her followers, but most of the Wrens are ordinary and normal – by that I mean our *sort of people. Not too posh like Lucinda but they've had a certain upbringing. Gosh, that makes me sound an awful snob, but actually, you know, I feel that initial training and being friends with Nancy has all been very good for me. When I was younger, I think I would've seen a maid or a road sweeper and imagined that their thoughts were quite different from mine – not better or worse, just somehow different. Now I know that people of all walks of life read books and think deep thoughts. It seems an obvious thing to say, but I think I probably was rather a dreadful snob myself without realising it. And I'm sorry for that, though I suppose I couldn't help it. I just want you to know that I do believe this war is making me a better person, in many ways. I now know that a person in any walk of life might well be constructing the most beautiful poem in their head whilst carrying out the most mundane of tasks. It sounds obvious to put it that way, but it's a bit of a revelation to me. Anyway, I couldn't admit this to anybody but you, because I know you never judge me, my dearest Mama, and always do your utmost to see the best in me. And I love you for that! And miss you dreadfully.*

Anyway, this was supposed to be a letter about our studies and instead I veered into waxing lyrical. Forgive me for that. I get all thoughtful when I hold a pen! Suffice to say, we continue with our rigorous schedule of Morse code lessons and soon, apparently, we will be learning more about electricity and waves and so forth. We have to understand the equipment we'll be working with once we're posted away. Still no news on when or where that will be, but I'll let you know as soon as I do, of course. Oh, I almost forgot – we had exams this week and Nancy was top of the class and I was third. Delighted with that! Lucinda failed three of the tests! Serves her right! So she'll have to retake, whereas we are free to go on to the next type of lessons and learn more every day. It's all rather tiring and wearing at times, but the countryside is pretty, the girls are good-natured, the food is good and the bathwater hot and – I really couldn't ask for more.

Please write again soon and tell me more of the goings on at Ravenscar and how the clan are doing. Thank you for news of Evvy – I'm not surprised at all that she got that cushy number painting propaganda posters for travelling exhibitions. She always was one to find the spot in the sun. I'm sure you miss her being all the way down in London, but at least she isn't in France. All we hear from there is bad news, so it's good to know she got out in time. I'm glad Connie and Twins are back at school and safe there. I am quite safe here too, Mummy, don't you worry. Tired and worn out, but safe. Could you send me more thermals and a hot-water bottle? The nights are nithering *here, as Nancy would say. Thank you, dearest.*

Much love always,
Grace

Chapter 3

February 1940

'So, let's take stock of who has already left my employ and who remains. I'll make a list. Women first, then men.'

Rosina sat in the servants' hall at the long table where the staff ate their meals each day. She remembered coming in here six months before on the morning of the Prime Minister's announcement, which felt like aeons ago now. After the drama of that moment, life had not changed much for Rosina, at least initially. There was much talk of gas and invasion to begin with, but this soon faded and people gossiped more about the war perhaps being a flash in the pan and it would all be over soon. But it was not and the most obvious effect on Rosina's life was the gradual depletion of her staff from the Hall. One by one, they had joined up or gone back home to family or left to contribute to some other part of the war effort. This table would usually be filled by the Hall's staff, but now so many had gone that she imagined it must be quite a lonely affair at mealtimes for the cook, Mrs Bairstow, who she now sat opposite.

'Well, head parlourmaid left this morning, as tha know, and has gone off to factory work. Head housemaid yesterday to join t'WAAF and kitchen maid went months ago to join t'Wrens along with t'housekeeper, of course, whose post I've been covering, as well as my own.'

Mrs Bairstow sighed and Rosina looked up at her. Though they called her Mrs, she had never married, wedded only to her job and Raven Hall. She was a small, wiry woman, fiercely hardworking and utterly capable. When the housekeeper had left to join the Wrens it had been a shock. Given her age of thirty, Rosina had not thought the housekeeper would be going anywhere soon, but off she went, soon after Nancy. Perhaps she saw excitement in such a life, after being cooped up here in domestic service. This, it seemed, was happening all over the country now. Not only were the men now conscripted, although the women had not been officially called up as yet, many were joining up of their own volition, as Grace had done.

'And a marvellous job you've been doing of both, I must say,' said Rosina, smiling at Mrs Bairstow, who gave a small smile in return, not entirely convinced. *But I don't doubt she welcomes the extra pay*, thought Rosina.

'Thank you for that,' said Mrs Bairstow, then continued

with the list of male bolters from Raven Hall. 'Butler, estate manager, footman and both grooms left with t'King's Own. Both under-gardeners and chauffeur gone with t'Navy. Mr Jessop will be quite on his own now in that huge garden.'

The list of staff now swallowed up by the war was starkly depressing when Rosina heard it all in a row like that.

'Yes, I'm going to talk to Jessop tomorrow morning about all this. I have a few ideas about the garden, how we can make it useful. And, as far as grooms go, I'll be selling some of the horses and keeping only two, so we should manage with the Head Groom who has his game leg keeping him out of war work, bless his heart for his sacrifice in the last war. He's done enough. And it's lucky my father taught me to drive, so as and when we need it, I can use the car we've kept, now the chauffeur has gone.'

'And t'maids? How will we manage with most of 'em gone now?'

'I've had a think about that. I think we'll probably need to hire dailies.'

'Dailies are more likely to be had. There might well be women hereabouts with bairns that'll need a bit of extra. We really need help with t'laundry and general cleaning duties. It's not only daily things, it's bigger jobs like washing stonework, wax polishing t'woodwork and oiling window frames. All these jobs take time.'

'Yes indeed, so let's hope you're right about the local

women needing a bit of extra money coming in. It seems staff are less keen to live in now. But it's still worth putting out an advertisement for live-ins and see what happens.'

'Yes, worth a go. In t'advert, tha should probably shine it up a bit by saying it's in a safe area, away from t'ports and other targets for Jerry. I hear people are looking out for that in a new job. And say "help" or "assistant", rather than maid or servant. It's t'new way of things, folk getting uppity about domestic service. They like new words for old things.'

She was a smart one, Mrs Bairstow. Sharp as a tack. Rosina put pen to paper. 'How about something like this? "Domestic assistants sought. All duties, help given. Comfortable home. Live-in or out. Country house. Safe area. Convenient access to railway station at Ravenscar. Between Scarborough and Whitby."'

'That should do it. I'll put t'word out locally to see if any women are interested. But t'fact is, factory work and suchlike is more appealing, as t'hours are shorter and more regular and they're given more free time. And t'pay can't compare. I heard factory girls in Scarborough are on a pound a week, not a pound a month, like a maid earns.'

'Yes, I see that. And I understand it. And with these young women, seeing their sweethearts and brothers and even fathers going off to war, they want to do their bit for Britain too.'

'They do. Parlourmaid said before she left, "Why don't

they give t'girls guns too and we can go and fight with our men?" Daft as a brush, that one.'

Rosina thought of her father shooting pheasants and how she'd discontinued the practice once she took over the Hall. Seeing those limp, lifeless birds smeared with blood always made her feel sick. But she could see that young people would feel like that towards the enemy. She didn't feel murderous towards them, just sad; sad that they were all in this position again, only two decades after the last bloodbath.

'Well, her heart is in the right place, I suppose. Defending her country. We're all doing our best. Right, I'll put the advert in and we'll see what turns up.'

Mrs Bairstow went on, 'But even if we do manage to get a woman in, it'll still be a struggle getting all t'jobs done, I won't lie to thee, ma'am. Right now we still have one young maid here doing dusting and laundry and so forth. Wun't it be a good idea to get a daily in to do heavy work and let t'young maid do front-of-house sometimes, do parlourmaid jobs of answering t'door and telephone and house bells, taking tea to t'drawing room and serving dinner at night? She's only young, tha see, and I think she's struggling with t'laundry on top of all t'other jobs.'

'Well, I've been thinking about this. All those front-of-house jobs you mention – I want to do away with them. I really don't need anyone to answer the door or any of those other jobs. And let's cut down on dusting by putting dust sheets on the furniture in all the girls' rooms while they're away, as well as the guest rooms and other unused spaces. We must also ensure that all rooms get a good airing regularly, as well as fires lit from time to time to keep damp at bay. The last thing we need at Raven Hall is dry rot.'

'All good ideas, ma'am. And before he went, t'butler told me some folk in big houses have sent off all their ornamental silver to be lacquered, which saves hours weekly on polishing.'

'Oh, that *is* a good idea. Yes, I'll arrange that. And I want you to know, Bairstow, that I have every intention of pitching in and helping with the housework.'

Mrs Bairstow frowned. 'Oh, I don't think that's right, ma'am.'

Rosina knew that her cook-housekeeper was the old sort, defined by tradition and knowing one's place.

'I know it sounds odd, but the times are changing and so must we. I will help with a range of duties. I've made a list here, look. Dusting, the polishing of all brasses and changing bed linen, which we'll do less often; we'll also launder things less often, especially table linen. I'll eat on a tray in the lounge from now on. To be honest, it will be a relief not to have to dress for dinner!'

Mrs Bairstow raised her eyebrows. 'Does tha know how to polish brasses, ma'am? Tha know it's not just t'fenders, but t'coal scuttle and other items, not to mention all t'doorknobs?'

'I'm sure the maid can teach me. And I want to learn other things too, from you, Bairstow. I would like to know how to cook some simple meals, so you can have weekends off. Now, I know what that look on your face means: you don't like all this. But needs must. And you are doing two jobs now and you're looking too tired for my liking. So I want to be able to cook for myself at weekends and for the girls when they are home from school or wherever and I'll be rounding them up to pitch in too when they're here. I fear teaching me to cook will be quite the task, I'm afraid, because I know little more about cooking than the odd glance I've given over the last twenty years or so to *Mrs Beeton's Book of Household Management* which, as you know, has been sitting on a shelf in the kitchen since my wedding. But I am determined to learn, if you will be so good as to teach me.'

Mrs Bairstow nodded. 'Thi mother would be proud of thee.'

Rosina took a sharp intake of breath. Mention of her mother made her eyes well up and she opened them wide and blinked to try to clear them. 'Oh, I don't know about that.'

'Well, I do, ma'am. She were a gem of a woman, thi mother. And she loved thee to distraction. And she were

53

always a queen with us staff and spoke to me like an equal, rather than a very young cook, as I was when she passed. And we spoke often. I do believe she got on better with me than with t'housekeeper she had back then. And when she were ill I told her I'd do all I could to look out for thee and so I shall. And if me teaching thee to cook is what tha want, then that's what we shall do.'

'Thank you, Bairstow,' said Rosina, still moved. It was wonderful to hear those little gems about Mama. Rosina had always tried to model herself on her mother, on her kind and gracious ways in particular. Even when the cancer ravaged her with pain, Mama had still said please and thank you to everyone that helped her in any small way. A marvel of a woman, really, and Rosina still missed her, over twenty-five years on. 'Thank you very much for that. And one more thing: I'd like to help with the washing-up too.'

Mrs Bairstow shook her head violently. 'Oh no, I draw t'line at that. A lady must never have a charwoman's hands.'

'Well, this lady doesn't care and wants to help. So you must let me.'

'I'll get t'maid to come and see thee later, show thee about t'brasses and so forth. Leave t'rest to me for now.'

'Thank you,' said Rosina and brushed a tear away from her eye. She was surprised at how emotional she'd become at the mention of her mother. Till now she had not felt she'd done anything to be particularly proud of, except

54

make a pretty good job of raising five daughters. Yes, that was a huge achievement for anyone, especially alone as she had been. And just last month, she'd also joined the local Women's Institute and helped to organise a dance in aid of the Nursing Association, with music played by the local quintet, and it had been rather a lovely evening.

But more was being asked of her now, more was being asked of everyone. And it was bringing people together, with their shared privations of utility clothing, rationing and petrol shortages. The separate worlds of upstairs and downstairs were shifting into one and, Rosina thought now, it was not entirely unwelcome.

She spent the rest of the afternoon with the maid, Sheila, learning how to polish brass and copper, also making a list of all the items in the house that would need it and how often. Then she asked Sheila to show her how to put up the blackout curtains, as she had decided this should be her daily task from now on. As it was February, this job had to be done before dinner due to the early sunset, so she went round and finished it herself while her tummy was rumbling. Every time she went through a door and looked at the shine on the handles she felt useful. She then had her dinner in the lounge as she'd requested and enjoyed it very much, propping a book on a cushion on the settee beside her and reading as she ate. She liked the informality. She also looked forward to when the girls were home and having them muck in.

Evelyn, in particular, would be good at all that, as she'd lived a bohemian existence since school and had chosen to fend for herself. It would be good for the rather unworldly Grace to learn some domestic skills too, although she guessed her eldest now knew rather a lot about scrubbing floors after her initial Wren training. Rosina looked forward to the time when her girls would be all round the table, serving themselves, not having to watch their conversations as servants came in and out, free to just be themselves and not having to change into smart clothes for dinner. The chaos of it was rather appealing to Rosina, who had lived most of her life amid layers of routine and expectation.

After dinner Rosina went round and turned all the lights off in the rest of the house, keen on saving energy where possible. She left a lamp on in the lounge, though; she was going to sit there for a while and listen to the wireless before bed and do a crossword, perhaps. She was just settling down on the settee when she was startled by a loud knocking on the front door. She put her newspaper down and went out along the corridor to the front hall, meeting the maid there who was pulling on her cap and apron, caught out by the unexpected visitor at this hour.

'Don't worry, Sheila. Remember I said earlier I would answer the door from now on. You go back to your evening and I'll see to this.'

'Yes ma'am. Thank you, ma'am,' said Sheila, looking shocked as more urgent knocking was heard at the door.

Rosina opened it to see a man in a tin hat and armband. It was the Ravenscar Air Raid Precautions Warden, Mr Albert Wigfall, scowling at her.

'Tha's got a light showing! Go and sort it immediately!'

'Surely not?' said Rosina. 'I did them all myself.'

'Well then, tha didn't do a very good job, did thee? It's in that room at t'front, round there. A chink of light, clear as day. Go and see for thissen. I'll wait.'

Rosina nodded at the man and pushed the door to in his officious little face, annoyed by his familiar tone and infuriated to be caught out when she'd done her very best with the blackout and had even gone outside to check all the windows afterwards to ensure she'd done it right. She went back to the lounge and inspected the curtains, to find the thinnest gap, the merest chink between them. Would Hitler's bombers really be able to see this from the skies? And would it definitely draw deadly bombs down upon her house? Whatever she thought of the likelihood of this, she rearranged them as best as she could and came back to the front door to find it open and the man standing impertinently in her hallway! She walked straight past him and out on to the front steps, turning to him and crossing her arms, as a signal for him to follow. He did so, with some slight loss of face, and joined her on the driveway.

'Let's see if tha managed it this time,' he said and led the way to the offending window, scrutinising it, as if his eyes were microscopes. The whole thing seemed ridiculous.

'Satisfied?' said Rosina.

'I am now, aye. I assume thi maids have all left, quite rightly, to take up useful war work. And that's why tha find thissen having to do such menial tasks. But that's no excuse for shoddy work.'

'I wouldn't call it shoddy at all. I bow to your greater knowledge of chinks of light, but when I did it earlier I could see no such thing. It took me a long while to go round doing them all and I tried my very best to do the best job I could.'

'Well, tha'll have to try harder to be up to scratch in future. When I think of all our countrymen in France and thereabouts, suffering under all sorts of horrible conditions and here th'are, t'lady of t'manor, complaining about having to put up a few curtains.'

'Well, I wasn't complaining until—'

But he cut her off. 'Dun't tha know this coastline is a prime target? Why, just along t'cliffs, t'RAF turned up a few days past, bristling with lorries and equipment, building strange constructions along t'coast, with concrete-reinforced huts and erecting aerials and so forth. And tha can bet that passing bombers will find that most inviting and we'll be right in t'firing line, believe me. So, better make sure thi blackout is perfect. And tha's got thi shelter organised. Have tha, then?'

How she wanted to slap the man in the face! But she knew he was doing his job and doing it well, as infuriating as he was.

'Yes, Mr Wigfall, I do have our cellar kitted out for all our staff and myself in case of air raids.' This was true, yet as she thought of it, she realised that in her rather blasé attitude towards the as yet non-existent air raids she had not put much down there for everyone's comfort. And that maybe she should add more provisions in the cellar, such as some nice biscuits and brandy and some tea-making facilities to go along with the chairs and commode behind a screen she'd already had placed down there. 'Now, if there's nothing else, I'd like to get back to my evening, please.'

'Not so fast, Mrs Calvert-Lazenby. There's t'small matter of a fine you'll have to pay. I assume tha can afford it, living in such a place?'

Rosina imagined it gave him much pleasure to hand out the fine to the lady of the big house. She accepted it and said she'd arrange payment of it the very next day. She also thanked him for his sterling service, at which he looked pompous and yet sceptical, assuming she was being sarcastic. And off he went, into the night, doing his duty. She couldn't really reproach him for that, but did he have to be such a bully about it? Perhaps he did. She knew she'd never take her blackout for granted again and would check it far more carefully from now on.

Getting ready for bed that night, she thought about the warden's news of the RAF constructing something along the coast and that did concern her. She'd heard of the forces requisitioning country houses and the owners made to move out to hotels in town or stay with family. She wondered if this would happen to Raven Hall and wondered, too, if she would fear it or welcome it. But actually, the thought of losing her home for the foreseeable future did fill her with dread and she hoped it would never come to that.

As she climbed into bed, Rosina felt alone again. Most of her time was spent enjoying her independence, yet at times it would hit her how very alone she was. But even at moments like these, she never missed her husband. George had been a bully, a spoilt child of a man, although he hadn't started out like that. When she'd first met him, he was full of wit and action, sweeping her off her feet through sheer energy. Everyone called him 'the puppy', as that's how he came into a room, full of jokes and tricks, making everyone laugh and shake their heads. But once he'd charmed her into marrying him, his true colours began to show: the tantrums he threw like a toddler when he didn't get his own way and his awful fits of temper which he referred to as being 'grumpy'. She could never hear that word now without feeling aggrieved.

'Grumpy' was George's euphemism for anger, a deep rage he'd get into when one of his black moods came over him.

And the sex . . . she hadn't known what sex would be like but the man had no interest in it at all. He clambered on top of her as if she were a distasteful chore and lasted for ten minutes, pushing her aside afterwards and sleeping, with not a single soft word or even a peck on the cheek. She knew enough from speaking to female friends (and reading a contraband, unexpurgated copy of Lady Chatterley) that there ought to be more to lovemaking than that. Now she had reached the age of forty-four without ever having had decent sex. When George had died, she remembered thinking that she never had to have sex again as long as she lived and that was a relief. But part of her pondered on why so many songs and novels and poems and films had been made about love and romance, if that was all there was to it. Surely there was more; with another man, maybe she'd find out . . . But she felt old and withered, though her daughters told her she was still so beautiful and looked at least ten years younger.

Yet the thought of being with another man was tinged with the fear of making another bad choice. She had been so blinded by George's charm and the way he'd showered her with love like a rain of incendiary bombs, that she had married him without thought. Then, within months of the wedding, she realised that it was all a dreadful mistake, that he was not the man she thought he was and that now she was pregnant with their first child, there was no escape. Thankfully, he knew that too and absented himself from their lives from then on, her family's money running through his fingers like dry sand.

It was obvious he'd married her for her money and land. He was far more interested in adventuring than in her and the children. But actually, that was quite a relief. Despite the enormous financial cost, it was worth it not to have him there most of the time and she still remembered the tightness in her chest that would come when she heard him barrelling up the drive in a flash car, home from his latest adventure. Even in that big house, she felt she could never be far enough away from him and his death in a skiing accident was a blessed release, though she felt terribly guilty for feeling such a thing, when it had robbed his daughters of their father. She just hoped they all realised how little impact he'd had on their lives, so hopefully they would not feel his absence as they grew older. She knew she had always been everything to them and hoped she would be enough, be both mother and father to them, so they would not go into womanhood feeling a hole at the centre of their lives.

She thought of them now – Grace in Hampshire, Evelyn in London, the girls at school – and suddenly wished with a huge pang that they were all home with her. She'd thought about bringing the girls back from school but, especially now she'd heard about the RAF nearby, she felt that school was the safest place for them, deep in the countryside. She missed them dreadfully these days; in fact, she had always missed them, had never wanted to send them away to school but George had insisted, because it was the 'done' thing. And now her girls were so used to boarding-school life, they probably wouldn't want to be schooled at home, except perhaps for Daisy. So it was better for them to be where they were, really, but Rosina felt sad that she had missed out on so much of their childhoods and this made her feel lonelier still.

'Oh, buck up, for heaven's sake!' she scolded herself as she plumped her pillow, ready for sleep. She had a pillow, a bed to put it on, warm blankets and a lovely house to live in. And a treasure in Mrs Bairstow to help her run it. Whatever moans and niggles she might have, she resolved to sleep knowing she was doing her best, that the girls were doing their best, that the nation was too. But she dreamt of avalanches and woke in the night with the pillow on her face, in a cold sweat. It was hard to be brave alone at the witching hour, however privileged you were, when you were haunted by bad memories and scared of what the future might bring.

Chapter 4

The next morning, Rosina went out of the side door and on to the lawn, feeling the crunch of frost under her feet as she crossed towards the greenhouse. Waiting for her was Mr Jessop, the head gardener of Raven Hall, who had worked there man and boy, joining the gardening team as a child, long before the Great War. As she closed the greenhouse door behind her, she wondered if Mr Jessop could ever have imagined he'd be the only gardener left at the big house, having to take on responsibility for it all, entirely alone. She hoped to allay any fears he might have with her talk this morning, and also wanted to inspire him.

'Jessop, how are you?'

'Well enough, ma'am. Chilly.'

He was a man of few words, carefully chosen.

'Indeed. Now, let's discuss the situation we find ourselves in and see if we can seek some solutions.'

He nodded. His face was lined and weathered, his eyes small and dark yet brightly shrewd.

'I have a plan I've drawn up and would like to share it with you,' she said.

He nodded again.

'See here.' She placed her notebook on the potting bench and Mr Jessop peered down at it.

'Do I need my specs?' he said.

'No, not really. I can explain it. So, my idea is this. I think we should now start running this place as a market garden. We turn the suitable garden areas and greenhouses over to the production of vegetables and we sell them to local villagers. I'd bet that others might come from further afield to buy them too. And we might even have a customer in the RAF, as I hear they're setting up in the area as we speak. So, no more houseplants and flowers in the greenhouses, only vegetables. And no more luxuries like asparagus. We'll replace them with potatoes and turnips and other essential vegetables. What do you say, Jessop? Can it be done?'

He was frowning and staring at her notebook, even though without his reading glasses she knew he would be able to see nothing of note.

'I'd need help,' he said.

'Of course. I was thinking of canvassing all the local farmers and seeing if they had daughters or sons below

66

conscription age who might want a bit of extra work. Maybe we might get a girl from the Women's Land Army, if we're permitted.'

Mr Jessop let out a long sigh and Rosina wondered if he disliked the idea of girls working in his garden, as he saw it. But then he said, 'Girls would be good. They work harder.'

And she remembered that Mr Jessop had three daughters, all long grown up and gone out into the world. 'Good,' she said. 'I'll look into that.'

'There is a boy. Evacuee. Staying at t'farm yonder,' he said with a vague gesture westwards. 'Mrs Bairstow's cousin's boy or summat from Hull. He's always skulking about.'

'Sounds like he could do with something to keep him occupied,' said Rosina with a half-smile.

Mr Jessop looked up and her and his eyes creased slightly, the closest he usually got to a smile. 'Aye, 'appen he does.'

'Good. We're in agreement, then?'

'Aye. And Mrs Jessop will pitch in too, when she can.'

'Splendid. Ah, and one more thing: I'm thinking of keeping chickens. What do you say to that?'

'Ugly, bad-tempered creatures. But useful.'

'And what say you to a cow?'

'I wun't say nowt to a cow. They're not known for conversing.'

Rosina couldn't help but laugh at that and Mr Jessop's eyes crinkled again.

'Could we keep one for milking, do you think?'

'If ma'am will milk it.'

'I shall, if one of the farmers shows me how.'

'Mrs Jessop'll show thee.'

'I'd be much obliged to her,' said Rosina.

'Tha might recall, we had cows here during t'last war.'

'Yes, I do remember that. I loved the sound of them.'

'They were nice beasts. Did tha know that in t'last war, in some of t'big houses, all of t'gardeners were lost and t'gardens went to seed and have never been rescued? All overgrown still now, with vines growing through t'greenhouse rooves and so forth, husks of their former selves.'

Rosina had never heard Mr Jessop speak so many words in a row at once.

'That will never happen here, Jessop. Not on my watch.'

'Nor mine, ma'am,' he replied, and there was that crinkle at the corner of his eyes again.

Rosina felt they understood each other perfectly.

'Splendid. So, if you'd be so good as to make a list of the seeds and equipment you'll need, with ordering details and costings, we'll get started as soon as we can.'

'Aye ma'am,' said Jessop, adjusting his cap, looking ready for action, as much as he could, with his face as expressive as a wall.

'Thank you, Jessop.'

Rosina picked up her notebook and left the greenhouse.

Mention of the Great War had brought a shadow across her morning, as it always did. For her two elder brothers – Basil and Douglas – had been lost to it. Such bright flames of life they both had, quenched by war. It had crushed her father so soon after the loss of his wife to cancer and he had turned to the drink that would later destroy him with liver disease. And after the deaths of her silly, funny, brilliant brothers on the battlefields of Flanders, Rosina had become the sole heir to Raven Hall, something which she had never expected or desired. In fact, she had wanted to run away to France (as Evelyn had done more recently), become a nurse and marry a brave officer. But she'd stayed, tried to console her inconsolable father – and when she met George, had to listen to her father's endless lectures about how George's family weren't good enough and he was only after her money. But, little fool as she was then, or at least she saw herself that way, she did not listen to her father and convinced herself that George was the love of her life, had ended up marrying that cad as a paltry rebellion against her father. She shook her head to rid herself of memories of her dear brothers, their untimely deaths too frightening to think upon in these dangerous times, especially with two of her own flock away from home and in the thick of it. Grace might be safe now in Hampshire, but what if the Navy posted her somewhere dangerous? And Evelyn in London. Surely it would be a target at some point, if not now then soon, very soon? She really must insist Evelyn come home. She could do with the help. Consumed by her thoughts, she stared at her shoes as she walked up the path and glimpsed another set of feet in the corner of her eye, which turned swiftly and trotted away. She looked up to see a boy running down the path towards the battlements.

'I say!' she called.

He stopped and turned, looking for all the world as if he'd been caught committing a dreadful crime.

'Are you Mrs Bairstow's relation? The evacuee?'

The boy nodded and Rosina walked up to him. He looked to be about ten years old or so, perhaps older but small for his age, his brown hair a bit too long over the ears and unkempt. It needed a cut, a mother's care, which Rosina supposed he did not have here, being away from home.

'What's your name, then?'

'Ronald Holt,' he said, his accent from the East Riding, rather than hereabouts. Then she remembered that Jessop had said he was from Hull.

'You shouldn't really be hanging about these grounds, Ronald. You're supposed to be staying at a farm, aren't you?'

He nodded again, looking terrified.

'Now look, it's all right. I'm the lady of the house, Mrs Calvert-Lazenby. But if you like it here, maybe you could make yourself useful. Would you like something to do when you're not at school?'

The boy nodded emphatically.

'Well then, you see that greenhouse over there? In there is Mr Jessop, my head gardener. He has lots of jobs that need doing because we're going to dig for victory. Would you like to help your country?'

The boy nodded again, this time so violently that he looked somewhat dazed afterwards.

'Good boy. And there will be a few pennies in it for you. I always pay my employees well.'

At this, Ronald Holt grinned, the smile changing his face completely. It was a charming smile.

'Off you go then. Mr Jessop is expecting you.'

Ronald ran off up the path without another word; in fact, the only words he'd actually said were his name, so a shy boy, but clearly eager. She was glad to think of Jessop having a helping hand. She'd read in the paper that the Women's Farm and Gardens Association were going to apprentice women to work under head gardeners for a few months before taking on the duties of under-gardener. She would write to them, as well as visit the local farmers to see about their older children too. Rosina smiled; she felt she was making real progress. And it was nice to see a child running about the Raven Hall grounds. It all felt so empty here without the girls and with so many of the servants gone. She liked the idea of a gang of young people working about the place. It would really cheer things up.

Youth had that effect.

She turned on to the lawn to cross it to the house, her mind filled with all the clerical jobs she'd set herself, as well as her cleaning duties for the day, so she did not see the young man standing at the end of the driveway, watching her, as she stepped off the frost-crisped lawn. She was only alerted to his presence when he started walking towards her and, hearing his unfamiliar footsteps, looked up.

He was RAF personnel of some sort, dressed as he was in the customary blue tunic, belted at the waist, blue trousers and blue forage cap, shirt and tie. She could see his hair was blond beneath his cap, really yellow and he was young, somewhere in his twenties. His face was more like a sculpture than human, with high cheekbones and a sharp jawline. Yet his expression was soft, almost amused, as he sauntered towards her. He did not have a military air, more the gait of a young man taking a pensive stroll on a Sunday afternoon. Rosina was so surprised to see this figure materialise here before her house, she did not speak at first, staring at him as if he'd stepped out of the very air.

'Morning,' he said, his voice not local. It had a softness to it, something of the West Country about it, she thought.

'Good morning,' she replied, then remembered Mr Wigfall's words about the RAF arriving along the coast. 'Oh, heavens, you're not here to turf me out, are you?'

She hadn't meant to say it, just think it, but it came out

anyway. He laughed and replied, 'Goodness, no. Whatever gave you that idea?'

She could hear now that his voice was educated, still with that soft edge, so he had clearly been sent away to school, as her daughters had.

'I've heard about requisitioning and thought maybe my time had come.'

'Well, not from me. I'm here about something else. Please, let me introduce myself. Sergeant Harry Woodvine.'

He held out his hand and she took her notebook in her other hand and stepped forward to shake his. He had a firm, dry grip and smiling eyes.

'Rosina Calvert-Lazenby.'

'Thought so. I'm here with a team that's working down the coast a bit. We're staying in wooden huts near the site and going to Mill Farm for laundry and meals, but the old couple there fell ill and so we need a new partial base for my men and myself, to use the facilities. We were told about Raven Hall and your name came up. I like a bit of a walk, so I came along the coastal path and here you are. It's a beautiful house, by the way. Quite extraordinary, the battlements there.'

'Thank you. Well, of course, we'll help in any way we can.'

'We'll come for breakfast each day and we'll require a packed lunch of some sort. Then we'll be back for dinner. And laundry once a week or so.'

Heavens, she thought. *That's a lot of food and extra work for Bairstow, the maid and me.* Of course, you had to say yes to these things – it was all part of doing your bit. But the thought of it all alarmed her at first.

'Will you need to sleep here too?'

'Goodness, no. We've got our digs back on site.'

'What are you building there?' she said, then immediately realised her mistake. It was very likely some kind of military secret and she was embarrassed she'd asked. She'd seen the posters like everyone else: Careless Talk Costs Lives and so forth. He didn't reply, just smiled at her. *Such a nice face*, she thought, *intelligent and kind*. Then she added, 'Please forget I asked that. Stupid, foolish question.'

'Well, it used to be normal to ask such things. It's about getting out of the habit, I suppose, stifling natural curiosity. So, could we start coming this evening, if that's not too much trouble?'

'Of course, whatever you need. How many of you are there?'

'Six of us altogether. Sometimes more men will come from elsewhere so there might be twelve or so on occasion, but mostly it will be just the six. And the RAF will foot the bill. Here, I've got our ration cards for you so that you can purchase supplies.' He handed them over and she slotted them inside her notebook. She might have to make a trip to Robin Hood's Bay to buy more supplies for this lot, she thought; the local shop might not have enough. Or perhaps Mrs Bairstow would commandeer the task.

'Of course. How long will you be here for?' At this, again he smiled.

'I see,' Rosina said. 'Well, no more questions. Forgive me.'

He stepped closer and she could see he had large eyes of a kind of cornflower blue, her favourite colour. 'There's nothing to forgive. It's a strange time for us all, isn't it? Having to learn new ways of being.'

'Yes,' she said quietly and stared at him. Then he held out his hand again and she shook it.

'Jolly good. I'll be off then. See you tonight, about five-ish, I suspect. We'll be in a van. All right to park it here, before the front door?'

'Yes, of course. Do you . . . want something to eat now? To take with you?'

He hesitated and felt in his pocket, pulling out an apple. 'Well, I have this for the walk back. But I'll be honest, since the couple at the farm have been poorly, we've been fending for ourselves and we're terrible cooks. Breakfast has been a haphazard affair to say the least.'

'Well, I'm sure I can rustle up a jam sandwich, if that will do.'

'That will be *proper jam*,' he said.

'Oh yes, it is proper jam. My cook makes it every year. Gooseberry, plum, summer berries.'

He laughed and she looked at him quizzically. He shook his head. 'It's a saying, from my old stomping ground. I come from Shropshire. When something is rather marvellous, we call it *proper jam*.'

'What a lovely idiom,' she said. 'I've never been to Shropshire. Indeed, I'm not even sure I know where it is.'

'That's what most people say. It's next door to Wales, if that helps.'

'Well, I know where *that* is. I'm not a complete ignoramus.'

'I'm sure you're not anywhere near such a thing,' he said and pushed his hands into his pockets, smiling at her and tipping back slightly on his heels. She stared at him again, distracted.

'Uh . . . so yes . . . a *proper jam* jam sandwich. Please, follow me, Sergeant Woodvine.'

She went into the house and he followed her. It was a while since she'd had a visitor here. Friends had come for bridge or dinner and drinks in the days before the war began, but since then she'd noticed that people had begun to hibernate somewhat. Friends had gone quiet, worried about the changes in their own lives, in their country and the world. There was a collective anxiety hovering behind every one of them. They had not been invaded, but it could be on the horizon and the fact of it was a shadow that lay across them all. Some were galvanised into action by it, to fight off the darkness, while others were paralysed by it.

As they turned right to go down the hallway past the ballroom, he said, 'I feel this place must have a fascinating history . . . am I right?'

'You are indeed,' she said, slowing her pace and turning to him, so they walked side by side. She knew the long history of her home very well and was accustomed to telling it. 'The house was built in 1774 and, when they were digging the foundations, they found a Roman stone showing there was a fort here once. There used to be an alum works along there, often raided by pirates from the continent. A captain was the first owner of the house and later it became an asylum. They say King George the Third and the Queen of Portugal both stayed here at different times. In 1820, the owner had the mock battlements built to surround the grounds and twenty years later, the same owner, a gambling man, lost the house in a bet involving a race of two woodlice across a saucer.'

Sergeant Woodvine laughed. 'How extraordinary!'

'Yes, it's my favourite part of the story! The new owner built the local church and a railway tunnel, which was too damp and difficult for trains to get up first time. They often had to reverse back and build up enough steam to try again. *That* owner was my grandfather. He nearly lost the house at that time, due to spending far too much on the railway tunnel, which was only built so as not to spoil the view. But some investments came good and my family kept the estate and it flourished. And now here I am, trying to keep it all together.'

'What a marvellous history. Is it just you then these days? It's awfully quiet.'

Rosina felt her cheeks go hot, though she wasn't sure why. She knew it wasn't meant as an insult, but somehow she felt embarrassed her home was so empty of life, as if it were a personal failure.

Sergeant Woodvine added, 'Gosh, I *am* sorry. It's my turn to feel I've asked a stupid question now. Please accept my apology. I am an awful nosy parker.'

'Not at all. It's a fair observation and it's true. My husband died a few years ago now and my daughters are either away with the war or at school. Most of the servants have left so we do find ourselves a quiet and rather lonely place just now.'

Why did she say lonely? She didn't mean to say it. And it wasn't even true. But then her cheeks felt warm again and she realised it must be. Yet this was the last person she should ever tell about it, some random, young, handsome serviceman, probably twenty years her junior. Ridiculous behaviour.

'Well, all that will change from tonight. You're about to be invaded and I'm afraid you'll be rather yearning for that quietude with six or more engineers in your house every day, morning and night.'

They'd reached the kitchen by this point and Rosina introduced him to a surprised Mrs Bairstow who took the ration books and assured them both that she'd take care of everything; in fact, she'd get off straight away to the shops and sort out extra provisions now, if Mr Jessop could take the car and drive her there, due to it being too much for her to carry back on her own.

'Of course,' said Rosina and off Mrs Bairstow went. Rosina had been worried that her cook-housekeeper would feel put upon to receive such guests, but she seemed all a-flutter and genuinely glad to help. Maybe it would make Mrs Bairstow feel part of the action or maybe it was just nice to have people to serve again, what with all the girls away and so many of the staff gone.

Rosina took Sergeant Woodvine to the servants' hall and he sat down at the table while she went back to the kitchen. She might not be able to cook as yet, but she knew where the bread, butter and jam were because she sometimes crept down late at night when she felt hungry in the early hours on those nights she couldn't sleep and bread and jam always did the trick. Now she used far too much butter on the bread, much more than she would usually do, considering the meagre rations, and spread the precious, jewelled plum jam on the bread far thicker than normal too. Somehow, she wanted to treat this young man, living in a wooden hut with only an apple to keep him going.

She came through with the sandwich to find him standing by the window, staring out at the grounds. He turned and the thin February sunshine lit up his face.

'This place is like something from a fairy tale,' he said, then took the sandwich from her and thanked her. He took a great bite out of it, and, still standing up, wolfed it down, crumbs dropping on to his front, which he brushed away with long, slim fingers.

Rosina stood beside him. 'How so?'

'Something about it is mysterious.' He took another bite and wiped his mouth with the back of his hand. There was a smear of red jam on his cheek.

'Not really. It's just an old house and grounds, a bit neglected and unkempt. A bit forlorn.'

'I totally disagree,' he said and shoved the last bit of the sandwich in his mouth. When he had finished chewing, he looked at her directly and said, 'It's beautiful. And it's full of secrets.'

Chapter 5

March 1940

The gruelling Morse code practice continued, listening over and over to patterns and writing them down as fast as they could. Grace was now up to twenty-two words per minute and Nancy was at twenty-four. But still this wasn't good enough. One afternoon, Grace was called out of the lecture room and presented to a Commander from the Admiralty who looked at her the same way she'd look at the cockroaches in the kitchen.

'During yesterday's transmissions you made nine errors. It simply won't do. The Navy requires total accuracy. Absolutely one hundred per cent. Buck up or you'll be out.'

With that, he dismissed her and Grace sloped back to the lecture room with a black cloud over her head. Nine errors felt catastrophic. She must have been the worst in the class. But as she sat down she saw others who'd been called out coming back with miserable faces. Even Nancy was called out. After class, she asked Nancy what had been said to her.

'Two errors yesterday,' her friend said, 'and it i'n't good enough. He said that I'd be thrown out if I carried on that way.'

'*Two*? Mine was nine!'

Nancy grinned. 'I reckon they're saying t'same to all of us then. Putting t'fear of God in us, so we won't mess things up.'

Along with Morse, they were now being given dictation classes, so they could improve their handwriting speed while keeping it legible. Sometimes senior officers from the Admiralty would again turn up and scrutinise their handwriting with a magnifying glass, chiding those whose script was not clear enough. So, the pressure was weighing on them all. The hours of training and lectures were beginning to become a strain.

What was needed was some light relief and, luckily, the local church committee came to their rescue by informing the Wrennery that they were putting on a dance at the church hall that weekend. Their studies had been so rigorous these past weeks that none of the Wrens had ventured out in the evenings, only having the odd expedition on their day off. After dinner, there was chatting in the bunks and then most were asleep 'early doors', as Nancy put it, so exhausted were they. So this local dance was a welcome distraction and the first time the whole cohort would go out en masse. Well, most of them; some had declined and were staying back at the Wrennery, including Lucinda and her clique – she had declared that she wouldn't be seen dead at such a paltry little venue. Grace had been planning to stay away from the dance too, until she heard Lucinda wasn't going. She hadn't been to many dances at Oxford and had attended none during initial training. She was too shy and at five feet nine assumed from her few previous experiences that all the men would avoid her and she'd be a wallflower. She had acute social anxiety and couldn't imagine that she'd ever be picked to dance, had hated standing at the side, being passed over by man after man, so in recent times she simply never went to dances. She had, however, learnt the modern dances at home with her sisters or university pals, dancing to the wireless or gramophone and thought she was actually quite good at them, but she had never practised them with a real, live man. So when Nancy asked her what she was going to wear to the dance, Grace had hummed and hawed about going and Nancy scolded her. This was their chance for a bit of fun, Nancy had said and added that if Grace wasn't going, then Nancy wouldn't either. So, Grace agreed to go, as long as Nancy stuck with her for a bit at the beginning, which Nancy promised she would.

Now, as they stood picking out their clothes and getting

ready, Grace was starting to feel horribly nervous. She looked at Nancy's pretty dress with its daisy print that hugged her lovely figure in all the right places. Grace picked out a white satin blouse and green skirt, the smartest thing she had with her. She really must ask Mummy to send some of her nicer things, she thought, if dances were going to be a regular thing. But there had not been enough time, so this would have to do. It did at least accentuate her waist and, if she tucked the blouse in properly, her bust did look quite shapely under it. But what to do with her hair or face? She had no idea, so she turned to her friend.

'Can you help me do something with . . . this?' She gestured vaguely at her head. Nancy's hair was pinned back in lovely, big, loose curls – natural curls; she didn't even need curlers or rags to get them but Grace's hair was dead straight. She had had it cut to shoulder-length when she joined the Wrens and she did wet it each night and pin it up to create some curls, but almost always she ended up just pulling it into a tight bun because she never knew how to style it properly. The night before Nancy had encouraged Grace to pin her curls in a different style, which she'd helped with. Now, Nancy brushed them out and grabbed one of her large blusher brushes, wrapping sections of hair around the handle to make large curls, then pinned these into shape on the top of Grace's head. At the sides, she rolled the hair into sausage shapes which she pinned at the nape of Grace's neck, then she took a navy ribbon from her sewing bag and tied it around the remainder of the long hair to form a low ponytail. She then tucked the end of the ponytail up underneath and secured it with pins.

Grace could feel all this happening, but had no idea how the finished look would be and she felt herself prickling with sweat at the thought of her hair being pinned back from her face when she was going to be seen by eligible men. She had seen Evvy create such masterpieces on herself, but had never felt confident enough to sport such a style herself. Of course, she had to wear her hair pinned back as a Wren at work, but if she had her choice she would have always left hers down to hang like curtains, behind which she could shield herself from the world.

Nancy passed Grace a hand mirror and she held it up with trepidation – and then she saw herself. It looked absolutely smashing! It seemed to change the whole shape of her face. She realised she had a nice, oval face with a curved jawline that was shown off perfectly by the hairstyle. It was so long since she had studied herself in a mirror and she thought she looked very different. In fact, she looked pretty.

'Well? Don't keep me on tenterhooks,' said Nancy. 'Love it or hate it?'

'I *adore* it. You are now my official stylist! What about

make-up? I never wear it, but I suppose one should to a dance.'

'Well, tha's lucky. Tha's got perfect skin. An English rose, as my mam used to say about colouring like yours. So tha don't really need foundation or powder, but I can put a bit on if tha want it.'

'No thanks,' said Grace, turning up her nose. 'I don't like the idea of it all over my face.'

'I'll just do a little touch here and there. Trust me,' said Nancy. And Grace did trust her, absolutely. She examined Nancy's own flawless make-up as Nancy's face was so close to hers while she pencilled Grace's eyebrows and put a smudge of eye shadow on and a lick of mascara. It was all very quick and light, as Nancy had said, Grace didn't need much. Then came the precious lipstick. All make-up was in short supply and Grace had none so thanked Nancy several times for letting her use hers. Nancy taught Grace how to apply the red lipstick just right to get a nice shape to the lips.

'We can do it like Joan Crawford if tha like, use a pencil to make thi lips bigger. But actually, tha've lovely full lips just as they are, so I think it'll do nicely. Here, have a look.'

Grace took the mirror again and was amazed at the visage that stared back at her. She looked like a glamorous film star – much better, she thought, than Joan Crawford, who Grace had always thought had a vicious face. She could not stop staring at herself, then felt her eyes fill with tears of joy.

'Oh no! Don't weep, for heaven's sake!' cried Nancy, laughing. 'Tha'll ruin it!'

Grace laughed too and stood up and hugged her friend.

'Ready then?' said Nancy with a wink. Grace glanced round at the other girls getting ready to go and felt that she matched up to them in glamour. She had never felt like this before.

'Nancy, thank you so much! You're so kind to me and generous with your skills. I wonder if I can repay it somehow?'

'Ah, that's just being friends, flower. That's what lasses do.'

'Oh, I know. But how about this? I know you love learning and reading. Perhaps I could tell you some more stories from the Greek myths sometime and we could discuss them. I could even ask Mummy to send some of my books from home for you.'

'Oh, that would be grand,' said Nancy, beaming a smile.

If only she had met Nancy years before! But she realised immediately that even if she had, they would never have been able to sit together as equals like this and learn beauty tips or tales from the Classics. War had levelled the ground between them and again Grace found herself strangely grateful for this fortunate side effect of the harsh fact of war.

'Heavens above, what a sight!' came a snide voice and Grace knew exactly who it belonged to. 'Look at these two! The local and the yokel!'

And there was Lucinda, her little gang about her, looking Grace and Nancy up and down as if their appearance were ridiculous. Grace froze, her usual feelings of gracelessness flooding back. What was wrong with the way she looked? She remembered hearing Bairstow once call a local woman who dressed rather young for her advanced age 'mutton dressed as lamb'. Is that what Grace was now? Did she look stupid with this lipstick on, her hair all done up? Were her clothes out of date, out of fashion? But even if she did look stupid, even if Lucinda and her pals were laughing at her, Grace knew that Nancy looked wonderful and had a marvellous eye for the latest fashions, if not the money to afford them. Then, something clicked in Grace's head at that moment and she knew she would not take any more of this from Lucinda or anyone else.

'Oh, do put a sock in it, Lucinda,' said Grace, amazing herself that the words had come out of her mouth. Lucinda turned her furious face to Grace, who swallowed nervously but saw that Nancy's eyes were bright with delight. So she carried on, 'It's so obvious to everyone that you're just jealous of us. You can't stand how well we're doing on the course and how little we care about what *you* think. And, let me add, when it comes to your stupid jibes about where

Nancy and I come from and what we wear, Nancy has every right to be here, more so than you. You're absolutely green with envy of Nancy because she's so clever and pretty and nice. So take your ill-conceived snobbery elsewhere because there's no place for it in the Wrens or in this war.'

A little peal of applause rang out from some of the other girls and Lucinda turned on her heel and stamped back to her bed, throwing herself on it and turning to the wall then grabbing a book she pretended to read. A couple of her coterie went over to her and whispered with her, stroking her arm or hair which she shrugged off. But most of the others turned from her and drifted over towards Grace and Nancy. A couple of them nodded at Grace, as if to say 'well done' then they moved off as a group and left the sulking Lucinda behind.

As they walked through the Wrennery, conversation bubbled up about their day, their lives, their clothes, their families and boyfriends at home or away with the war. Grace was quiet, still astonished at her outburst, at standing up for herself and her friend, something she'd never managed before in all her years of school or university. She'd seen bullying in action – and had suffered from it herself, being nicknamed Graceless at her school for years, a word she now detested as it brought back the humiliating memories. She had never stood up to the bullies, just slunk away and cried in private. Perhaps it was joining the Wrens that had given her this strength, but whatever had given her this new-found confidence, she was grateful for it. And so, it seemed, was Nancy. Grace knew her friend could easily have torn a strip off Lucinda with her clever tongue, but Nancy kept giving Grace knowing little smiles that she knew showed her delight at Grace's defence. She'd been ashamed she'd been so weak at Lucinda's cruel words about Nancy before, but now felt she'd put things right.

And so the chime of Wrens (Grace applied the bird's collective noun to her colleagues) made their way down the lane to the village church hall and, as they reached the doors, there was much excitable chatter about how many men would be there and of what quality. Once inside, Grace looked up, expecting to find herself in some kind of wonderland. Instead, it was a very ordinary church hall, with plank floors and no decorations of any kind. At the far end was a small stage upon which was a table with a gramophone on top. There was no band, only the vicar, sorting through a small pile of records. At one side was a table with jugs of what looked like lemonade on it, next to another table of bread rolls and the air smelt of perfume and mothballs. Chairs lined the other walls and, standing about in clumps, were some elderly men with their wives, a couple of middle-aged Home Guard types here and there and a few younger servicemen in uniform near the stage, but nobody handsome as far as she could see. Everyone in the hall turned and stared at the Wrens as they came in and, their faces fallen at the depressing interior, the girls shuffled off as one to the far side of the hall, away from everyone. They gathered in a huddle and started whispering about how disappointing the male contingent was.

'What a bunch of old gits,' said Nancy which made everyone roar and the rest of the hall stare at them.

Then the gramophone started up and the strains of Victor Sylvester scratchily unfurled, sedate and uninspiring. The older ladies – Grace guessed they were church workers – started waltzing with their elderly husbands and the Wrens went to get some lemonade. The younger servicemen – all in army uniforms – strolled over. There were five of them and the five prettiest girls were picked, including Nancy but not Grace.

'No thanks,' said Nancy and turned away, back to Grace.

Grace watched as the soldier frowned at this rebuttal but he soon recovered and asked another Wren who was delighted to oblige.

'Why did you do that?' said Grace. 'He wasn't exactly Clark Gable, but he looked all right and he was well under forty years of age.'

'I told thee I'd stick with thee at t'start. Once tha's found thi feet, then I might say aye.'

'Oh, but that's not fair on you,' cried Grace but was

dreadfully grateful and thought tears might spring up in her eyes again.

'Oh, aye, it is. Us girls need to stick together. Men are awful!'

They laughed at this and turned round to watch the dancing couples. The church hall door opened and a few more young soldiers came in. These weren't bad-looking at all and went straight to the lemonade table. Nancy and Grace giggled as they heard them complaining there was nothing stronger to drink. Then, after downing a glass each, some looked in their direction and two came over and asked Nancy and Grace to dance.

Grace's was shorter than her. *Just my luck*, thought Grace, as the other soldier had been taller and yet went for Nancy. Well, it was only one dance and maybe he would be nice. His name was Fred, he said, and he was from Essex. The dance was a gentle waltz, which Grace was relieved about; it meant she could concentrate on her conversation with the young man instead of worrying about her feet.

'Sailing round in boats then, you Wrens?'

'Oh no, not at all! We work with wirelesses.'

'Oh. Sounds boring,' he said and then did not speak again. Grace tried to think of something interesting to say, all the while heavily aware of his hand holding her hand and his other hand at her back. But as they danced, he was looking about at other couples and she felt he not only found wirelesses boring, but her too. So she thought she ought to make an effort to make scintillating conversation.

She said, 'Do you know where you're being posted next?'

'Nah. Abroad somewhere.'

More silence.

'Well, they asked us the other day if we had a preference as to where each of us might be posted. My friend Nancy told them Yorkshire, because her father's there and her little brothers and she would like to be close to home to help out when she can. But I said anywhere but Yorkshire! I grew up there, you see, and I want to travel and see the world a bit.'

'Which is Nancy?' he said. 'The pretty one?'

'Yes,' said Grace, and suddenly felt as big and ungainly as a dancing bear.

'You don't sound like yer from Yorkshire. You sound posh.'

'Well, yes, I suppose I must. I went to boarding school from an early age.'

He made no reply to this and they continued dancing steadily without a word.

Throw me a bone, thought Grace, but then thankfully the music came to an end and he said thanks and walked off swiftly. Grace slunk back to the wall, where some of the other Wrens had been standing without a dance since the beginning. *At least I got asked once*, thought Grace and decided that the evening wouldn't be a complete disaster then. But actually Fred came back and asked her to dance three more times, and each time the conversation was stilted and awkward, but he wasn't a bad dancer and suddenly it dawned on her that maybe he wasn't so much bored by her, as nervous. He did try to ask her a few questions about Grace's interests and told her he liked football and also that he collected jazz records, which he knew a lot about. But between dances he went back to stand with his mates and so it was hard to really get to know him. Perhaps she wasn't the only one lacking a bit of confidence around here.

So the evening wore on, with record after record of flat, dreary Victor Sylvester dance music, though there was great excitement when the vicar talked everyone through how to dance the Dashing White Sergeant and everyone joined together in circles, which was all rather jolly. Besides Fred, Grace was asked to dance by two of the elderly husbands, which she did and felt strange holding their papery hands, but at least they were taller than her. They were very good dancers, though, and she enjoyed that. As the evening came to an end, the vicar made a speech about everyone doing their best and reminding all that they must keep coming to church to pray 'for our brave boys across the sea' and so forth and everyone gave a round of applause and she saw Fred do a two-fingered whistle, which she had always admired and wanted to do, but had never learnt how.

Then everyone was filtering out of the hall into the night

and, once outside, she was looking around for Nancy when she felt a tap on her shoulder. She turned round and looked down at Fred, who took her hand and leant in and kissed her right on the lips.

'Wanna give me yer address then? We can write when I'm posted overseas.' He took a scrap of paper and stubby pencil out of his pocket and handed it to her. Still in shock from the utterly unexpected kiss, she wrote out the Raven Hall address – not knowing how long she'd be in Hampshire – and handed it back to him.

'Nice one,' he said and put his arms around her as she stood there stiffly. 'Anuvva kiss?' he said and grinned. Grace had no idea what to say and let him kiss her again, this time feeling something slip between her lips. His tongue darted against her teeth a bit before she found herself pulling away, as one does from an unpleasant smell.

'Yer hair's nice,' he said and grinned. 'And yer mouth.' Then he winked.

'Thank you,' she said, still too shocked to say anything useful.

'I'll be in touch, then. Cheerio.'

'Cheerio,' she said and tried to smile, but it must have come out as a grimace because he gave her a funny look, then turned and went off to find his mates and they all went off together, laughing and shouting about nothing.

'All right, Grace?' said a familiar voice and there was

Nancy at her side.

'That boy kissed me!' said Grace.

'Mm, yes, I saw that. I'd've belted him one. Why didn't tha?'

'I was too amazed! I wasn't sure if he even liked me. And now this! He even asked for my address so he could write to me. Truly, I do not understand men at all.'

'I hope tha gave him Buckingham Palace as thi address!'

'No, I gave him Raven Hall.'

'What on earth did tha do that for?!' cried Nancy and laughed.

'I really don't know. It seemed rude not to.'

'Did tha like him?'

'Not really. Well, he was all right.'

'Tha's mad!' laughed Nancy again. 'And green. Tha really need a lecture about men. Don't worry. I'll take thee in hand. Listen to Auntie Nancy and learn a thing or two about t'male of t'species. But now, let's go to Regal and get summat hot and comforting in our bellies.'

They linked arms and walked to the fish and chip shop with the other Wrens, everyone discussing their evening and the despicable lack of handsome chaps to dance with. It came out that Fred had not only asked for Grace's address but had kissed her too and the others were full of admiration, saying he was one of the best-looking there, despite being a little short. So Grace believed herself a success, despite spending most of the evening feeling like an utter failure.

They all got chips and ate them from the paper packaging whilst walking home, chatting and laughing. The taste of the salty, vinegary, hot chips was marvellous, yet Grace kept thinking about the feel of Fred's tongue in her mouth and how disagreeable it was, the way it had darted about like a little fish. Was all kissing like that? Oh, she hoped not, or she would swear off it for life. It was something to ask Nancy about when they were alone! She couldn't admit to the other Wrens that this was her first kiss. And she was secretly pleased that he'd done it, despite the rudeness of not asking first. And despite the fact it was a bit grim. It wasn't at all how she'd imagined it when watching film stars pressing their closed lips together. But it was a start at least, she supposed.

Back at the Wrennery, she unpinned her hair and brushed it out, sad to see the curls go and her straight, shapeless hair return. But at least now she knew how to style it better and, despite the prosaic surroundings of the church hall, there had been something rather magical about the evening, her first dance where she had actually danced. She told Nancy it was the best evening of her life.

'Oh, just tha wait, lass. That were nowt. The girls are talking about going into Portsmouth when we're on leave, to stay at a hotel and go to a proper ballroom. Are tha game?'

'Oh yes, absolutely!' said Grace, and went to sleep

dreaming of ballrooms and, strangely, aquariums.

There were weekly village dances after that and Grace went to every single one with Nancy. Fred never showed up again but some other fellows did and Grace was kissed by some more chaps who were better at it. Another soldier asked for her address but she knew better this time and wrote a fake one, although afterwards she thought she might have quite liked to have had letters from that one as he was at least well-educated. One night, she let a rather handsome soldier put his hand up her blouse behind the church hall, and another night, one with jet-black hair put his hand up her dress and she pushed it away but then let him caress her thigh, which felt rather marvellous. She was learning a lot and sharing every delicious moment with Nancy back at the Wrennery in their late-night chats.

As the dances went on, however, the servicemen attending them thinned out over the next few weeks and then disappeared completely as they were posted abroad. So the Wrens stopped going to the dances and looked voraciously ahead to their leave, when the famed trip to Portsmouth would take place, or 'going ashore', as the Wrens called going out on the town. Grace missed the weekly excitement of the church hall and the fumblings outside afterwards, but she used the time instead to improve her Morse code and to learn more about men, flirting and sex from the font of all worldly knowledge, Nancy, who shared such invaluable wisdom as, 'Beware flatterers. They want nobbut one thing from thee' and 'if they have a sob story about their childhood, they're usually lying to get thi pity, so tha'll feel sorry for them and let them kiss tha'. These things would never have occurred to Grace, who believed everything she was told, but she began to learn just how gullible she was, how trusting, and how she had to school herself out of this when it came to dealing with the opposite sex. It was all rather perturbing but also addictive and she was restless once they stopped going to the dances. So she eagerly looked forward to their leave when they would go to a proper venue with – hopefully – a better class of men.

It was all planned to happen on the Friday of their next leave. They were being given a long weekend off, not long enough to go back to Yorkshire, but there was definitely plenty of time for a night or two in a Portsmouth hotel and lots of fun on the town. And then, the Thursday before they were due to go, just after lunch, everyone was called in by the nurse to have their inoculations against typhoid. They were told it was nothing and they'd be fine to go back to classes afterwards. Some cheeky Wrens pretended to be ill by putting their heads on the desks and then winking at their neighbours when the kindly Scottish instructor asked if they were ill. Grace smirked at this but didn't dare copy it. Always a good girl at school, she was still one here. But then she did begin to feel unusually tired and thought putting her head down might be quite welcome. Then she felt hot. Then cold. And then incredibly sick. She glanced about her and the whole room looked as if it were underwater. She did put her head down and heard some girls nearby giggle.

'She's just putting it on!' said one.

'Come on, Calvert-Lazenby,' said the instructor in a grumpy voice, though he was usually a kind man.

But she couldn't lift her head, she really couldn't. Someone else said she was pretending, then she heard Nancy's voice close to her ear.

'Are th'all right, lass?'

She tried to speak but her mouth wouldn't open and neither would her eyes. Everything felt like the most tremendous effort.

She heard Nancy again, this time saying, 'She wun't make it up. She's no actress. I think she's really poorly, sir.'

A glass of water was brought and Grace managed to lift her head, to the sound of a room full of gasps.

'Oh, she looks like death!' said someone, as she felt sweat dripping down her face. Grace indeed felt like death; in fact, she found herself inwardly begging for death, as surely it would feel better than this. She was taken back to her bunk, very unsteady on her feet and Nancy sat with her as she slept fitfully. She remembered broth being brought and generally being encouraged to drink water and she woke up at some point in daylight, feeling weak as a newborn kitten. But at least the hot and cold and the nausea had gone. And she could see straight as the room wasn't swimming, at last.

Nancy was beside her, reading a book.

'What day is it?' croaked Grace.

'Tha's alive, then?' said Nancy and smiled. 'It's Saturday, lass.'

'Oh no,' whimpered Grace. 'Portsmouth. The ball. We were going yesterday.'

'It's all right, lass,' said Nancy and stroked Grace's hair, damp from sweat.

'But I missed it, I missed it. And so did you.'

'Hush now. Stop fretting and look around thee.'

Grace did so and saw she was not the only Wren in bed. There were several more, all with other girls sitting beside each bunk, pouring a drink or reading or playing patience with cards on the bedside table.

'Leave has been moved till everyone's better. Going ashore will still happen, so don't tha worry.'

'Oh, thank bloody heavens for that,' whispered Grace and fell back to sleep, thinking that she had wished for death when she first fell ill but now she wanted to live just long enough to go to a ritzy dance in a big ballroom. After that, she would die quite happily, thank you very much.

Chapter 6

Grace and the others soon recovered from their injections and they also had a smallpox one, the result of which was a sore arm and a day or two spent with everyone saying 'My arm!' whenever anyone came near them when exercising or in a crowded space. Lectures went on as usual and then one day they were instructed to report to a different room, in which stood a haughty-looking commander. An absolute silence fell as he introduced himself and began to explain his presence.

'I have to inform you of the true nature of your instruction here and the kind of job you will be called upon to do when you complete your training. You will be working for Y-Branch as Special Operator Intercept Telegraphists, abbreviated to Tels (SO). This entails listening in to enemy ships and naval signals traffic from the Kriegsmarine – that is, the German navy. You will be recording enemy messages that will then be decoded elsewhere. Your station will be called a Y Station. The Y stands phonetically for WI, the acronym for Wireless Intercept. The information you intercept will then be sent on and decoded at another location, Station X. You will be searching the airwaves for all transmissions from German ships and this information will lead to your colleagues hopefully securing the location of said ships, using high-frequency direction finding or HF/DF, about which you will learn in the coming weeks. Once the location of the enemy ship is found, the hope, of course, is that it will be sunk by our chaps. So be in no doubt that your work will have a direct and very real effect upon the enemy and the course of the war. Due to the highly secret nature of your work, you will today be required to sign the Official Secrets Act and never speak or write to a soul of the work you will be doing, either now or in years to come. If the terms of the OSA are breached by you in any way, the punishments are severe, including death.'

As he spoke, the atmosphere in the room grew charged. Nobody moved a muscle or even breathed, it seemed, and Grace felt proud that she and her fellow Wrens would be involved with actions that would have a direct effect upon the enemy, something she had never imagined. The whole point of the Wrens was to free up men to go to sea; their very motto was 'Never At Sea', which had the double meaning that nothing would faze a Wren but also that they would never see active service at sea. Now they knew that their work could sink ships, the war was suddenly at their feet – or, in wireless telegraphy terms, in their ears. Now they knew precisely why their ability to listen to Morse code and transcribe it accurately was crucial and that their job, once this training was completed, was to listen in to messages from the German Navy and relay them to those who would use this information to protect Great Britain from the enemy. It was thrilling to think that all those dits and dahs could one day mean a British life saved.

After the lecture, they were led to another room where they had to queue up in silence to sit at tables and sign the Official Secrets Act. It was a solemn moment. As she took up her pen and was about to sign, Grace momentarily stared at the nib before putting pen to paper, feeling a prickling sensation take over her whole body, at the implications of this work and the secret nature of it. She knew, as they all did, about careless talk costing lives. But now she knew that she would never be able to speak to anyone – not even her family – about the crucial work she was going to do. She would have to lie or simply keep mum, perhaps saying she was a secretary or other harmless profession. This rankled a little but she did not question it. She knew the importance of the necessary confidentiality. It seemed like the kind of spy stuff she'd seen in movies and been thrilled by, yet now it was real and it was her.

She swallowed down her trepidation and signed her name. There, it was done. And everything felt different.

After that day the nature of their training changed too. It was much more focused on the mechanics of the work they would be doing once they left Hampshire. They were told that their job would largely involve sitting for hours before radios, tuning in to different frequencies, searching the airwaves for enemy transmissions. They would have to learn about the disciplined procedures of the German naval wireless stations and the U-boats. They would not understand the coded messages they would then transcribe but they did have to understand the difference between those coded messages and so-called 'operators' chat'. This usually happened immediately before the coded messages were transmitted and consisted of the German Morse code operators discussing things like signal strength.

This chat used something called the international Q code, which Grace and the others would now have to memorise. For example, CQ meant *calling all ships* and R meant *I am receiving you*. Another pile of new information to commit to memory, alongside Morse. From the day the Wrens had signed the OSA, all of their notebooks were taken in every evening for safekeeping. They were told again they must never mention the nature of their training to anyone or be careless with their notes and while they were permitted to keep a diary, they must not record in it any information about their work. They would be allowed to inform friends and family where they were posted, but nothing more. Every night, handing in her notes, Grace would again feel very slightly irked that she was doing such important work and yet the world would never know about it. However, she knew that her duty was not only to do the work and to take pride in it, but also that it was right and proper that she should never be able to boast about it. She must learn to be stoic and silent; just as soldiers and sailors and airmen had to accept the harsh realities of their new work, so must she. They were directly in harm's way, she at least was not, for now. And she taught herself to be mindful of this, whenever she felt annoyed about the secrecy.

Thus, their work intensified and again put strain on their minds. Grace's Classics books had arrived from home, sent by her mother to give to Nancy. But neither of them had much time in the evenings to read or talk about them, as they were so worn out from the day. Most girls went to bed earlier than ever at night through sheer exhaustion and the need for escape clamoured within them all. Thus, when their next long weekend of leave was announced, plans for the Portsmouth trip were instantly revived.

Grace had already written to her mother to ask her to send her best two dresses, from which she'd choose one for the night at the ballroom. When they came, she found that

Navy food had filled her out a bit, but luckily the dresses still fitted and actually they now hugged her figure in the right way. In the past, she'd always gone for clothes that were a little baggy as she found comfort from her shyness in their looseness. She now decided that the best one to wear would be the lovely deep orange one with a sash belt that tied in a pretty bow at the back. She'd wear it with an emerald silk scarf around her neck because the combination of green and orangey-red set off her russet hair beautifully. She'd only worn it once before, on a trip to Aylesbury to visit a university friend, Patricia, and go with her to a church dance there. That was in the old days when she'd wanted to hide herself away in drab clothes, but Patricia had given her the orange dress, one of hers, and insisted Grace wear it, then said it looked so good on her that she must keep it. Grace had never had the confidence to wear it again, so put it away. But now she felt that it was time for it to have a new outing – and be noticed and, hopefully, admired.

The Friday came for their trip to Portsmouth. Grace and Nancy were going along with around ten or so other Wrens and they all packed small bags with their overnight things, as well as stuffing their gas mask cases with make-up and other essentials. They began to walk out on the road to Portsmouth but before long all the Wrens had managed to hitch rides in cars and trucks, Grace and Nancy on the back seat of a car driven by a middle-aged grocer and his wife. They were asked about their work in Hampshire and this was the first time Grace found herself lying about it. They said they were being trained in administrative duties, to which there was a slightly disappointed 'Oh' from the grocer's wife. *Ah well*, thought Grace, *I'd better get used to it.*

Once in Portsmouth they were dropped on the street where their bed-and-breakfast was situated and were told by the landlady that there was a 10 p.m. curfew. Since the dance they were going to ended at eleven, this was rather annoying, but then a girl in the room next door told Nancy that there was a window in the bathroom downstairs that the residents left open so that they could climb through after curfew. That would be ideal, they decided, so got themselves glammed up and off they went, walking into town and asking a passer-by for directions to the Empress Ballroom. Nancy had a flyer about the dance which read:

Empress Ballroom. Hot Swing Band of 8, under Dynamite Johnnie Lynes. 7.30 to 11, entry 1s. Hot Night!

That phrase *Hot Night* echoed in Grace's head whenever she thought of the dance. What delights would await them?

As they approached the venue, they saw a queue of girls dressed up to the nines outside, some in uniform, and lots of men, also in uniform. They joined the queue, meeting their other Wren friends, who had walked in from other guest houses and small hotels. The queue moved quite quickly and soon they were inside where the sight that greeted them was beyond Grace's expectations by a mile. The hall seemed vast and had a café at one end with a balcony filled with tables above from where you could watch the dancers below. There was a broad stage at the other end where the band were playing and lavish settees lined one wall, alongside more tables and chairs. A standing area was on the other side of the hall and a dance floor in the middle of it all was already crowded with dancing couples. The people there were made up of an incredible range of types: tall and short, fat and thin, all services represented and quite a few different uniforms from countries around the world. The music was hot indeed, reminiscent of Glenn Miller and other swing bands Grace had heard on the radio. The ceiling was domed and around it shone many spotlights that changed colour. In the centre hung a huge mirrored ball with a spotlight from each corner of the hall shining on it as it turned. A rainbow of magical colours moved gracefully over the crowd and would light up a couple for a moment then move on, the air filled with smoke and heat.

'Oh, Nancy! It's bloody marvellous!' cried Grace, having a new-found delight in rather racy language these days.

Nancy was grinning and tapping her feet to the band's rhythm and, arm in arm, they went to the café and bought some lemonade; there was no alcohol again, as at the village dance. More groups of men and women were piling in through the entrance the whole time, some clearly the worse for wear in terms of alcohol consumption, and Grace realised that it seemed to be the done thing to get sozzled before you came. After finishing their lemonade, Grace and Nancy went to find some of the other Wrens in the standing area but within minutes both had been asked to dance.

The dances were fast and tiring – speedy waltzes, foxtrots and quicksteps, among others. Grace found herself with a different partner for each one, shouting stilted conversation with each partner before she realised it was much more fun to just dance. After a couple of numbers, she felt loosened up and really let herself go, throwing herself with gusto into each dance, which seemed to delight her partners. Their dancing prowess was mixed and she found that she was more interested in the better dancers than the better-looking ones. It was a joy to be moved around the hall by a nifty dancer who was light on his feet and it was deadly to find oneself in the arms of someone with two left feet and so even if a bad dancer was handsome, Grace would avoid him afterwards. Before long, she was worn out and went back to the standing area, where she found Nancy, and together they went for a breather at the café to drink more lemonade and eat an iced bun.

Then one of Grace's favourite songs came on – 'Don't Sit Under the Apple Tree with Anyone Else but Me' – and she and Nancy squealed with delight and headed for the floor. They were soon snapped up by a couple of sailors in their bell-bottoms. Grace's was a dreadful dancer but she didn't mind too much, as she was singing along with the song just as the whole hall were, hundreds of voices raised together filling the atmosphere with jollity and togetherness. Then the bandleader announced a gentlemen's excuse-me quickstep and within seconds a tall army officer with an unfamiliar uniform was tapping the sailor on the shoulder and Grace was within his grasp, looking up at him.

He had platinum blond hair. She'd never seen a man with such a colour, only film stars like Jean Harlow. He was extraordinarily tall, maybe six foot four or even five, towering above her, which made for a delightful change. He smiled down at her and led her expertly through the quickstep. They did not speak at all, just danced and glanced at each other. She studied his uniform to guess at his nationality. It was a greenish-grey colour with dark piping. As the quickstep ended, the band struck up a tango. With every other dance she had changed partners, but this time she stayed with the officer and he clearly had no intention of letting her go either. Now the music was slower and sparser, she could talk to him a little.

'I'm Grace.'

'And I am Erik, with a k.'

His voice was European, certainly northern, but she couldn't place it.

'Where are you from?'

'I am Dutch.'

'Ah, from Holland. I've never been.'

'I come from Utrecht, a university city. One of the oldest universities in the Netherlands.'

'How smashing! I went to the University of Oxford.'

'Also smashing,' he said and smiled at her. *Gosh, he's handsome*, she thought. *Perfect teeth*.

They carried on dancing, the sensuality of the tango bringing them close together.

'You're a very good dancer,' she said.

'And so are you. But you're a little stiff for this tango. Let yourself go. Dance as if you were making love with me.'

She felt her cheeks colour deeply and avoided his gaze. What a shocking thing to say! But soon she couldn't resist looking up at him and found he was staring at her intently. The coloured lights flitted across them, colouring them both pink momentarily and she felt light-headed. The song came to an end and, despite loving every moment, she was a little relieved because she felt rather dizzy. He took her to the café and bought her another lemonade, then led her upstairs to the balcony where they stood and watched the dancers circling about the hall in organised chaos.

They talked a bit about their friends here at the dance, as well as their families and where they came from.

'Your English is excellent,' she said.

'Thank you. I do my very best to speak well to a beautiful and intelligent English lady such as yourself.'

She smiled shyly. 'Thank you. But really, I am impressed. When I was at Oxford, I noticed how often foreigners spoke better English than a lot of English people could claim to. I'm embarrassed to admit that I know very little of modern foreign languages, just a bit of schoolgirl French to get by. Although I can write in Ancient Greek and Latin, it's not very useful.'

'But impressive. You are both extremely pretty and academic. Very unusual. And I love this fiery-coloured dress of yours. Most becoming.'

She looked up at him, feeling rather faint from all these compliments. It was intoxicating to hear such nice things said about herself, things she'd never heard directed to her before.

'Shall we go for a walk?' he said. 'It's very loud in here and hot.'

Grace glanced around nervously, looking for other Wrens. She had lost sight of them several dances ago.

'That would be nice . . . maybe a short walk?' she said, hesitantly.

'Yes, just a short walk.'

'But first I really need to find my friend Nancy to let her know.'

'Then let us go on an adventure. The Search for Nancy!' he announced in mock-epic style, throwing his arm out dramatically for her to go first. They both laughed and she led the way, making her way through the crowd, looking for familiar faces. She saw a Wren friend in the café queue and asked if she'd seen Nancy but she hadn't.

'If you see her, will you tell her I'm just going for a quick walk but I'll be back soon?'

The Wren, a dowdy girl called Joyce, took one look at the tall officer behind Grace and rolled her eyes. 'We won't hold our breath,' she said and turned away. Grace was annoyed by this but also a little proud that she had bagged such a good-looking partner.

'All right?' said Erik and Grace nodded.

Eric took her hand and led her through the crowd to the exit. The feel of his strong hand around hers was exhilarating and she let herself be led, liking the pull of his strong frame as they went. She wondered if he'd pull her around the back of the ballroom and kiss her, as others had at the village hall, but once outside he held out the crook of his arm, through which she laced her own arm and they began to walk, just as he'd suggested. They talked easily of their university days – he had studied law, he told her. He was a musician too, he said, playing both violin and piano in quartets and quintets, and he had read many English classic novels too. It was fascinating to really talk to such a well-read, educated man. She had had some male friends at university, but none for whom she felt this physical pull, this desire to touch and be touched by him. Her lips as she spoke to him felt tingly, wondering when he would stop walking and kiss her. But he carried on talking and she enjoyed it so much she didn't mind waiting for the kiss. The anticipation was all the more delicious.

Then she became sharply aware of the effect of all that lemonade earlier. She was desperate for a wee. She said, 'Could we make our way back now? I really do need to powder my nose.'

'Powder your nose? But it looks beautiful to me. You have a perfect little nose.'

'Ah, no. This is a language problem. Erm . . . I need to . . . answer a call of nature.'

'Nature? What kind of nature?'

'Oh, dear me,' she said, exasperated. 'I must visit the Ladies' Room.'

His frowning face lit up. 'Ah, you need to—'

'Yes,' she said quickly. How dreadfully embarrassing it all was.

'I understand. But look, we have walked quite a way from the ballroom. And just along here is my hotel, not far, at the end of this street. There is a lavatory you can use there in the front hallway.'

She peered down the dark street, then turned to look back in the direction they'd come. Lost in their conversation, she hadn't noticed how far they'd walked or even the direction and she had no idea where she was. But she knew that she must go for a pee urgently or very soon it would be trickling down her leg if she wasn't careful. She looked at him and he smiled pleasantly, awaiting her answer. He was educated and civilised, as well as being an officer. Surely she could trust such a man? Yes, surely she could.

'Yes, all right then. That would be very kind of you.'

'It is my pleasure,' he said and they walked down to the last house on the street, a tall, narrow building called the Spitbank Hotel. He went up the steps and looked down at her as she stood uncertainly in the street. He held out his hand and she took it. He drew her to him and touched her hair, their lips an inch away from each other. Then he turned and retrieved a key from his pocket and unlocked the front door, holding it for her. She went in first and he said, 'There is the necessary room. Second door on the right.'

'Thank you,' she said and made her way down there as he stood in the open doorway.

Once on the lavatory, Grace relieved herself gladly and as she washed her hands and checked her face and hair in the mirror, she could not stop thinking of his lips that had been so close to hers on the steps, but then he had turned away. Was he shy? Was he being a gentleman? She admired him for that, but hoped he was not so much a gentleman that there would be no kisses tonight. She *needed* him to kiss her, she realised, wanted him to more than she'd wanted to kiss any man ever. She realised her red lipstick had mostly rubbed off, but Nancy had the one they shared and so she could not retouch it. Her hair still looked good and her cheeks were a little flushed from the cool March air they'd walked through . . . and perhaps a little through the stimulating company of the tall Dutch officer.

She came out into the hallway, to find him inside now, the front door closed. He walked straight up to her, striding down the passage, and when he reached her, he took her in his arms and kissed her. Oh, it was the most glorious kiss! Lips against lips, firm and passionate. They broke off to breathe and then he was back again. She found her lips opening and there was his tongue. But none of the flickering, fishy movement of Fred or the clumsiness or roughness of the some of the others. This one moved slowly and sensually, melting her. It was the best kiss she'd ever had and she never wanted it to end.

But someone was putting their key in the front door and they both gasped.

'Come!' he said and, grasping her hand, pulled her down

the corridor to one of several doors where he quickly took out a key and opened it, gesturing for her to get inside, which she did excitedly and he followed, pulling the door to with mock care, uttering 'shh' as he did so.

'We are not allowed young women here,' he whispered loudly. 'For calls of nature or powdering noses or any other purpose!'

'Oh, I see!' she said, laughing.

'But . . . ' he said and stepped up to her again, taking hold of her hand softly, with his other hand sliding into the small of her back, 'I cannot help but break the rules for you, beautiful Grace.'

His lips were on hers again and more glorious kisses followed. He pulled off her gloves and threw them to the floor and she pushed her fingers through his hair, so soft against her hands as she pulled his head towards her, wanting him deeper and deeper in her mouth.

Oh, the things he said to her, how stunning she was, the prettiest girl in England, how deeply blue her eyes were, how lovely her hair was, how womanly her curves. How he blessed this war that had brought them together and cursed the same war that would draw them apart one day. And she let herself drown in that river of praise and found herself willing to be led to his narrow, single bed and lie down on it, his weight on her overwhelming and thrilling, as he tried in vain to touch her breasts through the double layers of her corset and vest. He gave up and fumbled at his fly, then pulled up her skirt and, yanking her knickers down eased her thighs open with his knee, his mouth still hard on hers, his tongue still soft in her mouth.

And she lost her virginity there, in that squalid little hotel in Portsmouth, on a chilly March night in 1940. It only lasted half a minute, if that, then he groaned and collapsed on top of her and his weight did not feel thrilling any more, only heavy and cumbersome. He rolled off her and stood up, pulling up his trousers and buttoning his fly, as she pulled up her knickers and pulled down her skirt. And now he was cold and business-like, said he'd take her back to the ballroom, and they walked in total silence all the way, not touching. Gone was the charming conversation about books and music and she had no idea what to say and he made no effort. As they approached the ballroom and could hear the swing music seeping down the street towards them, he said only, 'You know the way from here, yes?'

She nodded and he gave her a quick peck on the cheek and said, 'Goodnight' and turned and walked away. She walked on a few steps and turned the corner, then broke down, leaning against a shop front and weeping. She knew her make-up would be running down her face but she couldn't stop. She shuddered with the shame of what she had just done – not the fact of it, because she had often thought about sex and was quite eager to try it if she met the right man –

but the regret that she had given herself to an empty flatterer such as Nancy had warned her against. And suddenly, slicing through that shame was a cold blade of fear: what if she were to fall pregnant and be thrown out of the Wrens in disgrace, never to achieve her destiny of becoming a wireless telegraphist, all for a quickie with some Dutch bastard with pretty hair and good teeth? *Hot Night*, the flyer had said. But all Grace felt was cold as she shivered alone in the street and, realised she'd left her favourite chiffon evening gloves on his floor. With bare, icy fingertips, she wiped her tears away and pulled herself together to go back into the Empress Ballroom and find her best friend.

Chapter 7

April 1940

'It's downright irresponsible, that's what it is.'

'Please, Mr Loftus, do tell me exactly what happened,' said Rosina, standing outside the front door, trying to placate one of her tenant farmers whose face was puffed up with rage. He'd come up that evening and sent word via Mr Jessop that he needed to speak to her urgently.

'Tha know t'tanks that are stationed in t'village? Well, two of 'em took a shortcut to Station Square and drove straight across two of our fields, destroying our winter crops! With all this rain recently, t'land was sodden and those damn tanks – excuse my language but I reckon in this case, it's necessary! Well, they churned up t'soil summat awful and destroyed a barley and wheat crop. We'll have no yield at all in them two fields. As I say, it's downright irresponsible what with us digging for victory and so on.'

'I agree, it's appalling. What on earth were they thinking? I'll look into this for you, don't you worry about that.'

'It's a bloody liberty, ma'am! Excuse my language again!'

'I quite understand your anger, Mr Loftus. I assure you I will look into it thoroughly and see about compensation.'

'We're already run ragged, what with t'wife overloaded with t'burden of providing meals and lodging for t'farm workers and those land girls they foisted on us.'

'I thought the land girls were working well, or so Mrs Loftus said to me.'

'Well, one of 'em is. Two, I suppose. But t'third is clueless.'

'She'll learn,' said Rosina. 'I'm sure she will. And we're all in the same boat with so many changes. We're feeding RAF personnel every day here too and I know it's not easy. But I will get straight on to this destruction of the crops – that's absolutely not on.'

'Much appreciated, ma'am,' he said with some relief. 'But if I get my hands on any of those tank drivers—'

'Brave boys all, I'm sure,' she interrupted quickly, with her eyebrows raised, trying to keep his morale up, 'who soon may be driving those tanks through enemy territory.'

Mr Loftus nodded begrudgingly and then, with a quick goodbye, he turned and walked off up the avenue of trees stretching along the driveway to the hall.

Rosina walked swiftly back to the house, a fire in her belly. Those fools! She understood the need for the army to practise manoeuvres, but to be so destructive at a time when every seed mattered was madness. She knew she would have to write some army commander a letter that would probably be ignored and, in the meantime, she had some other servicemen in her very kitchen at that moment eating her out of house and home. Bairstow enjoyed their company, it was obvious. It was as if she were Mother Hen to the lads. They teased her and made jokes, all under the watchful eye of Sergeant Harry Woodvine, who kept them in line if they got too cheeky. Rosina enjoyed their company too and had joined them for dinner on several occasions, mucking in with the preparation and the clearing up. She liked to think that by doing this she was continuing to do her best to make Bairstow's life easier. But the truth of it was that she loved the company. She'd been interrupted during dinner to see Mr Loftus and was eager to get back there.

Approaching the kitchen, she heard the good-natured chatter of the men and Bairstow. Whenever she entered the room, there was always a hush that descended and a little hiatus in the conversation, which she hated, wished they'd treat her as one of their own. But she knew that was unlikely and so had taken to making a joke of it, as she did when she walked in that evening, saying to one and all, 'Lady Muck is back.' Everyone laughed, albeit a bit nervously.

Rosina glanced at Sergeant Woodvine and they smiled at each other, then he stood up and said, 'Off we go then, lads. We've taken up far too much room in this kitchen with our feet and our stomachs already today.'

Six chairs were roughly pushed back and the men trooped out, thanking Bairstow and Rosina as they left.

'Sergeant Woodvine, could I have a word?' said Rosina, catching him just as he was nodding goodbye to her in the open doorway.

'Of course.'

Rosina was aware of Bairstow behind her beginning to clear away and wanted to help, but she had to catch him before he left.

'It's one of my farmers. He says two tanks drove across our fields and destroyed winter crops. I want to complain but don't know who to write to. I was just wondering if you had any idea.'

'Well, I'm assuming they would have been under orders to go in that direction, for whatever reason, though you're right, it was an unfortunate path for them to take.'

'Worse than unfortunate, I'd say. It's pretty disastrous and, as my farmer says, irresponsible, considering crops are so vital.'

'Of course, of course. I'm not trying to excuse it. But

I do know orders are orders and must be followed. I do understand your position, though, and it *is* bad form. As I'm Air Force and they're army, I don't know exactly who you should write to, but I'll do my best to find out, if that helps.'

'That does help, thank you,' said Rosina, who saw that Bairstow had by now cleared most of the table. 'Now I must help clear away.'

But Bairstow said, 'Chickens need feeding, ma'am. I can manage this.' Rosina noted how Bairstow still hadn't got used to the idea of her helping out with the washing-up. She'd accepted Rosina's burgeoning efforts at cooking and dusting, but often found an excuse to shoo Rosina away from the more menial kitchen tasks.

'That's true,' said Rosina, turning to the sergeant and saying, 'Sorry about that. I'm trying to help wherever I can and Bairstow takes on too much.'

'No apology necessary,' he said. 'Can I help?'

'Oh no, absolutely not. You're already doing your duty.'

'With the chickens, I meant. I like chickens. They remind me of my grandfather.'

'Why? Did he look like a chicken?'

He guffawed at that and said, 'Lord, no. He was a devilishly handsome man, just like my father. Something went wrong along the way when it came to me, of course.'

'Don't be ridiculous,' she said, without thinking, then

127

caught his eye and turned away. 'Bairstow, do you have the bucket of scraps?'

'Under t'sink, where they always are,' said Bairstow knowingly and Rosina felt her cheeks redden. He wasn't the only one being ridiculous; Rosina felt ridiculous too, sharing banter with this young man in front of the servants. She busied herself fetching the bucket and when she got to the doorway, Sergeant Woodvine reached out and offered to take it and she let him.

As they reached the front door, she heard the men chatting as they waited in the van for him. 'What about your lift?'

'Oh, I'll let them know I'll walk back,' he said, putting the bucket down outside the front door and trotting over to the van to send them on their way, taking up the bucket again when he was back beside her.

She led him across the lawn and past the greenhouses to a shed where they kept the rest of the chicken feed.

'Do you get a ration of feed for them?' he asked.

'Yes, actually, we do, as we're keeping six. We get a ration of corn, but they're always hungry so we boil up potato peelings with other kitchen scraps for them too.' Getting a bucket of seed, she took him down the path to the coop. 'Neither the gardener nor I could get hold of any wire netting, so he built them a house and run out of some old planks and driftwood. They do escape sometimes though and we find them on the washing line, on the fence or even the windowsills. They are a pain, but I find them absolutely hilarious!'

'So do I! Ludicrous creatures. But I am very fond of them. As I was trying to explain earlier,' he said with a humorous tone, 'my grandfather kept chickens and adored them. When he first had them, someone gave him three chicks at the pub and my grandmother warned him they'd all be cocks though he had been assured they were hens and, sure enough, they grew into three fine cockerels, scratched up all his grass and pecked everyone and everything that came their way, including their poor old dog, on whose back they'd perch as he went up the garden to relieve himself. They pecked him on the neck till he got a bald patch.'

They both laughed at this. 'The old dog had his revenge though when my grandmother fattened those three monsters up and we had them all for Christmas dinner. Such huge legs they had! And the dog got his portion too, eating his old enemies.'

He's so easy to talk to, she thought. *It's as if we've known each other for years.*

'You sound very fond of your grandparents,' she said, as she scattered the corn and the hens came running, bumping into each other and making a commotion, acting as if they'd never been fed.

'Oh, I am. Well, I was. My mother's parents were dead

before I was born, both of natural causes. My father's mother is still around though pretty ancient but her husband with the chickens died a few months back.'

'I'm sorry to hear that.'

'Well, he lived a long life. He was a teacher in Shrewsbury and my grandmother came from Ironbridge. She lived there but was born in Coalbrookdale, the birthplace of the industrial revolution, as I'm sure you're aware.'

'I wasn't aware. How so?'

'Oh well, the town of Ironbridge grew up around the first iron bridge built in the world. And Coalbrookdale was where they pioneered the new techniques in ironworking that made it possible to build such a structure.'

'How marvellous,' said Rosina and watched him pour the boiled-up scraps into the trough for the birds.

'It is. As I said to you before, most people don't know where Shropshire is but they have a lot to thank it for. It's beautiful country there too, with the Severn Gorge and marvellous geology.'

'You make me want to visit.'

'You should!'

They stood and watched the chickens feed voraciously, their human shadows long in the evening sunshine, falling across the path of the chickens and merging.

'Have you named them yet?' he said.

'No. I hadn't thought to.'

'Well, we should. How about . . . film stars?'

'All right, then. Hmm . . . those two are always together, like sisters. Let's call them Olivia de Havilland and Joan Fontaine.'

'Excellent. And that one has a dangerous glint in her eye, so let's call her Barbara Stanwyck.'

He winked at her and she laughed and added, 'And this one is so grumpy *she* should be Bette Davis. And this one's the most graceful, so she can be Ginger Rogers. And lastly, that one, is my favourite and the most beautiful. Who's the most beautiful star, do you think?'

'Oh, Hedy Lamarr, no question.'

'You're right. Hedy Lamarr it is.'

'You have a hint of Hedy Lamarr about you,' he said, quietly.

'I wish!' she cried. 'She's dark with sparkling green eyes and I've this reddish-brown hair and blue eyes, which can't compete.'

'It's the mouth,' he said and looked straight at her. 'And the perfect skin.'

'I've never heard such nonsense!' she said unconvincingly and picked up the bucket. 'Let's fetch the eggs. Bairstow will be wondering what's happened to us.'

They collected the eggs and put them carefully in the bucket with a bit of straw to nestle in, then made their way back to the kitchen. He started up a conversation about the extraordinary quality of eggshell, how it was nature's perfect engineering, the ideal balance of protection and fragility.

What a mind he has, she thought. *What a pleasure it is to speak with him.* He was so knowledgeable about so many different topics and it made her want to quiz him for hours. How did he know so much? He couldn't be much older than Grace, but he seemed to have lived a lifetime longer than her daughter. Grace was full of book learning but naive and Rosina had the feeling that with him he was worldly somehow, though she had no particular evidence for it. There was a quiet confidence about him, a knowing look in his eye that wasn't smug, more as if he were at home with himself wherever he was.

They reached the door to the hallway that led to the kitchen and, as she opened it, she turned to him and on a whim asked, 'How old are you?' then knew instantly it was quite the direct question and probably rather rude.

'I'm twenty-six.' *Only five years older than Grace*, she thought. Somehow she'd been hoping he'd be older than that, she realised, though she didn't question why she'd hoped such a thing. He certainly seemed older. *He's an old soul*, she thought. Then he added, 'I won't ask you the same.'

She laughed and said, 'Oh, I don't mind. I'm ancient. I'm forty-four.'

'Don't be preposterous. You're not a minute over thirty.'

'Flatterer!' she said and went inside.

'I'm not,' he said, catching up to walk beside her. 'I never flatter. Don't see the point. I just say what I see. It's my scientist's brain, you see, no imagination. And you, from a scientific point of view, resemble a person in her early thirties. It's a scientific fact and you can't argue with that.'

'Scientific flatterer,' she said and smiled at him with raised eyebrows.

'I promise you, I'm not. I have many faults. I'm a highly unsociable person and I have too much of a fondness for whisky, but a flatterer I will never be.'

'You don't *seem* unsociable,' she said.

'Oh, I'm a mimic. I can copy small talk from talkative people, but at heart I'm an introvert. I'm only truly happy one-to-one and only comfortable in the best company.'

He seems comfortable with me, she thought. 'I have an excellent whisky in the drawing room, if you ever need a snifter.' What was she doing? Inviting him for drinks, now?

'I would give my right leg for a good whisky.'

'That settles it then,' she said, as they reached the kitchen. 'Wait here one moment.' Bairstow wasn't in there, thankfully, as Rosina did not want her to witness that she was still with the sergeant. She put the bucket back under the sink and washed and dried her hands, then came out to find him and lead him down to the drawing room.

'What whisky do you have? I'm agog to hear!'

'It's a Macallan single malt. Acceptable?'

'Oh my lord, that's heaven. Are you sure you don't mind sparing a little?'

'Of course. Anything to bolster the war effort.'

She poured a measure into each glass. She'd had this bottle from before the war started and it had lasted as it wasn't her custom to drink whisky. She preferred gin, but didn't mind a warming tot of malt from time to time, especially when poorly.

He sipped, then licked his lips and screwed his eyes shut. 'It's fruity . . . it's oakey . . . it's peaty!'

'Oh, do shut up,' she said and they both laughed and sipped again. It was going straight to her head and she resolved not to take another sip. And to send him packing as soon as he'd finished his. There was something not quite proper about this situation, but alongside the warning flags she felt light-headed and happier than she had in months. Years? Yes, it was years.

He was musing now about the qualities of different whiskies, when her ears pricked. She could swear she'd just heard Evelyn's laugh, far away and she'd recognise her second daughter's high-pitched giggle anywhere. But it was impossible. Evelyn was in London. No, it must have been a seagull, flying close to the house. She tuned back into what he was saying and allowed herself to look at him. His first name was Harry, he'd said when they met. Should she call him that? Of course not, because then that would invite him to call her Rosina and that would be beyond everything. Quite scandalous. But she could call him Harry in her mind. What was the harm in that?

'Mummy?' came a voice from the other end of the house.

'Oh my goodness,' she said. It *was* Evvy. What on earth?

'Mummy! Mummy!' came another voice, moving closer. Constance's! And soon Dora was calling too, but not Daisy, characteristically quiet.

She glanced at Harry, whose face betrayed that he, too, knew there was something somewhat illicit about this moment and it was about to be blown apart by the entrance of the bunch of young, rowdy females who were coming down the passageway towards them now, laughing and calling all the way.

'In here, my darlings!' Rosina cried and swiftly put the whisky down, as did Harry, then he pushed his hands stiffly into his pockets and cleared his throat.

Then there they were, four of her five girls materialising in the doorway, the three younger ones in their somewhat shabby school uniforms and the elder in a fashionable pair of slacks and a tight-fitting sweater that showed off her figure perfectly.

'Mummy!' came the general cry and Rosina was about to be rushed by the four of them when, in a comical moment, they all clocked the presence of the RAF officer by the window and stopped dead.

'Girls, this is Sergeant Woodvine. He and his men are working along the coast and eating here each day. I wrote about them in my letters to you, remember?'

'Oh yes,' said Constance. 'How jolly!'

'Splendid,' said Dora, gazing at Harry.

Daisy was silent, as usual. Yet unusually for her, so was Evelyn. She seemed to be sizing up the two of them and the situation all in one glance. Then a sly smile came across her face, which Rosina did not like the look of one little bit.

'These are my daughters, Daisy, Dora, Constance and Evelyn.'

'Charmed, I'm sure,' said Evelyn and stepping forward, held her hand out to Harry, who took it firmly and shook it without speaking, nodding and giving a stiff smile. Rosina remembered what he'd said about small talk and suddenly felt terrible for him, foisting four rowdy girls on him, an introvert.

'Sergeant Woodvine and I were discussing Mr Loftus's field, which has been trampled by two tanks today. He's going to help us get in touch with the right people.' It was partially true. Well, that was how the conversation had started, all those aeons ago in the kitchen. So much ground had been covered since then . . . but the girls did not need to know that.

'How fascinating,' said Evelyn, languidly, dropping on to

a sofa arm and staring pointedly at the two whisky glasses on the sideboard.

'Aren't you going to ask us why we're all suddenly here, Mummy?' said Dora excitedly. Rosina could tell she longed to throw her arms around her mother, but was holding back because of the unexpected company.

'Well, it's Easter weekend soon, my darling. But you weren't supposed to be home until Thursday.'

'They let us out early!' piped up Constance.

'Oh, you rotter. I was going to tell her that,' said Dora.

'And we met Evvy on the train by complete and utter coincidence. What are the chances of that?' cried Constance, again cutting off Dora, who looked close to tears and who added, just for something to say, 'We all walked from Ravenscar station and left our bags by the front door,' but nobody really needed to know that and she looked cheated.

'I ought to be going,' said Harry quietly and Rosina replied, 'Of course, of course.'

'Oh, so soon?' said Evelyn. 'Or perhaps you've been here quite a while.' She smiled insincerely at them both.

Rosina laughed nervously and said, 'Now, now, Evvy. None of your London humour here. Say goodbye to Sergeant Woodvine now, girls. He's got lots to do and can't hang about here.'

'Goodbye, Sergeant Woodvine,' chorused the younger

girls, to which Evelyn added, 'Ta-ta.'

Rosina stepped awkwardly out into the passage and said, 'Thank you, then, Sergeant.'

He looked at her, a little nonplussed by the scene he'd just found himself in. She didn't know what else to say. Well, what was there to say? Their little bubble had burst and she felt clumsy with him now. He evidently felt the same, because he joined his hands stiffly behind his back and nodded, then turned and walked off down the passage. She knew she should have accompanied him to the door but she felt rooted to the spot, watching his long legs stride hastily away from her. The sound of her daughters' impatience to be properly alone with their mother spilled out noisily from the drawing room and, of course, it was a delight to see them and she wanted their company too. But she stayed in the passageway until Harry turned the corner and was gone.

Chapter 8

Hugs and stories of the journeys were swapped and Evelyn explained her unexpected presence: she had decided to make a quick trip home for the Easter weekend to see everyone. Rosina took the girls to the kitchen to make a late supper. There was some winter cauliflower in cheese sauce left, which she put in the oven to warm through with some mashed potato.

'Food is so depressing these days,' said Constance, picking at the cauliflower cheese. 'How am I supposed to grow strong with no meat?'

'Firstly, Connie, you are extremely strong already. And secondly, we must get used to far less meat now, girls. I give the lion's share to the servants and the RAF men, as they work harder than me.'

'Well, that doesn't seem fair!' said Dora.

'I actually think it's very fair,' said Rosina. 'And anyway, eating less has improved my figure, so I'm not complaining.'

'I can see that, Mummy,' said Evelyn, wolfing down the meal, used to such food from living in digs in London. She finished and pushed her plate away. 'And I'm sure I'm not the only one who's noticed.' And she winked at her mother, which Rosina frowned at, taking Evelyn's plate and turning away to hide the fact that she felt her cheeks reddening and didn't want her daughter to see it.

'Do we have any pudding, please, Mummy?' asked Daisy.

'Yes, darling,' said Rosina, standing at the sink. 'There's jelly in the pantry. Help yourself.'

'Anything else instead of jelly?' asked Constance. 'We have that all the time at school.'

'It's either that or water ice made with fruit pulp. Or I have a bit of fruit curd you could have on toast.'

'Jelly will do, I suppose,' sighed Constance and the younger girls ate it quickly and excused themselves to go and unpack, but Evelyn stayed.

Rosina was delighted to see her but somehow felt awkward with her. She just wanted to put her arms around her and hear all the gossip from London, but she carried on at the sink washing the crockery.

'Can I help, Mummy?' said Evelyn and Rosina replied, 'You can go and unpack if you like, darling. I'm fine with this.'

'Oh, that can wait. I want to hear all about this Sergeant Woodvine. He's absolutely delicious!'

Rosina was glad she was facing away from Evelyn over the sink, so her daughter couldn't see her face. 'I suppose so,' she said, noncommittal.

'No suppose about it,' said Evelyn, coming to stand beside her mother and leaning against the side so she could see her mother properly. 'What are they doing here anyway?'

'I'm not sure. Building something along the coast. The ARP man said there were aerials involved, so it sounds secret to me. The RAF men won't talk about it, anyway, so I suppose it must be classified.'

'How exciting!' said Evelyn. 'Well, I think he's taken a shine to you, Mummy.'

Rosina shot a glance at Evelyn, who was grinning at her with eyebrows raised.

'You've been hinting that all evening and it's ridiculous,' she said, shaking her head. She put the last piece of washing-up on the side and wiped her hands on a towel.

'Why is it ridiculous? You're a beautiful woman!'

'In my forties!' said Rosina and laid the towel out flat to dry on the side.

'So what? In France, an older woman and a younger man is quite acceptable amongst certain areas of society. And in London, in the arty set I move with, lots of young men have affairs with older women. They love the mystique of them and their experience. And the fact they don't want to nest, don't want to get married and don't want to have babies. In fact, I'd say men in their twenties and women in their forties or even fifties are the ideal match in that way.'

'Oh, really?' said Rosina, in a mock-interested tone. 'Well, we don't live in such circles here. Not that it is even worthy of consideration, as what you're saying is nonsense. And quite scandalous! So please keep your London ways to yourself. It won't wash here.'

'Don't be grumpy, Mummy,' said Evelyn and came to her mother, wrapping her arms about her. Rosina leant in for a stiff hug, then relaxed as she felt her lovely daughter squeezing her tight. She had longed for Evelyn to come home, but the girl knew her too well and had caught her out doing something she'd known was folly. Now she was embarrassed. But it was more than that: she was annoyed, that something she'd enjoyed as her secret pleasure was now open to scrutiny.

'I'm just weary, darling,' said Rosina, hugging her daughter back.

Evelyn pulled away a little and kissed Rosina on the cheek. 'Don't feel odd about it, Mummy. There's no reason why you shouldn't enjoy yourself. It's been a few years now since Daddy. You deserve a life too, you know.'

'I do have a very full and busy life, thank you. And really, you must put this ludicrous idea to bed. I was just being hospitable to Sergeant Woodvine because he's helping us with a complaint to the army. That is all. He's a pleasant young man and is probably missing his mother, away from home.'

'You make him sound like a child!' laughed Evelyn. 'He's much older than me. In his mid-twenties, I should say. And you're only forty-four. Hardly ancient!'

Rosina wanted to say that he was twenty-six, but stopped herself because it would sound as though she knew too much.

Evelyn added, 'He's a full-grown man, in every way.' And she nudged her mother and there was that cheeky grin again.

'Oh, do put a sock in it!' said Rosina, smiling despite herself. 'He's a very nice young person and that's that. Stop imagining things. Now, tell me all about London.'

They sat back down at the kitchen table and Rosina was glad that the conversation had moved on.

'Well, it's going swimmingly so far. The two jobs keep me extremely busy.'

'Two? I thought you were working for that firm who put on propaganda exhibitions.'

'Yes, I'm still doing that. We're doing a display for Harrods at the moment, posters recruiting for the Land Army and warning people about lights at night, that sort of thing. Rather dreadful paintings, really, but we do our best. But I'm also painting scenery for a local theatre, mostly at night. Sometimes we stay up all night doing it. They're still putting on shows. Afterwards, sometimes we go to the Ivy for a late supper. They can't charge more than five shillings for a meal, of course, so we use our ration coupons and have a good dinner. It's a wonderful feeling, after painting for hours and then sashaying down to the Ivy for food and drinks. And there are the most splendid actors in there too. Why, the other night, Larry Olivier and John Gielgud were sitting just across from us! Can you imagine?!'

'Gosh, how splendid! I'm glad you're having fun.'

'Oh, we are. There's a wonderful atmosphere in places like that. In London, generally, I'd say. It feels like a community, as vast as it is. People are kinder than they used to be and they look out for each other more, neighbours are talking more. Because you're all thrown together in this strange situation and there's a lot of passion and fondness, in a way there wasn't before the war. You meet a chap and you know you'll probably part soon, so there's an urgency about everything. It's like when you have a fling on a summer holiday and you know it's finite, so you throw caution to the wind and go all in.'

'Are you being careful, though? I don't like to think of you taking risks, on the streets of London.'

'Yes, Mummy. I can look after myself, you know that. Tough as old boots, me. Yet with the face of an angel!'

Evelyn laughed as she said this and put on an innocent expression, her hands together in mock prayer, blinking her eyes rapidly while looking towards heaven.

Rosina laughed too and said, 'I try not to think about what you get up to. I'm sure you're a terror but I do know that you're very savvy. Not like your older sister. From what I hear, she's had rather a rude awakening in the Wrens. All that marching and scrubbing floors and so forth. But she's enjoying it.'

'It'll be the making of her,' said Evelyn. 'She needs to live a little. She'll come out of her shell, you'll see. I think this war will be good for her, as hateful as it is to say such things. But I do think that about Grace. And myself. I'm having a riot! I know it's evil to say so, but it's true!'

Rosina looked at her daughter's beaming face, so cheeky and beautiful, her eyes sparkling with naughtiness.

'Oh, I am so glad you came home for the weekend, darling. It's joyous to see you. We need a bit of life in this house.'

'Me too. I've missed you all, even Connie! I even miss her throwing that damn ball against my wall! Funny, the things you miss.' Evelyn yawned luxuriously at this point, her arms thrown up in the air, mouth wide open.

'Time for you to go and rest. I have a few things to finish up. Off you go.'

And off Evelyn went, swishing across the kitchen in

her slacks, her curled hair bobbing on her shoulders. It was lovely to have her back, so unexpectedly. Rosina felt ashamed that she had wished her away earlier, just to save her embarrassment about Harry. And now she thought about what Evelyn had said about younger men and older women. It all made sense, in bohemian circles at least. But that didn't apply to her. And she still felt ridiculous, whatever Evelyn insisted. Harry Woodvine was just a nice young man and they could talk easily, that was all. And she was sure that's what he thought about it too. Or did he? At the thought that he might admire her – even desire her – she felt a lurch in her stomach. And then a fear came, that now the seed was planted in her head, she would say or do something and make a fool of herself and he would recoil from her. She couldn't imagine anything more humiliating than a woman in her forties throwing herself at an unwilling and uninterested young man. How utterly dreadful! She felt the whisky was probably a mistake. Whatever her daughter thought, it was not a good idea to mix business with pleasure and having the RAF in her house was the business of wartime and she must keep it that way. It would be simpler all round if she distanced herself a little from Harry Woodvine and reminded him and everyone else that she was the lady of the house . . .

After going upstairs to help the girls remove all the dust sheets from their rooms and then seeing them all to bed that night, she went to her own room, worn out from the day's emotional merry-go-round. But she lay awake for a long time, as sleep evaded her and thoughts swirled around her head.

In the morning, Rosina did not see Harry and his men at breakfast, as she deliberately had an early breakfast and avoided it. She heard laughter coming from the kitchen and wondered if Harry was wondering where she was, but put it aside immediately. She must get on with the business of her life.

The girls all went out for a long walk and it was just before lunch when they returned – but they were not alone.

'Mummy?'

Rosina turned as she heard Constance's voice. Rosina was writing a letter to the as-yet unknown army officer she would have to complain to about the fields. She had left the address blank and a gap next to 'Dear'. Rosina saw in Constance's face that something odd was going on.

'What's happened?'

'Oh, nothing really. We just found a man, that's all.'

'What man? What's wrong with him?'

'Oh, nothing really.'

'Stop saying "nothing really". You look guilty. What have you done this time?' Constance was always one for getting into scrapes. Far too curious and too bold, that one.

'Nothing really, I mean, well . . . something. We brought a chap home with us. He's not got a home, you see.'

'What man? Where?'

Constance beckoned to Rosina, who put down her pen with a huff and followed Constance down the passage and outside. There, in the front drive, stood Daisy and Dora, holding hands and looking awkward, sometimes glancing up at a very shabby-looking man, dressed in a filthy pair of baggy trousers, a buttoned-up tweed jacket that looked too small on him, a scarf tied tightly around his neck, muddy boots with wooden soles and a flat cap. His hair was long, sticking out from under his cap over his ears, and he had a bushy beard. It was difficult to tell how old he was because so much hair covered his face, but there was no grey or white in it. Evelyn was sitting on the low stone wall nearby, smoking a cigarette and grinning at the whole thing.

'Can I help you?' Rosina asked, walking towards the man.

'I don't want to be no bother,' said the man.

'What's going on, girls?' Rosina said, nonplussed.

'This is Mr Throp,' said Constance. 'We found him living in the brickworks.'

'Did you now?' said Rosina and looked back at Mr Throp, who said, 'It were closed down last year at start of t'war on account of t'furnaces lighting up t'blackout.

I wasn't troubling folk there. It's been empty these past months.'

'I know that about the brickworks, Mr Throp. But what can I help you with?'

'He didn't ask to come here, Mummy,' piped up Constance again. 'But we found him in this destitute state and as Christians and Englishmen we couldn't bear to leave him there like that.'

Mr Throp looked down at the ground.

Rosina said, 'I'm sorry to have wasted your time, Mr Throp. But since you're here, perhaps we can bring you something to eat and then see you on your way.'

'He's looking for work,' said Dora, letting go of Daisy's hand and stepping close to her mother. 'Honest work, he said. And Daisy remembered you'd said in your letters that Mr Jessop was looking for help in the garden. And Mr Throp says he was a gardener in the parks in Scarborough when he was younger and then we thought . . . '

'Then *I* thought,' interrupted Constance, 'that we should bring him back here and see if he could have a job.'

'Well, that was very naughty of you, girls. And very thoughtless. Dragging Mr Throp all the way here from the brickworks.'

Then a stifled sob came from Daisy, who had tears running down her face. 'I'm sorry, Mummy,' she said and sobbed again. Rosina gave her a hug and smiled awkwardly at Mr

Throp, who took off his hat suddenly, perhaps thinking he should've done that already, or doing it in honour of Daisy's tears. Daisy looked up at her mother, eyes filled and said, 'But his dog had died and we saw the little grave. And we couldn't leave him there alone. It was too, too dreadful.' And she sobbed some more.

Rosina glanced over at Evelyn, who was shaking her head and dragging on her cigarette. She'd be having words with that one, letting the youngsters get in such a situation. But she guessed, too, that wilful Constance had commandeered the poor man and masterminded the whole thing and it was difficult even for Rosina, as her mother, to stop Connie in full flow, let alone her sister.

'Right, you girls go inside and get washed up before lunch. I'll have a chat with Mr Throp and we shall see what is to be done.'

'Yes, Mummy,' came the chorus and they all traipsed inside, Daisy snuffling and wiping snot with the back of her hand, whilst Evelyn stubbed out her cigarette under a shoe.

'Put that in the ashtray in the hall, please, Evvy,' said her mother, giving her an *I'll deal with you later* glare as she sauntered by.

As the girls were retreating, Rosina had a chance to have a good look at Mr Throp. He was younger than he seemed, his prodigious hair and beard not obscuring his bright eyes, which looked about him with interest.

Once they were alone, Rosina said, 'Mr Throp, I can only apologise for my daughters' rash behaviour in frog-marching you all the way here.'

'No apology necessary,' he said, with dignity. 'Thi girls are champion and've shown me nowt but kindness.'

'I'm glad to hear that. And I can bring you some food and . . . ' She thought of her husband's clothes, still hanging in the closets, untouched for years. Both men were of average size so perhaps they might fit Mr Throp. 'And some clothes.'

'And th'are that kind, I am speechless,' said Mr Throp.

'Not at all,' said Rosina, looking at how filthy his face and hands were and imagining him getting changed into clean clothes back at the brickworks or wherever he went next. And it bothered her to think of him putting clean clothes on to such a dirty frame. 'And . . . and perhaps you would like a wash here?' She looked at his beard and his hair and thought of how she'd given all her girls haircuts from an early age and couldn't quite believe herself saying the words but she did say them. 'And a haircut and shave, if you wish?'

After all, as Evelyn had said, war had created a new kind of community spirit. And as hard-nosed as she sometimes had to be as the lady of the big house, she had always had a soft heart. It was where her girls got theirs from. But Rosina was no fool. Feeding, washing and clothing the poor chap was one thing. But a job? That was not on the cards.

'Could you wait here a moment, Mr Throp?'

He nodded and Rosina went inside and along to the kitchen, where she found Bairstow preparing a simple lunch of cheese sandwiches for the family. Rosina explained the situation to Bairstow, who received the whole thing with raised eyebrows. Rosina finished by asking Bairstow if she would prepare one of the servant's old rooms with hot water, a flannel and towel for Mr Throp, while she would fetch some of Mr Calvert-Lazenby's clothes.

'I know Throp,' said Bairstow. 'He has a sad story.'

'Well, now, you must tell it to me, but on the way to see him, as he's been waiting outside a while.'

As they walked, Bairstow told Rosina that Mr Throp – first name Lionel – was in his forties and had been an upstanding member of the community at one stage. He'd been born in Robin Hood's Bay and, as Dora had said, used to work as a groundsman for the council in Scarborough. His parents both died when he was a young man and then he had a wife and child and they died too, of influenza. 'And it turned him queer,' said Bairstow. 'He's not a drinker nor a gambler, they say. He had t'flu too, which left him with a bad lung, but he were otherwise fit. He just couldn't cope with t'loss of his nearest and dearest, though, and he disappeared for years, wanting nowt to do with nobody. And then folk said they'd seen him around and about, wandering. His wife were from Ravenscar originally, y'see. So they say he's hoping to see her ghost. I'm not sure about that part of it, but he's harmless enough, I'd say. And worthy of help.'

These last few words were said as Rosina and Bairstow crossed the threshold to Raven Hall, to find that Lionel Throp was not standing where he'd been left. He was not along the driveway either.

'Oh,' said Rosina. 'Perhaps he's wandered off.'

Bairstow cleared her throat and tapped Rosina on the shoulder and she turned to see that Mr Throp was kneeling beside a bed of rose bushes that bordered the front lawn, delicately pulling out weeds and leaving them out on the grass to shrivel up in the sunshine. Rosina and Bairstow exchanged a smile and watched him for a moment, the finesse of his movements not lost upon them. Rosina made a decision and said to Bairstow, 'I'll finish the girls' lunch. Can you see to Mr Throp? If you could feed him first, then get him washed, I'll lay out some clothes. Then when he's done, we'll take him to Jessop, shall we? He can sleep in the servants' quarters. There's plenty of room, after all.'

'Will do,' said Bairstow, smiling approvingly.

The afternoon passed in a tumble of jobs and dealing with the girls and helping Mr Throp settle in. After he'd washed, dressed and shaved his beard completely off, he looked quite altered. He told Rosina he was fifty-one and she noticed that his hair had not one grey strand in it, which was unusual for a man his age, although his skin was more weathered than a normal man in his fifties, but no wonder, considering his years in the wilderness. And once Rosina had cut his hair, he looked utterly different. He had nice eyes and bad teeth. He was a bit taciturn but could talk knowledgeably about topics he favoured, such as gardening, about which he clearly knew a lot.

It was odd to have a strange man about the place and Rosina made it very clear to him that there would be a probationary period, to see how he was as a gardener and about him living in the house. Bairstow had vouched for his character and background, but the rumours of the vagaries of his mind did perturb Rosina somewhat. Yet, in wartime, it seemed the right thing to do to help one's fellow man and Jessop could certainly do with the help. No women from the area or girls from any sort of government scheme had turned up and Jessop had been struggling with only Ronald Holt, the evacuee, for company. So Mr Throp could well be a bit of a godsend. Also, Rosina had an innate trust of the twins' liking for him, as she'd noticed they had always seemed to have a foolproof judge of character. And the twins had warmed to him instantly. So Mr Throp could stay, at least for a while, and she'd see how things went.

Later, when Rosina introduced him to Jessop, the gardener said, 'I know Throp.' And that seemed to settle it. Jessop also handed over four dead rabbits in a sack to

Rosina. 'Mrs Jessop shot them this morning on thi land.'

'Then you must keep one of them for yourself, Jessop,' said Rosina and held the sack open for him to retrieve one. He thanked her and she was delighted with the bounty. Good old Mrs Jessop! She was a terror with a shotgun, so they said, had a perfect aim. They'd all have rabbit stew for dinner and Rosina knew the perfect recipe, as she'd recently made a study of rabbit recipes for this exact purpose. She'd braise it in dark beer with prunes. They'd got both those ingredients in, just waiting for some rabbits to turn up and now they had.

Rosina was pleased with the day, despite the unexpected turn of events. The girls had been entertained; they'd done a kindness as a family; they had a new under-gardener and now they had rabbit for tea. Bairstow helped Rosina prepare the animals; she was a little squeamish about such things, but was getting more used to it now she was helping with the cooking more and more. The kitchen smelt marvellous as the stew bubbled away in their biggest pot, enough to feed the six RAF men as well as her own brood with actual, real, proper meat! What a feast!

Rosina heard the van coming up the drive with the men and decided it was much the best idea for everyone to eat together in the servants' hall. After all, what was the point in them retiring to different rooms when they were all eating out of the same pot? So that evening, around the long table that had once been filled with servants, sat Sergeant Harry Woodvine and his five men, Bairstow and Throp, the five Calvert girls and Rosina at the head, dishing out the stew that had turned out so well. Conversation was ropey at first, but Evelyn was marvellous and soon got everyone talking by asking about their favourite songs, to which the RAF lads vied with each other to impress her, gorgeous as she was. The younger girls were giddy with all the male company and teased by Bairstow, whilst Rosina noticed with approval that Harry and Throp talked quietly for a long time and that Harry was charming and gentle with him, which seemed to set Throp totally at ease in what could have been a difficult experience for him. It warmed her heart to see Harry's kindness, politeness and sensitivity with the man and – if it were possible – it served to endear Harry Woodvine to her even more.

Rosina watched all this with some pride, feeling that of all tables in wartime Britain, this was perhaps one of the most unusual and yet typical of the way life had been reshuffled these past months. Servants replaced by servicemen and the divide between the classes crossed. She smiled as she thought of it and, looking around the table, she turned her gaze to Harry Woodvine, who was watching her. On impulse, she held his gaze and did not look away. Neither did he. It was a still, quiet, intense moment in the hubbub of the rowdy dinnertime and she thought of it all evening, long after everyone was in bed and she was alone again, wide awake.

She recalled Evelyn at the dinner table, dazzling all the boys with her beauty and wit. Rosina thought of the young woman she herself used to be, before her brothers died, before she met George. She had been beautiful once, and young, full of dreams and aspirations. She had written short stories and wanted to write a novel one day. Not for the first time, she found herself somewhat envious of Evelyn's freedom, of Grace too and all her girls, at the beginning of their lives. She wished the very best for them, of course she did. She'd die for them! But she mourned too for her lost young womanhood. She'd been a wife and mother for so long, she'd forgotten that girl even existed. But she realised at that moment that this girl had returned – this young Rosina, who loved to talk all night and think deep thoughts; her true self had come back whenever she spent time with Harry Woodvine, when she talked with him and looked at him and even thought about him. And it brought her joy to think of it. A joy tinged with doubt that troubled her that night and sent her downstairs to the empty, blacked-out kitchen with a lit candle to ensure no late-night visits from Mr Wigfall. She sat at the table in the servants' hall, the same chair Harry had used, the candlelight flickering strange shadows across the walls. And she ate bread and jam and when she'd finished she said aloud to nobody, 'Proper jam.'

Chapter 9

May 1940

WRNS Training Depot,
Bramshott,
Hampshire
Wednesday evening, May, 1940

Dearest Mummy,

*This letter is being written to you by an Acting Petty Officer
Special Duties (Linguist) Y! Yes, I passed all my tests! I can
now read Morse at 30 words per minute. Nancy passed
too and quite a few of the other girls. (Mean old Lucinda
didn't – ha!) We received our new uniform – it has brass
buttons with anchors on; crossed anchors on the sleeve and
the gloriously stylish tricorne hat. We will be saluted by*

all those beneath us. What a turn-up! We had to get the bus to another training depot to receive our new uniform and to be photographed and approved. They will send the photograph on and I'll make sure you get it. So, I am now an A/PO with a significant pay rise! I'm particularly thrilled for Nancy with this. She deserves a decent wage. She is sending some of it home to her father and brothers, but I've persuaded her to keep enough for herself for a little luxury now and again, not that there is much luxury one can buy for oneself these days! I can't tell you anything about what we are doing as I have signed the OSA and won't ever be able to tell you, as it is also binding after I leave the Wrens, but be assured I am working hard and doing my best.

All my love to you, darling.

Yours,
Grace

It was a brief letter. Grace had hovered over the final paragraph trying to think of something else to say, but everything she wanted to tell her mother was either classified or were things she felt she couldn't share with her, not in a letter anyway and perhaps not ever. She read over it again and, still dissatisfied with the lack of news, she added a postscript.

PS the Navy has such hilarious names for things. One of my favourite things they cook for us here is tinned tomatoes on fried bread. Oh, it's so delicious! And comforting. But the name is hellish and very funny. They call it 'train smash'! I think you can imagine why from its mangled, bloody appearance!

Grace thought, *At least there's a bit of personality in there.* The secrets of war and the confidences of a young woman made for rather dull letter writing these days. For instance, she longed to explain the fact that she'd got her monthly bleed a week after her night with Erik and had never been more grateful for anything in her whole life. Only passing her tests was akin – and yet even that did not have the same level of relief as feeling the blood leak into her knickers. Wren knickers were nicknamed 'blackouts' as they were so thick and dark, so she could not see the crimson blood when she rushed to the lavatory, but she knew what the dark stain was and could feel the familiar monthly twinge of pain beginning inside her. She wanted to shout 'Hallelujah!' and sing from the rooftops. She vowed inwardly never to have sex again and knew, as she thought it, that it was nonsense and of course she would.

She had told Nancy all about her awful experience with Erik, back at the Portsmouth guest house afterwards and

Nancy had commiserated with her for having had such a rotten first go at it. She had lost her virginity a year before the war began and had lots of advice for Grace about it, even though she was younger. Nancy also told her about making the man pull out before he finished, as well as how to douche afterwards, and she explained that many chaps might well be in possession of a French letter, as some were given out to servicemen from different nations, so it was always worth asking if they had one and insisting they use it, if so. And the most heartening thing to hear was that sex could be much, much better than Erik had given her. It could be overwhelmingly marvellous, according to Nancy's graphic and shocking descriptions, and it gave Grace heart that she'd had a dud for her first experience and that a better one was out there. Not only with someone who had a better technique (apparently some men lasted more than half a minute) but with someone who actually cared for her and was tender and sweet as well as passionate. But the problem remained: how would you know until you were 'at it', as such? She wished men had a resumé, not only for their work but also for their sexual prowess, with references from former lovers as to duration, skills and so forth. How useful that would be!

She wouldn't dream of telling her mother any of that, of course. The other thing that had consumed her recently – and which she couldn't tell her mother about either – was the new equipment they'd started working on. They were learning to operate the Navy's high-frequency wireless equipment, called the HRO, an American high-frequency radio receiver, a big cube with a dial at its centre. They had to learn to find a signal amongst the noisy airwaves and would keep turning the dial backwards and forwards until they located one. They were told the likely frequencies where they'd find most of the German naval traffic and once they found a signal, they could use smaller dials to make it clearer. If there was a thunderstorm, there would be electrical interference that would be hell to listen to. But there were other, sweeter sounds, that could drift in. There might be dance music from faraway places like South America, haunting and exotic. Or the sound of American taxi drivers, even Turkish, Hungarian or Russian voices bouncing back off the atmosphere. The world seemed to become one as they listened to these remote sounds from above the earth. What a curious and mysterious world she now found herself in and she couldn't tell anybody a word about it. Thank heavens for the other Wrens, for only they understood what it was like and it created a deep bond between them, sharing and keeping such secrets.

The day came when those who hadn't passed their tests were to be sent away to other jobs in the Wrens and Lucinda was one of them. Over the months they'd been thrown together, Grace and Nancy had come to a grudging toleration of Lucinda and her clique. She was clearly the richest by far of all the Wrens there and never let anyone forget it, but all her expensive education hadn't helped when it came to learning Morse. On the day the results came, Grace had watched as Lucinda's face fell when it was announced that she had failed.

Grace said to Nancy afterwards, 'I actually feel a bit sorry for Lucinda now. She did put quite a bit of work into this last round.'

And now they were all 'in bunk', sitting on their beds and chatting, when the word filtered through that Lucinda as well as the others who had repeatedly failed the tests were out of the programme. A hush descended as the unfortunate ones packed up their stuff. Grace felt awful about the silence. It wasn't only Lucinda, of course. Some of the nice girls had also failed and it was hard to watch them pack. Grace felt someone should say something. Her previous self – pre-Wrens – wouldn't have dreamt of it being her but these days she had developed more of a backbone and she felt it was the right thing to do.

Focusing on a Wren called Irene in the next bunk, who was one of the unlucky ones, Grace said, 'I am sorry to see you go. Do you know where you're off to next?'

Irene replied, 'To do clerical work in Belfast, apparently. I'll be going with Lucinda.'

'Belfast?' said Grace. 'Gosh, that sounds exciting.'

'Exciting?' said a voice from across the room. It was Lucinda. She leant her elbow on a top bunk in that infuriating way she had of holding court. 'It sounds like the dreariest place on earth. I'll be surrounded by idiots with an impenetrable accent and rained on every day and night. It's just my luck to be sent there, to a place with no culture and no decent nights out.'

'Have you ever been?' asked Grace, surprised at Lucinda's vehemence.

'No, of course not,' said Lucinda.

'Then maybe reserve judgement until you do. It might be fascinating.'

'Well, at least it's not home,' said Lucinda. 'If they sent me back there, I'd kill myself.'

Lucinda turned away and shoved some more things in her bag, then left the room. Grace glanced at Irene, who leant down to Grace conspiratorially and said, 'It's not a happy home, Lucinda's.'

'Why not?' asked Nancy, who had been listening to it all. 'They're rich as Croesus, aren't they?'

Irene shook her head. 'I don't know the details. But Lucinda truly hates going home. Something about her mother being horrid and her stepfather . . . well, let's just say he sounds too *friendly* as far as Lucinda's concerned. She never talks about it in detail, though. But it must be bad, because it's a life of luxury there and why would anyone avoid that, unless something really rotten is going on?'

Grace looked round in the direction Lucinda had gone. 'Why indeed?' she said, pensively. Then she stood up and followed Lucinda's path out into the hallway. Perhaps she'd gone to the toilets. There was a block of three down the hall, so Grace headed for them and stood by the door a moment. Sure enough, she could hear the sound of sobbing come from inside. She went in quietly and the sound stopped immediately, followed by a couple of sharp sniffs.

'Lucinda?' Grace said softly.

No reply.

'It's Grace. I've come to see if you're all right.'

'I'm fine, for God's sake!' came Lucinda's sharp tongue. She came out of the cubicle, trying to adjust her hair and wipe her eyes to pretend that her face was not blotchy with crying. 'Can't a girl get any privacy in this bloody place? I'll be glad to get out of here.'

'Lucinda, there's no shame in being upset.'

'Shame?' spat Lucinda and turned her face to Grace so violently, that Grace gasped. 'You don't know *anything* about shame!'

Grace waited a moment for Lucinda to splash water on her face, then turn the tap off.

'It's good that you joined the Wrens, Lucinda. It gives

you the freedom . . . to escape things. And just because wireless telegraphy wasn't your bag, it doesn't mean that you won't find your niche elsewhere.'

Lucinda was now staring at her face in the mirror above the washbasin. 'My niche?' she said, in a quiet, hollow way.

'Yes, exactly. The place where you belong.'

Lucinda sighed and looked at Grace's reflection. 'But this is just another thing I've failed at, isn't it? The latest in a catalogue of Lucinda Pryce-Masterson's myriad collection of disappointments!'

'How could anyone see Lucinda Pryce-Masterson as a disappointment?' said Grace. 'Look at you! You're beautiful and rich. You have the world at your feet.'

Lucinda turned to the real Grace and looked at her, wide-eyed. She almost looked frightened. 'You don't know a thing about me. There are . . . there are things . . . My mother . . . She's cruel. She used to beat me with a riding crop for not having the correct deportment.'

'Oh, that's awful,' said Grace, genuinely moved. 'I'm so sorry to hear that.'

'Daddy used to stick up for me. But then he got ill . . . And after Daddy died – he was a sweet, kind soul, you see. After that, she married again, when I was twelve. And my stepfather . . . well, I don't even call him *that*. I just call him The Devil.'

Lucinda actually shuddered at her own words. She put her arms about herself and Grace noticed how slight she was, how vulnerable.

She put her hand on Lucinda's shoulder. 'Listen, I've never felt comfortable in the world. I've never found my niche. I've always been on the edge, an outsider, looking in. This is the first time I've ever felt that maybe I can achieve something beyond my own selfish needs. Perhaps Belfast will be that for you, who knows? As you say, it's got to be better than going home when you feel like that about it.'

Lucinda stared into middle distance for a while, in a kind of blank reverie. Suddenly, her face looked so young and Grace said, 'Lucinda? Are you all right?'

'There was a child,' Lucinda said softly. 'They took it away from me and I never saw it again. I don't even know if it was a boy or a girl. That's bad, isn't it? That they didn't even tell me that?'

Grace was utterly shocked and rendered speechless for a moment. Then, 'It – it's atrocious. It's unspeakable.'

'I've never told a soul that.'

'Then thank you for telling me. Listen, why don't we write to each other? I'd love to hear about Belfast.'

Lucinda came back to herself at that moment and looked at Grace as if she'd just appeared and the previous conversation had never happened. Her customary sneer reappeared on her face. '*Me*? Write to *you*? Don't be ridiculous. Let's not pretend to be friends now, just because you pity me. What an insult. Thanks – but no thanks. Have a nice life.'

She pushed past Grace and left swiftly. Grace stood for a moment and gathered herself, then she went back to their room, to see Lucinda continue her packing and snap at one of her friends who tried to help.

Nancy gave Grace a little pat on the shoulder which comforted her. She had tried her best and it just went to show that you never knew what was going on behind closed doors in someone's seemingly perfect life. But did it fully excuse Lucinda from being so unpleasant to everyone? After all, Nancy's mother had died young and it hadn't turned *her* sour. Grace's own father had died, of course, but she didn't see her father's death as evidence of her having had a difficult life, because she had money which she felt precluded a person from ever saying their life was hard. Yet now she saw that you could be very rich and be unhappy, that indeed you could even end up in a living hell, such as Lucinda's homelife sounded. But once you escaped from that, though, it was *your* choice how you turned out. You could either be bitter or you could choose to be a better person because of it. Yes, she had sympathy for Lucinda, but she could not fully forgive her nastiness. So, off they went, the failures, to their new postings and the other Wrens heaved a collective sigh of relief because, sympathetic though they were to most of them, now they could really celebrate their success and look forward to news of their next posting.

That news didn't come straight away. They were waiting for quarters to become available for them at the Royal Navy Shore Wireless stations they were being sent to and then they would be able to pass out. They were all offered extra classes to improve their skills and, if they completed a few weeks of these and passed the tests, they would become Chief Petty Officers. Not all the Wrens chose to do it and were thus posted off quicker but Grace, Nancy and a few others decided to stay and complete the course. They had to study the theory of wireless transmission, with concepts such as cycles and wavelengths and frequencies and oscillations – such a strange collection of new words – testing their brain capacity every day and, by the end of it, seven of them were told that they had fully qualified as telegraphists – Grace and Nancy among them. Grace was over the moon and dashed off another letter to her mother, telling her all about it . . .

I am now officially rated a Chief Petty Officer, known colloquially as a Chief Sparker! This apparently accords great respect from others and I've sewn the sparker's badge on my right sleeve, which has wings with a flash of lightning through the middle. We all went out for lunch in

Portsmouth to celebrate and were treated like queens in the restaurant. Afterwards, what we wanted most of all was to salute a real officer in our uniforms as we'd not done it yet, not with our sparker's badges on, anyway. So, Nancy and I walked about Portsmouth for a while, trying to find a likely sort and eventually in a park we saw a handsome, older naval officer. We stood up tall and both gave him our best and brightest salute and though he looked a bit surprised he reciprocated immediately and then we felt like proper officers too!

I hope you're proud of me, Mummy. I must say I'm really rather proud of myself. Getting a degree at Oxford was, of course, an achievement of merit and I'm proud of the work I did there, but somehow, Mummy – and I'm not sure if you'll understand this – somehow this work we're doing here is so alien to me, to anything I've ever thought about or tried before, that it feels much more of an achievement. Also, knowing I will be serving my country by using these skills makes me prouder than ever. I know I may never in my life be able to talk about it, but it's a knowledge I can put in my pocket and take it out at sad or difficult moments and bolster myself. And that's rather wonderful, isn't it, Mummy?

Soon after this letter was sent, Grace was called in to her supervisor's office and told about her posting.

'You will be going to the RN Shore Wireless station at

Scarborough.'

'Oh!' said Grace, not able to hide her disappointment. Scarborough was only a few miles down the coast from home at Ravenscar and as she had once wanted to run away to sea, similarly now she had a desire to be posted somewhere far away from home. It felt as if she were to be posted to her very doorstep. She walked back to the bunk in a huff. But then Nancy came in and said with delight, 'I'm off to Scarborough!'

'Oh, Nancy! Me too!'

And then everything was all right.

Chapter 10

The Wrens were allowed a week of home leave before they began their new post. It was handy, both Grace and Nancy living nearby each other, as it meant they could travel home together. The bus and the trains they took were busy and tiring, followed by a severe delay which led to them getting a night train that would arrive in the early hours of the following morning and travelling by train at night was a little unnerving. The train was blacked-out, of course, with the blinds drawn and only a muted blue light to see by. All the names of the stations were removed and sometimes there were baffling stops of long duration before moving on. They were surrounded by many others in uniform and at first there was plenty of chatter and camaraderie. If there seemed to be no room, some chap or other would say something like, 'Room here for a little one, Jenny.' Most servicemen called them Jenny Wrens, which

Grace found endearing. Just being in uniform was enough to make you warmly welcomed anywhere by others in the same garb and Grace had never felt more a part of a team than now. As the night wore on, the chatter lessened and it was not uncommon to see servicemen and women with their heads resting on someone else's shoulder as they snoozed.

They arrived in Whitby at three in the morning and the passengers disembarked and scattered to the four winds. Nancy needed a lift to Robin Hood's Bay and Grace to Raven Hall and a soldier taking an empty army truck south to Scarborough had said he'd take them both, which was a huge relief because the thought of waiting around at Whitby railway station for hours until the buses started was miserable.

Grace and Nancy climbed into the front seat beside the driver, a chap called Vic. He was very good-natured and chatted away with them on the journey. He dropped Nancy at the top of the hill in Robin Hood's Bay, although she lived down near the sea in the warren of narrow streets, but he didn't fancy getting his truck down there and back up in one piece and she was quite all right about it.

'See thee in a week in Scarborough,' said Nancy and they had a quick hug before she climbed down and walked away down the hill and into the night. Vic started off again and trundled along the high-hedged roads of the farmland between Robin Hood's Bay and Ravenscar. They continued to talk about Vic's adventures in the army so far, which were clearly not under the OSA as he told her everything in detail, whereas she could tell him virtually nothing. He didn't seem to mind, though, as he liked the sound of his own voice, that was clear. But Grace wasn't bothered; she was tired and it was quite comforting to listen to him droning on about manoeuvres on the moorland and angry farmers. She found herself in danger of nodding off, her eyelids drooping, with the rhythm of the truck and the lateness of the hour. But she knew she must stay awake to give him directions. They were coming towards the turn-off to Ravenscar and she forced herself awake and said, 'This is it, just here on the right.'

But he drove straight past it.

'I say, you missed it. The turning was right back there. Didn't you hear me?'

But Vic didn't reply and kept driving on, his face like stone.

'Can you turn around, please?' Grace was almost shouting now. 'You missed the turning!'

Then, without a word, Vic slowed the truck down and turned left into another road and went up it a bit, Grace thinking he was going to stop and turn round at some point, but he didn't. Instead he pulled into a lay-by and, parking up, switching off the engine. He still had not said anything.

'What's going on?' said Grace and Vic leant over to her

175

and grasped her by the waist and pulled her in for a kiss. A few months ago, Grace might have let him, out of shock and curiosity more than anything. But she was a different Grace now and she was having none of this. She gave him a hard shove, which seemed to shock him.

'Eh?' he said and leant back in.

'I say, get off me!' she said firmly and pushed him in the chest, so his side hit the steering wheel and he cried out, 'Ow!'

'How dare you!' she shouted at him. 'How dare you try to take advantage of a fellow servicewoman! Have you no shame? What would your mother say? Your father? You, with your nasty, gropey hands all over an unwilling Jenny Wren? You should be disgusted with yourself. Turn this truck around this instant and take me to Ravenscar railway station. Now!'

He looked at her, his eyes like glass. Then he sat back in his seat and started the engine. Without a word, he drove her to the station as she'd requested. She didn't want to tell him where she lived, so wasn't going to say to take her to Raven Hall. As he pulled up in Station Square, she quickly opened the door and climbed out, slamming the door behind her and marching off, looking purposefully towards a house in the corner of the square as if it were hers. She was aware the truck was turning around, but still in the square as she turned the corner of the house and walked down the passageway beside it. She hid behind the wall until she heard the truck draw away and finally leave. She was shaking and a bit breathless, but she was all right. After waiting a good few minutes, she came out into the silent square and had a look around to make sure he hadn't parked up and crept back. Then she ran down the road, gardens transformed into allotments on one side, farmland on the other. A thin line at the horizon told her dawn was coming and she could hear a few birds gently beginning to tweet their chorus as she turned into the driveway of Raven Hall and slowed to a walk, out of breath. She'd never been so relieved to see home, though just the day before she'd been rather dreading it, as she had become so used to Wrennery life. But now it looked like the most beautifully safe place on earth and, despite the scare of Vic's assault, she felt proud of herself that she had stood her ground and had made him do the right thing. But she was sickened that a serviceman would act in such a way. She had felt that they were all in it together and any uniform commanded instant respect, but then she thought of Erik and now Vic, and sometimes the way the naval officers at the training depot looked through the Wrens as if they were invisible . . . and she realised that the comradeship of war was all well and good, but the battle between the sexes was not over by a long chalk and perhaps never would be.

When she arrived home, she went round to the kitchen

entrance and saw, through the window, that Bairstow was already up, preparing her own early morning cuppa. Even on her days off, that woman was always up at dawn, or long before it in the winter. Grace knocked on the window and Bairstow looked so startled Grace worried she might give her a heart attack, but when she saw who it was, she smiled broadly and rushed to unlock the door to let her in.

'Miss Grace!' she exclaimed. 'What a surprise at this time of day!'

'Thank you, Bairstow,' said Grace. 'You have no idea how happy I am to see you!'

Grace was poured a cup of strong tea which tasted like heaven, then Bairstow soft-boiled a real egg from the Raven Hall hens, which was comforting and simply delicious. How good it was to be safe and warm. How good it was to be home!

'Thi mother will be up soon or would tha like to go and surprise her?' said Bairstow, pouring Grace another cup of tea.

'Ah, no. I'll let her sleep. Sounds like she needs it with all the extra jobs she's doing. And I hear you have company for mealtimes these days? A bunch of RAF men? What are they like?'

'They're champion,' said Bairstow. 'Nice lads, all of 'em. Polite but cheeky and their sergeant is a kind man.'

'That's good to hear. What work are they doing in the area, do we know?'

'Nobody but them knows owt about it. And they're keeping mum, as is right and proper.'

'Of course.'

'All we know is they're building a series of summat. Folk have seen aerials go up, but what that means is a complete mystery to me.'

Grace thought about what this was likely to mean. She couldn't share it with Bairstow or anyone, of course, but from her training she guessed that the men were constructing stations along the east coast equipped with the latest RDF equipment. RDF – Radio Direction Finding – involved using short-wave radio waves to find out the position of objects, such as aircraft. The Wrens had been told briefly about its existence but little more. She shook her head; the marvels of modern science were astonishing – and vital in this war.

'Oh, it's a complete mystery to me too,' said Grace, but Bairstow narrowed her eyes at her briefly, making Grace feel she'd been too obvious. She was still getting used to all this secrecy and was learning that it was much the best thing to say nothing at all.

'They'll be here soon, so tha might want to make thissen scarce, unless tha want to meet 'em. But anyway, you'll see 'em all here tonight for their tea.'

'Yes, I think I'll wait until then. I'm awfully tired so I think I might go straight to bed. Could you ask Mummy to let me sleep? Tell her I'll see her when I've woken up.'

'Yes, of course, miss. Tha must be dog-tired.'

'That I am. Thank you, Bairstow – particularly for cooking a whole egg just for me.'

Bairstow smiled and Grace went up to bed. She'd sent word ahead that she was coming but wasn't sure exactly what time or day it would be and so she found her room ready, dust covers gone and clean sheets on the bed. She took off her uniform and laid it out carefully, taking off her underwear but putting her slip back on to sleep in. She couldn't be bothered to find her nightie in her bag and she was desperate for bed.

She awoke sometime in the afternoon. It was difficult to tell the hour at first glance as the blackouts were still up. She found her watch and saw it was gone three. She looked up to see that her jacket was gone, most likely squirrelled away by Bairstow or her mother to be cleaned and pressed. So she washed then went to her bag and put on clean underwear and her Wren skirt, shirt and tie and she tidied her hair. Then she ventured out to see her mother, who she found writing letters at her desk.

'Hello, Mummy!'

It was an emotional reunion. Her mother had tears in her eyes, which Grace found touching.

'You silly thing,' she said, gently, touching her mother's

cheek. 'I've not been away that long. Just since January. Like an Oxford term, really. Just a bit longer.'

'It feels much longer!' said her mother and smiled through her tears. 'It's just so good to see you in the flesh, darling. How smart you are! And goodness, you've changed so much. It's extraordinary.'

'Have I really?'

'Well, your hair is much shorter, of course, and has a bit of a curl to it. And somehow you look . . . I don't know, even taller?'

'Oh dear, I hope not! I'm already far too tall for a girl.'

'No, it's something else. I know! You're not stooping any more. You're standing up perfectly straight.'

'Did I stoop?' said Grace carelessly, though she knew perfectly well that she used to, because of rather wanting to disappear altogether.

'You and I both know full well that you did. But you don't any more at all. It's marvellous to see, darling.'

'It's all that marching, I suppose,' Grace said. 'Forces one to stand up straight.'

But as her mother smiled knowingly at her, they both knew it was more than that. Grace had grown in confidence these last months and it shone from her.

They chatted a bit about the goings-on at the hall, the RAF chaps, the farmers, Jessop, Throp and Ronald. All the news. Then her mother said, 'Oh, I nearly forgot. A letter came for you. Here.'

Her mother retrieved it from her desk. At first, Grace thought it might be from Lucinda. Perhaps she'd taken up her offer after all. But seeing the handwriting, she knew it couldn't be. It was scruffy and utterly unfamiliar. She turned it over and saw the sender had the initial F. Who did she know with an F? How peculiar. She opened it up while her mother watched.

'Who is it from?' said her mother.

'I truly have no idea. Hang on.'

It was a short letter and she scanned it quickly to the end to find it was signed 'Fred'.

'Oh my goodness!'

'Who is it? I'm agog!'

'It's from Fred.'

'Who's that?'

'Hang on,' said Grace and started reading.

It was very brief and to the point, beginning with a *Dear Grace Calver-Lazenby* and going on to say very little, as Grace supposed he wasn't allowed to say much.

Im in France and its warm. Ive never been here and there is pretty country. I remember our dance and your dress. If youd do me the honor of writing to me and that that would be smashing.

(He'd crossed out the second that and then written it again.)

It was good to meet you and that. Maybe I could see you if I ever get leave. Are you still in Hampshire? If youve been posted on can you send your new address. Or Ill just keep writing to this one. I wish I could of kissed you more than twice I think. You had a nice way about you.

All the best and cheerio.

Fred.

Her mother had been fiddling with things on the desk while she read. *Oh dear*, Grace thought. She felt a dreadful snob but knew she could never give her heart to a man who didn't understand apostrophes. But then, this boy was miles away. And it was sweet of him to keep in touch. What harm would it do to write back to him and do her bit to keep the forces happy, including Fred? She thought of Erik and his coldness, then of Vic and his hands on her waist. Fred was nicer than either of them, after all. Although one thing she was learning was that a man is never as sweet to you as before he has bedded you. Perhaps that was the truth of all men – or maybe it was just some of them. Surely there must be some men who were still nice after sex. Nancy had certainly said some were, but Grace hadn't met any of those yet.

'Is he your sweetheart, darling?' said her mother, smiling.

Grace thought about Erik, Vic and the others. How she longed to confess to her mother about her dreadful first time and the relief of her monthly coming soon after; about all the ones who'd kissed and felt her up outside the village hall; even about that idiot last night in the truck. But what good would it do? Her mother would only worry about her. Or chastise her. Or look at her differently and not in a good way. After all, her mother had loved and married one man and never been with another, as far as anyone knew. What could she know about sex and men and desire and love and all that?

'Yes, he is. Nice chap called Fred. I met him at a dance near the Wrennery and he promised he'd write.'

'That's nice, dear. Tell me about him.'

But Grace realised she knew virtually nothing about him. It just seemed simpler to keep her mother happy this way, thinking she had a steadfast chap in the army to keep her out of trouble.

'Oh, there's not much to tell. He's just a good chap and we like each other. Anyway, how are you? How is everyone? I've had one letter from the twins and Connie but nothing from Evvy.'

They talked then about her sisters and Grace was relieved to have moved the conversation on.

'And tell me about these RAF fellows who invade the house every day. Are they awful? Bairstow likes them.'

'They're very good men,' said her mother. 'We all enjoy

their company. The sergeant is highly educated. Studied physics and maths at Cambridge.'

'Gosh, he sounds interesting.'

'Yes,' said her mother and paused. 'Look, I have to go and help Bairstow prepare dinner, darling. The hordes will be here soon.'

Grace went with her and helped too. It was nice to feel useful and when the RAF chaps came it was good to meet new people and gratifying to see some of them eyeing her up surreptitiously. She was annoyed her jacket was being pressed, so she couldn't wear it. She wanted to show off in it but she supposed the men were happier to see more of her figure in her skirt and shirt. The young sergeant barely looked at her, though, but spoke quite a bit to her mother. He would be interesting to talk to, as he must have a good knowledge of science and so forth to be in charge of constructing an RDF station. How Grace would love to quiz him about it. But it was impossible, of course, as he wasn't allowed to discuss it. Grace did find it hard to meet servicemen at the same intellectual level as her. Worse than hard, it was nigh-on impossible, of which Fred's letter was testament. She hated to write off a person due to their schooling or lack of it and tried not to judge people that way. After all, Nancy had had very little schooling and look how clever she was. Grace sighed inwardly, realising she was learning that education didn't really mean much when it came to natural intelligence and even the breadth of someone's knowledge. It was more about luck and opportunity than any kind of right or breeding. Maybe some of these chaps just needed more of a chance in life to prove themselves. Perhaps, for some, the war might give them this chance. And again, Grace felt that this war was making her a better person, dissolving some of her old prejudices and ignorance. With this in mind, she made an effort to talk to the chaps around the table and find out more about them. They were full of good humour and banter, which she enjoyed immensely and she could see why her mother and Bairstow didn't mind their imposition each day. It certainly livened up the place.

After dinner was over and the men had left, Grace helped clear up, impressed by how her mother had adapted to her new ways since the war had robbed her of most of her staff. Rosina seemed quite at home now with a pinny on and her hands plunged into the washing-up water, a sight that none of them could have imagined a few months ago. They played cards together after dinner and chatted a little, but there was a new awkwardness between them. As a child, Grace had shared everything with her mother. Not making friends easily, her mother had been her closest confidante. She would write epic letters to her from boarding school and go for long walks with her when home, telling her every fleeting thought that crossed her mind and all of her secrets. Now there was so much she couldn't tell her mother, their conversation felt somehow stilted and difficult and she was sure her mother felt it too, so that even though she was not tired by mid-evening, as she'd slept so late, she made her excuses and went to bed. Perhaps she was just exhausted, by the long journey home, the horrible incident in the truck and meeting all those chaps at dinner. But back in her room, she still felt out of place. Everything in it looked childish, as if it belonged to another person who no longer existed.

In the morning, she couldn't face all those fellows at breakfast and pretended to sleep in late. In reality, she was lying in her room, listening to the distant roar of the sea. How she had missed it when she first went away to school, then university and again down south. It was so good to hear it. But somehow it made her sad. Something had been lost while she'd become a Wren and she supposed it was her childhood. *War made one grow up rather quickly*, she thought. In those first few months of war, during her initial training and all the marching and scrubbing of floors, war had seemed like a bit of a lark, just something different from home and school and university life that was all a bit of jolly good fun. Then the Morse training seemed like a strange dream, so utterly unlike anything she'd done before, apart from grappling with Latin and Greek declensions, perhaps. But once she'd signed the OSA and they knew what their job was really going to be, she had felt herself change . . . No, that wasn't enough of a word to describe it. She had felt herself *evolve*. Yes, that was it. And learning that once she started at Scarborough next week, she would be listening in to the German navy and passing on that information to hopefully sink a few ships and save a few British lives, the war became more real, though as she hadn't started yet, it was still theoretical and somehow beyond her grasp. It still all felt a little like a game of battleships, but a very secret one.

The war had dragged on for months now and no invasion had come, as everyone had feared, before Christmas. So would it all be over by the end of 1940? People called it the Phoney War or the Bore War. But her superiors in the Royal Navy didn't act that way. Perhaps they knew something the general public didn't. It was all rather worrying and confusing and utterly beyond her control. She was ashamed to admit she was enjoying the war so far, but behind that was the knowledge that things might be moving in a sinister direction. And despite her secret status, she knew little more than the average person on the street.

Lost in thought, she realised that she had heard the men leave in their truck a little while before and so she got up and dressed hurriedly and went down to the kitchen, ready to apologise for sleeping in. She found her mother and Bairstow in the kitchen, a newspaper on the table, which they were examining in detail, in a concentrated hush.

'What is it?' said Grace.

'It's a miracle,' said Bairstow.

Grace walked swiftly round the table to look. She knew that in the past few days, the closing days of May, that the British Expeditionary Force in France had been retreating to the coast and that the newspapers had been full of the epic battle they were making to defend their ground. She'd read that the BEF were 'powerfully entrenched', but now the newspapers' top stories were all about how thousands of British troops were being evacuated from France via the coastal town of Dunkirk, many by Navy vessels yet others by an extraordinary armada of little ships piloted by ordinary British folk. *Trains Packed with Battle-Weary Men . . . BEF men returning from France were arriving yesterday in thousands at a south coast port . . . Train after train went down empty on South East Coast lines, many through the night, and returned full of weary figures in khaki . . .* '

Horrified, Grace read an account of one soldier's experience.

Nazi bombers were swooping down, unloading their bombs and machine-gunning the quay . . . When our ship was hit, we swam ashore, but when she did go down, we swam back again to take her out of the harbour. But she turned turtle and we had to swim again. Some of us were swimming for hours but then we were picked up by a warship. All of us were almost naked and we have had no food since Wednesday and no sleep for three days.

Grace immediately thought of Fred. His letter had been dated about two weeks ago, so that he could very well be on that beach, dive-bombed by German fighters or drowning in the water or left to rot on the sand. And what then, once the BEF were bravely evacuated? What then for France and Belgium? Thank heavens for the bravery of all involved in that heroic deed. But once they were back here or captured or – God forbid – dead, then the Germans would stand at the edge of France and they would look westward, towards Britain, towards the south coast and the east coast. Towards her home. And Grace knew that not only poor Fred and many other British lads just like him would be in terrible danger and might even have already been killed, but once that was over, then invasion was imminent. Would it come by air or by sea or both? Grace suddenly realised that, from June 1940, she would be sitting in the outermost reaches of the British front, at a shore wireless station above Scarborough, listening in to the German navy and potentially its invasion of the British Isles. No longer was it a Phoney War. Now, in the most real and most sobering sense, war was coming home to all of them.

Chapter 11

June 1940

It had been sunny, warm and very dry in the first few days of June. As Rosina left the church and walked up the street, it was only just before ten in the morning, but it felt like high noon, with the sun beating down and the air so close. She wondered if a storm was due. Well, that might at least give some relief from the heat. She thought about her meeting with the vicar as she walked. News had come that two local lads had been killed: a master mariner with the Merchant Navy and a warrant officer in the RAF, both younger than Harry. Rosina had visited the vicar to offer to pay for a plaque in the church dedicated to these two, which offer was gratefully received. It was horrible to hear about such young lives being lost, especially of those you knew, even if not well. Both young men had lived in Ravenscar and one of them used to play with the girls when they were younger. Gone now and dead, in the sky or in the sea or on the land. Should she visit the parents to give her condolences? No, they weren't her tenants, so it seemed intrusive. The plaque would be her tribute, she decided. More welcome, she hoped, than a visit.

Yet that morning she was visiting one of her tenants, a young mother called Phyllis Precious who lived with her little girl, Elsie, in one of the Raven Hall cottages. Rosina had been told that Phyllis had not received any letters from her husband, Wilfred, for some months and was distraught about his silence. Rosina had sent a card to enquire if Phyllis would like to come to tea, but the young wife had responded that she was expecting a baby any day now and was very cumbersome, so she would find the walk to Raven Hall difficult; would it be possible for Mrs Calvert-Lazenby to visit her instead? Rosina had agreed, of course, and instructed Phyllis that on no account should she worry about trying to drum up cakes or sandwiches or anything of the sort on rations. A glass of water would suffice.

By the time she arrived at Phyllis's house, Rosina's cheeks were hot from the sun, despite her sun hat, and her blouse felt sticky against her skin. The little front garden was lovingly tended with cheerful flower beds on each side and when she knocked on the door a small child answered, a little girl with thick, dark curls and big, inquisitive eyes, her mother following close behind. Rosina could see why

Phyllis did not want to walk in this heat: her bump was as enormous as she was petite. Rosina wondered if it were twins – she herself had been huge with Daisy and Dora. Pleasantries were exchanged and Rosina followed them into the sitting room and the little girl gazed with open curiosity at the visitor, one hand permanently grasping her mother's skirt, the other curled into a fist with her thumb jammed in her mouth. Tea was poured and comments made about the weather. Then the conversation dried up and Phyllis gazed off into middle distance, lost in thought.

'Is there any news of your husband?' Rosina asked, tentatively, wondering if this was a bad idea. But it was the reason for her visit, to see if her tenant needed any help in her husband's absence.

'Nowt. Not a word. For five months and nine days now. When he first went away, he'd write all t'time.'

'Well, that may mean nothing at all. As I understand it, the post is often held up from active servicemen. You'll probably find a big bundle of letters will turn up at once and you'll struggle to find the time to read them all.'

She hoped this had been comforting, but Phyllis didn't answer and just carried on staring into space. The girl tugged at her mother's skirt, a silent plea as she still had her thumb in her mouth and hadn't made a sound. Her mother did not move, did not respond.

'I'm going to guess your name,' said Rosina to the little

girl. 'I think it might be . . . hang on . . . let me think . . . is it . . . Elsie?'

The girl's eyes widened even further and she ferociously nodded her head and let her thumb drop from her mouth.

'Would you like to show me your room, Elsie? Then Mummy can get some rest while we play.'

She saw a glimmer of a smile in Phyllis's face but other than that, she still made no response. Rosina stood up, put down her cup and saucer and stretched her hand out for little Elsie to take. The girl did so obediently and then led her to her bedroom. It was a box room, really, and Rosina felt the child should have a bigger room and felt a little stab of guilt that this cottage, which she owned, wasn't bigger or better equipped for a family. There was a single shelf on the whitewashed wall, with a few clothbound books of stories and poems. On her bed was a dolly and on the floor was a pile of multi-coloured wooden bricks, with some minor constructions having been started and abandoned. Rosina knelt down and started building a wall. Elsie sucked her thumb again and used her spare hand to help, crouching down in a wobbly fashion, her fat little fingers grasping each brick with care and moving it to add to Rosina's wall. This preoccupied them for some time, until Elsie decided it would be more fun to destroy it and pushed the whole lot over with one sweep of her damp hand, the thumb still gleaming wet from its constant sucking. She grinned at Rosina and they both giggled.

'Would you like to read a story?' said Rosina.

Elsie nodded solemnly and they sat down on the bed and read some Winnie the Pooh poems for a while. Elsie was fascinated by the picture of the little sprite called a brownie who hid behind the curtain. She kept jabbing her finger at it and staring at Rosina. Then she clambered along the bed and gingerly reached out to touch the curtain that hung just above it, swiftly turning round to Rosina, who got up and whisked the curtain away from the wall, saying, 'Look, no brownies.' Elsie smiled but kept her thumb in her mouth, her smile vanishing as she started sucking on it again.

They sat down again to read some more and Elsie's little dark head nodded a bit, then rested gently on Rosina's arm as she read. Soon, she had nodded off. Rosina sat still with the little sleeping form for a while. No sound had come from the living room and she wondered if Phyllis was sleeping. She remembered the exhaustion and isolation one sometimes felt when raising small children alone. She'd had a nanny, which had helped, once Evelyn came along, but she had refused to have one when she only had Grace, insisting that she wanted to raise her girls as much as she could herself. George's absences had already begun before Grace's birth and so she was used to a solitary existence, just her, the baby and a house full of servants. Sometimes, cousins or friends would come to stay for a bit, which was comforting and fun, but they always went away again and determined though she had been not to have a nanny for Grace, she had found the long hours of entertaining a baby or small child relentless.

She had not minded the baby days, because although Grace did wake up at dawn, Rosina would pick her up and put her on her chest and the baby would go straight back to sleep and not surface again until elevenish. Then she would wake up, screaming hungry, and Rosina would put her straight on the breast. After that, Grace was usually awake until quite late at night and those long hours of the afternoon and evening, as Grace grew into a toddler and beyond, were filled with attempts to amuse her child, who seemed to have an insatiable curiosity about everything and never wanted to nap. So she gave in when she found out she was pregnant again and hired a nanny to help. But she was still very involved in all her girls' upbringings and remembered clearly how lonely it felt to only have conversations with small people all day when it was easy to forget you were an adult who had once had scintillating discussions around the dinner table. She loved having babies – after all, she had five of them – but she knew that deep down she was trying to do two things: first, gain George's attention by giving him a new child (which failed five times but she had hoped that one would be a boy, who never came) and second, to fill the ever-deepening chasm of loneliness that was gaping inside her. And the noise and activity of children filled the silence but never managed to plug the gap . . .

Rosina shifted the hot little package that lay against her arm, mouth wide open now, eyes fast closed. She carefully put her hand under Elsie's head, heavy with sleep, and settled her cheek on the pillow. It was too warm for a blanket so she let the child be and walked softly into the living room, expecting to see Phyllis also nodded off in the chair, but the young mother with the huge mound of a belly was wide awake, sitting in exactly the same position as when she'd left her, still staring in exactly the same way at nothing but her mind's eye.

Rosina felt a shiver go up her spine. *Someone's walking over your grave*, her own mother used to say to her with a wink, which always intrigued and rather terrified her. She stood for a moment in the doorway and Phyllis seemed utterly unaware of her presence. Rosina wondered if Phyllis's husband was indeed dead, lost at sea, in a watery grave. Then, suddenly, an image of Harry Woodvine leapt into her head and she thought of what might happen to him if he were sent away abroad. He was safe enough round here, of course. But Harry had told her that their current project would be ending soon and that his team would be split up and sent on to other places and he wasn't sure where he'd be going next. He said it was likely that would happen in a matter of days. So, after his project here was done, he would go and then heaven knew where he'd end up. The thought of Harry dead made her feel sick, actually nauseous and a little dizzy. She inwardly scolded herself to pull herself together. This poor young woman had most likely lost her husband and Rosina was keening about some young man she barely knew who was perfectly all right? It was absurd.

She broke the spell of her own maudlin thoughts by coming into the room. Phyllis noticed her at last and went to stand up, putting both hands on the chair arm for support, but Rosina said quietly, 'Don't. You stay there and I'll bring you another pot of tea, if you like. I wish you'd slept while I played with Elsie. She's napping now if you wanted to get your head down for a while?'

Phyllis shook her head absently then went through the laborious process of standing up and winced, her hand at her chest.

'Heartburn,' she said. 'Summat awful. Never had it last time. Too many bairns in my belly.'

'Is it twins?' said Rosina.

'Aye. So, I'll have three bairns to cope with. On my own.'

'You'll probably get a letter from him tomorrow, you'll

see,' said Rosina, smiling, knowing it was wishful thinking but praying it would be so.

'Nay,' said Phyllis, distantly. 'He's gone. I know it.'

Both women stood there, silent, the weight of the young mother's knowledge heavy in the room like the close air.

'If there's anything I can do to help, you must let me know. Send me a note or just come to visit. Really, I want to help.'

'Thank you, but nay. We'll be all right. I've stacks of jobs to do now, if tha don't mind.'

Rosina took the hint. It was tiring to deal with guests when you were pregnant and had a little one too. She remembered her own lack of patience or tolerance in the same position. But at least she had shown her face and hopefully helped a little, giving Phyllis a little break from responsibility. But they were not friends and both knew it.

'He were a good man,' Phyllis said suddenly and stared urgently at Rosina, as if this had been doubted. 'A kind and gentle man. I thought all men were poison till I met 'im. Me father used to beat us, but Wilf Precious were as gentle as t'lambs in t'field. He loved bairns and animals and growing things. He were not made for t'Navy, seasick and homesick, and he loved to write. He would've written by now. He wrote every chance he got. He were a diamond, that man. Precious by name and precious by nature, he were.'

'I'm sure he still is,' said Rosina, wanting to reach out

and touch Phyllis's shoulder but was shocked to see her shaking her head violently from side to side.

'Nay, nay,' she muttered and Rosina felt she could not say the right thing and decided she could do no more good there.

'I'll leave you in peace,' she said. 'Try to get a little rest before Elsie wakes up, mmm?'

But Phyllis wasn't listening any more and wandered off into the passageway. Rosina heard her go into Elsie's room and then came the sound of the little girl stirring, her mother shushing her and the bed springs creaking. Then all was quiet. Phyllis must have climbed on to the bed to rest with her little one. Perhaps the last thing she'd wanted was to be away from her child, even for a break. Rosina felt it was time to go, so she put the cups and saucers on the tea tray, took it out to the kitchen and washed them up as quietly as she could. Then she left, pulling the front door to as silently as possible.

Rosina's walk back up the lane was sombre and hot. She thought of when they'd brought the news that George was dead and she'd felt nothing, absolutely nothing. She'd believed at the time that it must be shock, that soon she would break down and cry for her dead husband. But the tears never came, and she almost envied Phyllis Precious, though she knew it was wicked to think such a thing. At least Phyllis had loved and been loved by a good man for a time, whatever the truth of his current condition. At least Phyllis had known kindness and gentleness. Rosina wondered what that must be like, for a man to be sweet to you and to really mean it, not just utter honeyed words to get what he wanted. Simply nice and good and caring, truly caring. She realised that she could not imagine how that must feel, because she'd never had it in her life.

Chapter 12

That evening Harry hung about after dinner and helped Rosina and Bairstow with the clearing up, as he sometimes did. They were all comfortable with each other now and chatted easily about the progression of the war. Rosina sensed he wanted to stay longer and suggested a walk around the grounds. Now the heat of the day was gone, it was a lovely evening, with a sea breeze that cooled the face and yet left the air still warm and pleasant.

They stopped at the front door, Harry lighting her cigarette and one for him. They crossed the lawn in a comfortable silence and stepped on to the pathway which was bordered by small violet flowers. Beside them was a low stone wall, safe and secluded, the cliff jutting above them on the other side, gulls crying beyond it. In this part of the grounds, small lawns were bordered by trees and the cliff itself, from which the battlements had been hewn.

The garden was laid out in tiers, with stone steps leading up to layers of battlements with narrow walkways and hidden seating areas. It was a garden of stone, grass, paths and, as Harry had once said, secrets. Back near the house, the sea was a distant rumble, but there in the grounds it was a constant, rushing roar, the perpetual waves rolling in and rolling in and rolling out and rolling out, forever.

Harry said, 'Tomorrow is our last day with you.' Taking a deep drag on his cigarette he looked at her.

'No, really?' said Rosina and stopped dead. Then, noting the drama of her reaction, she cleared her throat and carried on walking. She took him up to the first layer of battlements. The steps were worn in the centre, showing the wear of a century and the rock wall beside them was mottled with white lichen and fringed by creeping ivy.

'Yes, I'm afraid so. The chaps are all grumbling about it as they've grown accustomed to your hospitality. I'm sure wherever they're sent next will be hard-pushed to live up to it.'

'So, you're not all going to the same place?'

'No. The team are done with the local construction work and they're being sent off elsewhere. I'm going to be about for a while longer, as I'll be setting up and running some things hereabouts. Not sure where, but on this coast. Not far, I shouldn't think, as they've arranged digs for me in Whitby.'

A wave of relief swept over her. *He's not leaving, he's not leaving!* Well, the daily meals would end but at least he would be around and about. Would he still come over to see her, she wondered? There was no way she felt able to ask. Surely it would be inappropriate to do so. 'Whitby isn't far,' was all she felt able to say and took a quick puff of her cigarette.

'These walkways and battlements are extraordinary,' he said, changing the subject. Did he think she was suggesting something when she said it wasn't far? And changed the subject out of embarrassment? She hoped not.

'Yes, they were crafted from the cliff itself, using dynamite in some places. The locals thought it was madness, apparently. But it actually works, doesn't it? The battlements suit it. Apparently at that time there were iron trees in the gardens with metal leaves that would clink musically in the breeze.'

'How bizarre!' said Harry and laughed.

Along from the top of the steps was a viewing platform which gave a clear view over the trees to the sea beyond. It jutted out from the path in the shape of a triangle, laid with grass and bordered by a wall just above waist height, beyond which was a steep drop to another lawn below. In two corners were triangular seats made with slabs of stone.

'When the girls were little, they would play kings and

queens on those seats and their minions would sit on this wall with their legs dangling into the chasm and frighten me. They'd do it all the more, just to rebel against me, the little terrors. And I did the same with my two brothers when we were little.'

'That's the role of children, surely, to rebel against their parents and terrify them? It's how we grow up.'

'I suppose it is.'

'I imagine it must have been an idyllic childhood, being raised here.'

'In many ways, yes,' said Rosina, leaning over the wall to feel that old pull of the fall. 'Isolated, though. Separate from the world.'

'And that's why it seems idyllic to me.'

Rosina looked at him. He was leaning on his elbows on the wall too now, staring out to sea. He stubbed his cigarette out on the stone, making sure it was dead cold before putting the butt into his pocket. She appreciated this small kindness. She did the same with hers.

'Is the world so distasteful to you, then?' she said.

'Mostly, yes, it is. I like a few people, a selected few, but most people I find difficult. I like my own company. Books, whisky, as you know. I like trees. And the sea . . . Undemanding, out of reach.'

She was watching him as he spoke, loving his thoughts and the way he put them. Then, he looked round at her.

'I say, Whitby isn't far. But I don't know anybody there. Would it be all right if I came to visit here when I can? Seeing as you're my only friend in the area? I'll understand completely if not.'

'Of course,' she said and had to stop herself from beaming. 'You must come to see me . . . and Bairstow. For jam sandwiches, obviously.'

'Obviously,' he said and smiled at her. 'For jam sandwiches.'

They watched each other's faces and it seemed to last an age, though it was probably only a few seconds. And then the moment was broken, by the unmistakeable whine of an aircraft approaching behind them.

They both stood up straight and whipped round, scanning the skies for it.

'There,' said Rosina.

'Bloody hell, it's a German fighter!' cried Harry. 'Quick, get inside. Which is the quickest way?'

The plane was still far away, but Rosina wasn't going to argue. 'Follow me,' she said and took him up the next short flight of stone steps to the upper level of the garden, from where she could run around the hedge and across the lawn to the side door of the house. The plane's engine grew louder as they ran across the grass, then they heard the guns engage and Rosina ducked and put her hands over her head, as if that would make any difference. But she could hear that the plane was not overhead, instead a couple of fields or so away. They reached the back door and hurled themselves inside, Harry turning round to stand in the doorway and scan the skies. The engine's drone lessened and it sounded as though it was moving away. Harry went out on to the path and looked up.

'Come back!' Rosina said in a loud whisper, as if the pilot could hear them and would turn his guns on them at the sound.

'It's going,' he said. Rosina came out and they watched it reduce to a speck in the far distance. They stood a while to see if it might return, but it was gone.

'I think it was over my land,' she said. 'That's Popplewell's farm in that direction so I ought to go and look, see if it did any damage or – God forbid – hurt someone.'

'You're staying here,' he said firmly. 'It might be back. I can go with Jessop.'

'Certainly not!' she said, taking umbrage. 'It's my land and my responsibility. And Jessop is away for the day, visiting family with his wife. I've a shotgun in a locked cabinet in Jessop's shed – we each have a key. We can take that with us, just in case.'

'I'll carry the gun,' he said when she'd loaded it and she let him, never much liking guns, despite her father's insistence that she learn how to shoot animals that had to be put down. She led him beyond her grounds along the path beside the first field bordering her garden.

'There's a searchlight two fields on from here,' she said, 'so it might have been shooting at that.'

'Possibly so,' he said. 'Have you seen German aircraft here before?'

'Never. It's my very first one.'

It was actually exciting, she thought. She remembered when the ARP chap had scolded her about her blackout and now she saw he'd been completely justified in his wrath. It was worrying – and somewhat scary – to think of German planes just turning up over British land like that. But it also felt exhilarating, the way her heart was thumping in her chest, as they trotted up the path together, wondering what they'd find. Then they heard something that shocked them – the sound of cows bellowing in fear and agony. They followed the distressing sound and saw a clump of petrified animals huddled beside a fence and, in the middle of that field were large, brown shapes and the ground churned up. As they crossed the field, her eyes focused in on what lay in the middle. Then came horror: she was looking at several cows that had been shot to pieces.

'Oh God,' she said. 'It's Popplewell's cows.'

Closer still, she could see that the bull was lying on its side, showered with bullet holes and bleeding to death, still alive, its breathing laboured. Three other cows were dead while one had a severed foot and was lying half on its front, its neck twisted to the side, lowing miserably. When they reached them, Rosina knelt down and stroked the bull's soft ears. Its mouth was opening and closing slowly, as if it were trying to call its last sounds but was too weak to utter them.

'They need putting out of their misery,' said Harry. 'I'll do it.'

'Yes,' she replied. 'Just a moment.' She went to the cow that was still alive and fondled its ears too. Its breathing was ragged and its sounds of pain were dreadful to hear. 'Go ahead,' she said and stood up, walking away from the animals to give him plenty of distance. She wanted to turn away, but felt it would be cowardly to do so and watched him lift the gun and shoot each one in the head. He did well, as each animal was instantly gone.

They stood and stared at the dead beasts.

'At least they're at peace now,' she said.

Harry still held his gun as if he were going to shoot another, then broke it open and held it over his arm. And he looked at her and said, 'You might see me as very young. But I'm a man and I've had experience of life.'

Surprised by this, she gazed at him a moment, then replied, 'I can see that. You dealt with shooting those beasts brilliantly. Thank you.'

In that moment, she could see both his strength and his vulnerability.

'I was in Spain during the civil war. I joined the International Brigade. I killed Spanish men and I saw many others killed. It changed me.'

'Oh, Harry,' she said and did not know what else to say, this revelation rendering her speechless. To think, this man had been to war already and come back and now here he was, in the second war of his young life. It was then then she realised she had called him Harry for the first time aloud.

He added, 'It's important to me that you see me as a man, not as a boy. Not as . . . akin to a son. Because I do not think of you as a mother. I think of you as a woman. A beautiful woman.'

There was tremendous tension in the air between them, an electric charge. It was broken only because they heard someone call and Rosina turned to see Popplewell running down the lane beside the field and coming through the gate. He said he'd been at Ravenscar railway station putting his wife on the train to visit her poorly mother and they commiserated with him about the cows, berated the Germans for the murder of the innocent cattle and the general pointlessness of war. And all the while the air between her and Harry fizzed with meaning. She glanced over at him and thought how strange it was, a charged moment surrounded by carnage. She knew it would never leave her, the memory of him standing there, looking glorious with the shotgun over his arm, his blond hair ruffled and his cheeks pink, then beside him the brown of the cows' hides and the red of the gore.

Chapter 13

June 1940

The Wrens posted to Scarborough were all put up in the Hotel Cecil on Ryndleside in the north of the town. When they arrived, Grace looked up at what was to be her home for the next few weeks, months or even years – who knew how long? It was a square, smallish hotel, painted white, with steps leading up to the main entrance. Above, at the front of the hotel, was a wide balcony upon which some Wrens were standing who waved down to them. The hotel was set in a curved road opposite a wide green area, fringed with tall trees that led down to a park below. It looked quite a new build, the same as some other hotels on the street. Once inside, the rooms had two or three beds in each and Grace managed to wangle a two-bed room for her and Nancy, so they didn't have to share with anyone else. It looked out over the front and from there they could see the park itself, so it was a nice, verdant view. The other Wrens were from all over the country and they spent the first afternoon chatting in the corridor and in and out of their bedrooms, introducing themselves and having a bit of a lark. They renamed the hotel's areas and routines with Navy slang – the bedrooms were the cabins and teatime was tea-boat – and a Wren called Muriel, who'd been there for a couple of months already, told them that just next door was another hotel called the Outlook, where a few of the male naval ratings, who were also working at the Scarborough Y Station were based.

Grace was allowed to tell her mother she was in Scarborough but nothing else about her situation. This secrecy bonded her closer than ever with Nancy and the other Wrens because they were the only ones who really understood her feelings. Grace found that not everyone would be doing the same job as her and Nancy. Muriel, for example, was trained as a radio mechanic. She told Grace about the work she did, fixing the radios on which Grace and Nancy would be listening, explaining how they'd test for faults, solder loose joints, replace broken parts and so on.

'We're in the wireless workshop, which looks a bit like our old school chemistry lab. Sometimes we make cheese on toast over the Bunsen burners! The gents have a lavatory inside, but we have to go to an outside lav, I'm afraid, and so will you. The men who work here are all right, I suppose. Some treat you like a minor annoyance and some are kind. You'll see.'

Grace thanked her for the advice and was very impressed by Muriel's obvious technical knowledge. She was glad she'd been put down for Morse code and telegraphy, as she feared she'd be hopeless at anything so practical and hands on as Muriel's role. Another Wren there, Audrey, was a dispatch rider. She'd take the coded messages and other information from the Y Station and whizz around on her motorcycle, delivering it to other centres across the country, as well as maintaining and fixing the motorcycles if they broke down. Again, Grace was glad she would be sitting at a desk. She didn't fancy the idea of riding a motorcycle in all weathers, armed with crucial documents. It all sounded rather stressful and Grace admired both Muriel and Audrey hugely for their skills.

'I think it's marvellous that both of you are so mechanically minded.'

'Well, I was never any good with reading and writing,' said Audrey, with a shrug. 'But I understand engines. They just make sense to me.'

'Same with me and radios,' said Muriel. 'I look at one and it . . . I don't know, it sort of looks obvious to me, I suppose.'

'I'm so impressed,' said Grace. 'Do you like the job here? Do you like Scarborough?'

'It's all right,' said Audrey. 'The seafront is restricted and some of the people are a bit miserable. But I like it enough. I wouldn't mind them sending me down south for a while, though. I'd like to get a look at Station X.'

'I've heard Station X mentioned but I don't really know anything about it,' said Grace.

'Oh, it's the place the messages are taken. It's in Buckinghamshire somewhere or so I've heard.'

'It's at Bletchley Park,' said Muriel. 'My auntie lives not far from there, in Beaconsfield.'

'Oh, I know where Bletchley is,' said Grace. 'I had a university friend who lives near Aylesbury and I used to visit her there.'

'It's the secrecy of it,' said Audrey. '*Station X . . .* ' she added, with a magician's flourish of her hands, to suggest its mystery.

'Oh, it's not very mysterious,' said Muriel. 'I mean, what they do there is shrouded in mystery, yes, and who knows what they're up to? But the place itself is just a Victorian mansion. My auntie told me last year that lots of Foreign Office girls were going to Bletchley and why didn't I go and work with crowds of jolly girls there? I said, "I don't want to meet crowds of jolly girls, thanks. I want to meet Navy boys!"'

'Quite right!' said Grace and they all laughed.

'Speaking of which . . . ' said Audrey and took Grace

out on to the front balcony off the shared landing. As they stood there, Grace could see over the trees of the park to the sea behind it, which was flat, grey and mysterious, glinting in the late-afternoon sun, as well as Scarborough Castle, perched on the cliff overlooking the town. Audrey said, 'See that green stuff opposite? That's Peasholm Park and it has a jolly nice boating lake and a pagoda and long walks on winding paths all over it. It's a great place for a jaunt with a Navy boy! Or any nice-looking feller.' Audrey winked at Grace.

It all sounded rather delicious and Grace was looking forward to meeting some nice-looking fellers, if any were to be found. As a child, living just over ten miles or so from Scarborough, they had visited now and again, as well as spending quite a bit of time in Whitby. She was fond of both places and knew their town centres reasonably well, had visited Whitby Abbey and Scarborough Castle several times. But she hadn't spent any time in Peasholm Park or been out socialising in Scarborough since becoming an adult. So, despite her initial misgivings at being sent a stone's throw from home, she was beginning to warm to the idea. She thought their hotel was a vast improvement on the rural setting of their previous Wrennery and that there might be lots of fun to be had here, if they ever got much time off.

Word came that evening that all the new Wrens would start their first shift at the Y Station in the moorland above

Scarborough at 8 a.m. and they were to be ready at least an hour before. The next day, at 7 a.m. sharp, the Wrens waited on the kerb with the tin hats they had to carry everywhere and their transport arrived to take them to work. It was an army lorry, no more than an open truck, which had a hatch at the back that swung down. They had to climb up and pull each other on to the back where there were wobbly benches placed down each side, but not enough for everyone to sit down, so when some other male naval ratings got on further on in the journey, they had to hang on to the metal posts to which a canvas awning was attached. It was a cool morning but, being June, not too cold. Grace wondered how it would feel to be jolted along in that open truck in the winter months; she would have to ask her mother to send extra woollies for then, she guessed. The mood was lightened by some of the cheeky, forward naval ratings starting up a sing-song and soon they were all singing along to 'She'll Be Coming 'Round the Mountain', which seemed particularly apt for all these Wrens being driven up onto the high moorland.

The truck trundled through the town before turning towards the higher ground of the moor and after a long straight road edged by a patchwork of farmers' fields, they arrived at the site of the Y Station Someone had said this was where the old racecourse used to be and Grace imagined it would be a fine site for such entertainment, with the wide vistas across the moors as a backdrop. These days, the site was far less picturesque. The entrance was guarded by Naval Police with light machine guns and dogs and everyone had to show their papers before being gruffly allowed entrance to the site. Grace followed the exodus from the truck and found herself walking behind the naval ratings, who knew where they were heading, for a rectangular building, submerged into the ground like a bunker, the roof covered with tons of earth and topped with turf – Grace presumed this was for camouflage purposes, but nothing could hide the array of radio aerials on the site and she shuddered at the thought that they might well be an obvious target for enemy bombers. At this point, the ratings went off in one direction, while the radio operator Wrens and dispatch riders went off in another. This left the group of new wireless telegraphy Wrens standing in a huddle, unsure of how to proceed.

Then a Wren First Officer came out of the bunker and approached them and they all saluted her, right hand with palm face down and she responded in kind.

'I am First Officer Ludlow. Follow me,' she said and led them down into the bunker. She took them to a small room with some desks and chairs in it, but nobody sat down, just stood smartly waiting for the First Officer to speak. She told them the chain of command at the Scarborough Y Station: they should report to her in the first instance, then beyond that to a civilian, Mr Tweed, who was in charge of the day-to-day operations in the wireless telegraphy section. The officer-in-charge of the station was Lieutenant-Commander Rodger. Also, when they were on duty, there would be a chargehand who was a naval signalman and he would be in charge of all technical aspects of the station. He would also be responsible for conveying the frequencies to other stations whenever anyone heard a ship through their headphones. Lastly, the Wrens were told that they would be in the minority here as most of their colleagues were male naval ratings, with a few Wrens doing the same job as wireless telegraphists. There were also some members of the Civilian Shore Wireless Service, or CSWS, and these were all male too.

Ludlow went on, 'You'll be working in a watch system. The station is manned every minute of the day and night because the German Navy never sleeps, so neither must our Y Station Day One is 0800 to 1300, then off that afternoon to return at 2300 until 0800. Day Two you will have off to sleep. Then Day Three on duty from 1300 to 2300. Day Four is a Stand Off, where you will have some free time and then Day Five has the same hours as Day One. Understood?'

They all responded in the affirmative, though the strings of numbers and days were swimming in Grace's head. She was sure she'd get used to it soon enough, but her impression was that it sounded exhausting, especially Days One and Five, with those two long shifts. Nobody asked any questions, so then Ludlow told them that presently they would go to their sets and begin work.

'The chargehand will give you certain frequencies to scan. The vast majority of the traffic you'll hear at Scarborough station is going to be U-boats. Rarely, you might hear a signal from a surface ship. But your main focus must be the U-boats. Their messages can be rare and will certainly be short because U-boats must surface to transmit and they don't want to spend a second more up there than they need to. Sometimes you might hear a little squeak as the transmission begins and that is your cue. As you will know by now – but just to remind you! – the call sign used for U-boats is always the same: dah dit dit dah, repeated, otherwise known as the B bar. The moment you hear this, you must shout "ship!" to the chargehand and then call out the precise frequency. From there, your chargehand will take over in transmitting those frequencies to the D/F control, with the intention of locating said ship via triangulation. At the same time, of course, you must be transcribing every last scrap of Morse you hear – and transcribing it with total accuracy. I cannot stress this enough, the absolute necessity of accuracy. These messages will then be conveyed to other stations via teleprinter or dispatch rider, such as Station X. In order to decode these messages, every letter must be 100 per cent correct. There is no room for error in wireless telegraphy. Understood?'

Everyone again replied positively, though Grace noticed

that their voices sounded a little quieter this time. It was a lot to take in and it was approaching eight in the morning, so it was time for their first shift. They were starting off with their shortest shift, only five hours, which was a blessing.

All the Wrens were led into the main operations room where the male naval ratings and CSWS men were on one side of the room and a bank of radio sets on the other, all manned by Wrens they'd not met before. It was a long, wide room with quite a low ceiling, filled with meandering tobacco smoke as well as the noise and damp heat from the machines and so many bodies at work. Most of the CSWS seemed to have a pipe permanently clamped in their mouths and the naval ratings were smoking cheap-smelling cigarettes. In the centre of the room sat the chargehand at his desk on a platform. Grace saw a few of the men glance up when the new Wrens came in, give them a quick once-over, then go back to their work.

Grace and the others in her group each approached a Wren and the handover took place swiftly, so as not to lose a second of air time. Grace put the headphones on and they felt damp on her ears from the other woman's perspiration. With a grimace of distaste, she quickly whipped them off, wiped them on her skirt and replaced them, guessing it would be the same for whoever took over from her later. She glanced around to see if anyone knew which frequencies to start searching just as the chargehand stubbed out his cigarette and came over, handing out slips of paper with four frequency ranges written on it.

Grace took her slip and got to work, placing her left hand on the dial, a pencil ready in her right hand to write anything down. She moved the large dial through the frequency ranges, at times twiddling on a smaller dial to the left of it called the BFO (beat frequency oscillator), which searched around the frequency without leaving it and, for the next five hours, without a break, she searched the frequencies, hoping for that little squeak to appear and a U-boat message to begin. But she heard nothing of the sort, only the usual cacophony of noise of the airwaves, with random signals drifting in from here, there and everywhere.

A naval rating plonked a cup of tea down beside her at some point and she swivelled to say 'thank you' but his back was already turned and off he went. She wished she'd been able to go off and make a cup of tea, just to escape the stifling grey fug of the room and she told herself that she must find out about breaks and where to make a cuppa the next time they were on shift. Now and again she'd glance up to see how Nancy was doing, but none of the Wrens looked round much at each other, too intent were they on the job. One of the frequencies she was working didn't sound quite spot on and a nice CSWS man helped her put it right. At one o'clock, the shift was over and they went outside to find the truck waiting to take them back to the

Hotel Cecil. Feeling the sweet air hit them as they left the foul atmosphere of the bunker was delightful.

Once on the truck and moving off, the Wrens were full of talk about the work. Many were disappointed that they hadn't heard any U-boat signals and also that they'd hear few surface ships at Scarborough. It seemed the work would be incredibly intense but with little reward of actually hearing anything useful. There was also general consternation about the long hours of the other shifts. It was a strange feeling to know that they'd be back there tonight at eleven. This meant, of course, that they should sleep in the afternoon, but once back at the hotel, after a hearty lunch and back up in their rooms, sleep was the last thing on their minds. Grace drew the curtains in their room to encourage sleep, but as hard as they tried, she and Nancy tossed and turned and ended up laughing at their total inability to drop off.

'We'll be grand,' said Nancy. 'Think of all t'times we've stayed up late after dances or with boys, then had to work all day t'next day.'

That wasn't something Grace had ever really done, but she took Nancy's word for it. They gossiped all afternoon and heard the others doing the same, so eventually all doors opened and Wrens were chatting in and out of each other's rooms as usual. They had dinner and played cards and wrote journals or letters and some of the Wrens doing other jobs told Grace and Nancy to take sandwiches with them to get them through the night shift.

'But we've just had our tea,' said Grace, but Nancy agreed it would be a good idea. It would seem a long time till 8 a.m. So they found the kitchen where there were supplies left out for the Wrens to make beetroot sandwiches and then it was 10.30 and the truck arrived to take them to their next shift.

It was all rather exciting to be driving up to the moors late at night and there was an atmosphere of a jolly outing among the new Wrens as they arrived at the station. However, once back at their sets, Grace understood why sleep in the afternoon was so necessary. The night stretched ahead and crept at a snail's pace. She realised she'd forgotten to ask about breaks and tea, but saw that some of the men would tap another on the shoulder and leave, at which moment the other man would take over his headset and have one earphone from each set held to each ear, thus listening to two sets at once. Grace resolved to make this deal with the other Wrens at some point, because soon she would need a wee and surely the others would too. Later on, a CSWS fellow popped over and told them to go on a break.

Grace went outside with Nancy and they shared a cigarette with a couple of ratings and flirted a bit. The men rolled their own cigarettes and they made Grace's throat ache, so she was amused to hear that the nickname of these hand-rolled cigarettes was 'ticklers'! It was so good to get outside in the cool night air and escape the cloying, claustrophobic atmosphere of the operations room. But only a few minutes were allowed, so after a quick trip to the outside lav, they were back in and back on their sets. She noticed that some of the other Wrens wore more casual clothes at night – a pair of bell-bottoms or other navy-blue trousers and a shirt without a tie, as well as a pullover or cardigan instead of their jacket. She resolved to do this the very next night shift – sitting for long hours in full uniform was not exactly comfy.

Grace saved her beetroot sandwiches as long as she could, but by one she was starving and gobbled them down quickly, having failed in her resolve to eke them out all night. Around three, a naval rating put a cup of hot coffee next to her and offered her a fag, which she took with a smile. He put a cocoa tin lid down as an ashtray and she took a grateful drag on the cigarette, feeling the warm smoke fill her lungs. It invigorated her and now she understood why the others smoked so much because it kept her awake for a while; however, by 5 a.m. she was utterly exhausted. She cursed her stupidity at talking all afternoon and evening the day before and not forcing herself to at least rest. How desperately she wanted to lay her head down on the desk and sleep! There was no sign of a U-boat signal, yet still there was the incessant searching through the frequencies.

By just after six, she felt she was losing her mind. How would she be able to do this every few days for months or years even? And just before seven she could feel her head nodding and her eyes closing as her hand felt heavy and stupid on the dial . . . Suddenly the noise in her head went quiet and there . . . was it? A tiny, quiet squeak? Yes, it was! Then the Morse began. As she began scribbling furiously, she shouted out, 'SHIP!' her voice cracking through thirst and underuse, but the chargehand heard it. She added, '8290 B bar' which described the frequency and the fact that it was a U-boat. The chargehand leapt to attention and repeated the information into a microphone. The atmosphere was now electric in the room. Grace listened intently to the Morse as it came through, feeling as if all the hairs on the back of her neck were standing to attention as the sound of the enemy's hand tapping out its secret message filled her ears.

It seemed to Grace the most ominous sound in the world and she efficiently scribbled down all of the Morse before it ended as abruptly as it had begun. She slapped the page triumphantly on top of her set and an eager naval rating collected it from her and gave her a big grin. He took it off to the teleprinter room or to a dispatch rider, and Grace had to get straight back to work, but she looked up at one point to see Nancy giving her a smile and a nod. She smiled broadly back and nodded too. She knew Nancy was telling her 'well done' and Grace was so pleased with herself. Her very first U-boat! And at that moment, all the discomfort and exhaustion vanished, as she realised she had taken her first step in protecting the Royal Navy and defending her country from the deadly U-boats of the Kriegsmarine.

Chapter 14

After the first couple of night shifts, Grace and her group of Wrens came off looking like ghouls. Their eyes were sunken, their faces pale, their legs shaky and most complained of stomach ache, probably due to hunching over the set for nine hours, plus a headache from the metal bands of the headphones that pressed into their scalps. At the end of each night shift, Grace and the others would have to do a quick tidy up as the new shift arrived and took over their sets. They'd sweep up the sandwich crumbs, remove cigarette ash and the enamel mugs stained with tea or coffee and take down the blackouts. Somehow this seemed to be the worst part of the shift, that after all that work saving the nation, they still had menial tasks to do, which vexed Grace to an unreasonable level; she knew that, but exhaustion made people irrational, she knew that too.

But the night shift had one good thing about it – and that was that some of the cheekiest naval rating chaps worked it and were forever playing pranks on each other and sometimes the Wrens too, which caused great hilarity. One night a rating called Jim Cooke caught Grace's eye and winked at her, then pointed at another rating who had fallen asleep at his set. Jim got up, went to the chap's set and unplugged his headset then plugged in his own. He twiddled the dial until he found something that made him wince. It must have been an extremely loud noise, perhaps interference, from a teleprinter in the next room. Then he took out his plug and replaced the other one, leaving it only halfway in. Jim gave Grace another wink and tapped the sleeping man, who woke up with a start, saw his jack was half-out and pushed it in, only to have his ears assaulted by the terrific screeching. He nearly had a heart attack but Jim was back at his own set by then, looking as if butter wouldn't melt. Trying not to laugh was akin to torture! Jim was such a lark, Grace thought. He was staying in the Outlook Hotel, so he got the same transport sometimes when he was on the same shift. He usually held court on their truck, telling racy jokes to anyone who'd listen. Another day, she was coming in from a break and glanced at him. He put a folded note on top of his wireless set and nodded very seriously, indicating that she should take it. The male ratings sometimes asked the Wrens to assist them or collect things for them and Grace went over, opened the note and it read simply, '*Was your journey really necessary?*' She looked at him quizzically before she saw his mischievous smile. She went back to her set, annoyed she'd fallen for it but also having to stifle her laughter every time she thought of it.

Grace was keenly aware that if a Wren had been found asleep at her set or committed such a prank, she might have been sent away from the station permanently, but somehow the chaps got away with more. Some of them – including Jim – even took quick breaks to play tennis outside, leaving their rackets leaning against the wall afterwards and they were sometimes late coming back, which annoyed those who were left manning two headsets at once. Again, a Wren would never dream of doing this, but though Grace disapproved of some of this, the truth was that the headsets were never left untended and, despite their tricks and pranks, none of the staff failed to keep the frequencies manned at all times. Grace began to realise that sometimes one needed a bit of fun to get through the deadly dreariness of the job of an interceptor. It was deadly because it was so intense and one could never truly relax. She had imagined that it might have slow patches when you could take your headset off and do a bit of knitting, but, as their First Officer explained, Scarborough Y was not like that because it dealt more or less exclusively with U-boats, so there was no time for relaxing. Being bored working long hours in

231

any job was bad enough, but being tense and focused for long hours was worse. Everyone was working incredibly hard and, despite some grievances, Grace admired everyone who worked there for their dedication.

The chargehands were usually retired Merchant Navy Petty Officers and while some were polite and supportive, some were indeed petty and officious. Some clearly had an intense objection to women being in the Navy at all and made no bones about it. They would roll their eyes when the Wrens changed shift or criticise them for every little thing. Some would send the Wrens out to do menial tasks, such as making tea or sweeping up the corridor – one even sent Nancy and another woman out to wash his car and another to walk his dog! Secretly, Grace and her friends were always delighted to be sent on these little 'outings' because it got them out of the awful stink of the smoke-filled operations room for a short while, so it was not the demeaning punishment these men might have thought it was.

Mr Tweed was there each weekday, overseeing the daily running of things, and he seemed a nice enough chap, a civilian who wore brick-red plus-fours every single day to work. He was a bit shy of the Wrens and, behind his back, they would laugh at him, but always good-naturedly for he was not objectionable in the slightest and, in their more syrupy moments, reminded some of their middle-aged fathers at home, working in the Home Guard or wherever, and a few tears might be shed by the daddy's girls who missed them. The person they all had most trouble with was their First Officer, who was always difficult about leave and was forever scolding them about accuracy and attentiveness, which they knew perfectly well was crucial and did their very best to adhere to, at all times, day or night.

After a fortnight or so, the new pattern of working began to feel more like routine. They'd had to retrain their body clocks to adapt to this new rhythm of waking, sleeping and eating and, at first, after a night shift, Grace found she couldn't face breakfast; she just wanted to be left to curl up and die quietly in her bed. But as time went on she grew accustomed to it and found she was ravenous for breakfast back at the hotel. All of them still found it tricky to fall asleep in the middle of the day and much discussion was had amongst the Wrens of what to think about to induce daytime sleep, from pretending you were floating peacefully across the night sky, to picturing acres of black velvet, to imagining you were a dandelion seed floating on a breeze, to making sure your feet were warm, because who could sleep with cold feet? None of it worked – but their bodies needed sleep and eventually fell into line.

Grace found she was permanently hungry and yet all they could ever find for sandwiches was beetroot or the strong, hard kind of cheese that Nancy called 'mousetrap'. Now and again a bit of corned beef would be left out, which was soon snapped up. Grace wrote to her mother about the depressing sandwich fillings and was over the moon when she received a parcel from home soon after, with a carefully wrapped-up jar of Heinz Sandwich Spread, which although she felt a bit guilty for doing so, she kept a secret from the others except for Nancy and they made up their sandwiches in the privacy of their room and luxuriously licked the knife afterwards, so as not to waste a drop of the delectable concoction of crunchy veg in the creamy sauce. Before the war, Grace had never been that keen on the stuff, always preferring meat in her sandwiches, but now it seemed the height of decadence, even though it looked a bit like dog sick.

Another treat was hot chocolate, which Muriel had received from her family. Everyone in the Navy called it 'ki' and one afternoon, when Nancy and Grace were bored in their beds trying to get to sleep, Muriel brought in mugs of ki for them and they thanked her effusively. What a delight it was to taste proper, creamy hot chocolate!

'Oh, the joy of a bit of luxury!' crowed Grace, savouring the velvety taste on her tongue.

'It's nice we're saving t'world and all that,' said Nancy, 'but would it be too much to ask for a bit of nice food once in a while?'

'I know, I know. And yes, we are doing such an important job. But honestly, Nancy, sometimes I feel rather sick about it.'

'About what? Our job? Long hours?'

'No, not that. The fact of what we're doing. When we locate those German subs, that means someone out there might get the order to torpedo that U-boat and all aboard might be killed. So our action has led directly to all those German boys dying. It's a horrible thought.'

'But they're t'enemy, flower. Simple as that.'

'It's not that simple though, is it?'

'Aye, it is. When it comes to war, there's no room for looking at things in a complicated way. It's black and white, not shades of grey in between. Our island is being threatened and we have to defend it.'

'Absolutely, I agree, of course. But it just feels awful sometimes, targeting those German boys under the sea.'

'What about 'em? They know what they're doing, just as we do.'

'They're just following orders. They might not even like Herr Hitler.'

'It dun't matter. They're fighting against us, against our freedoms.'

'I know, I know. I'm just saying that sometimes, what we do, it leaves a bad taste in the mouth.'

'Not to me, it dun't. It's us or them,' said Nancy, who downed the rest of her now lukewarm chocolate and grumpily slammed it down on her bedside table and turned over in bed, facing away from Grace.

'I'm sorry, Nancy. I didn't mean to offend you.'

There was silence from the other bed. It was their first disagreement and Grace wished she'd kept her mouth shut. It was clearly something they'd never agree on.

A knock on the door came as welcome relief. It was Audrey, who opened the door quickly without waiting for a response, holding out a letter to Grace. She took it and saw it had been forwarded from home. The handwriting was unfamiliar. Inside she read the following:

Dear Miss Layzenby,

I found your name and address in my sons things. Im very sorry to tell you by letter and not in person but hes gone, Im sorry to say. Fred was lost at Dunkirk. Sorry for not telling you sooner. But we only just got some of his things back. I found your name and address written down in his things and next to your name Fred writ GIRLFRIEND AND LETTER WRITTER. So I wanted to tell you. Also I wanted to say your very kind for writting to my Fred. He was a good boy. Always kind and cheery. Well theres nothing more to say I think so Ill sine off.

Yours in morning
Ethel Miller, Mrs

Grace sat very quietly. That harmless boy was dead. Dead at Dunkirk. Maybe he drowned, maybe he died of injuries. And with a stab of guilt she recalled that she had never got round to writing to Fred, not even once. She'd kept meaning to, but somehow work and life in general had always got in the way. The pathos of Fred's mother thinking she had written to him made her feel even worse. She didn't know Fred at all, really, and had merely been amused by his letter to her. But none of that mattered now he was dead. She felt awful for not making the effort to cheer his last weeks by doing the minimal task of writing him a letter. Oh, that soldier far from home, waiting to hear from her! And she'd done *nothing*. Whether it was more from his death or her own guilt, she started to cry.

Nancy looked round sharply and said, 'Oh Lord, what is it?'

'That boy at our first dance. Fred. The one who wrote to me at home. It's from his mother. He's dead. At Dunkirk.'

'Oh, love,' said Nancy and came out of bed and sat beside Grace on hers, putting her strong arms about her, holding her tight while she cried. Nancy read the letter and they sat glumly for a while, with nothing to say. 'Now let's try to get some sleep, or we'll be wrecks tonight.'

Grace tried, but tossed and turned, unable to drop off.

She got a couple of hours eventually, but was too disturbed to sleep properly. She surfaced about twenty minutes before their alarm was due to go off and realised she did have something to say, something that had been burning inside her since hearing the news of Fred and reading the simple, grieving words of his mother, *Ethel Miller, Mrs.*

'Nancy?' Grace said, softly, not wanting to disturb her if she was really asleep, but loud enough so that she could hear if she'd already woken up.

'Aye?'

'Ignore everything I said before, about those German boys in the U-boats. I don't feel bad about it any more. I've not even a shred of pity for them. Boys like that killed Fred, probably without a single thought for what they were doing or who they were hurting. Without a care for him, his mother, or his young life. I hate them now – and I'm glad of what we do.'

Nancy said, 'Fair enough, duck.'

Grace dragged herself out of bed, feeing more exhausted after the brief, troubled sleep than before it and at work that night she felt like death warmed up and was terrified of falling asleep at her set. At one point she rubbed her eyes so hard she saw stars and couldn't focus for a moment. Then she blinked a few times to see straight and looked up to see Jim Cooke, the cheeky rating, smiling down at her. She wasn't in the mood for pranks. But he was holding a hot cup of tea and put it down for her, as well as a crumbly, misshapen biscuit he put next to it. She hadn't had a biscuit in ages. Then he took a note from his pocket and popped it next to the biscuit and went back to his desk while she read the note.

Mother sent the biscuits. She's a dreadful baker. But they've got to be better than beetroot sandwiches.
   Jim
   PS Fancy a walk round Peasholm Park tomorrow?

In the transport on the way home the next morning, Grace told Jim she needed to sleep first, as she'd got so little the afternoon before, but she'd be free for a walk the following morning and he called for her at ten. They crossed over the road from the hotel and entered the park by a steep, descending path through the trees. Walking beside him, chatting about the differences between the Outlook and the Cecil Hotels, in particular how much better the breakfasts at the Outlook sounded to Grace, she noticed a few things about Jim. At first glance, he looked quite ordinary, but he had big brown eyes that looked kind, but could also look wicked when he was in a mischievous mood. In fact, his whole personality seemed to emanate from his eyes and, once she looked at him closely, she realised they made him really rather handsome. He had a nice thatch of thick, mid-brown hair, which looked as if it might be soft to touch and he was the same height as her almost exactly, maybe half an inch taller. Usually, she wanted a man who was tall enough for her to look up to, but she actually found it somehow comforting to look a man straight in the eye when they were talking, especially when the eyes were as nice as Jim's. And anyway, since the tall Dutchman, she had gone off the idea of tall men for a while. They weren't all they were cracked up to be. Or rather, she was realising that her schoolgirl ideas of what constituted the perfect man were woefully ignorant. Height, frame, eyes, hair colour . . . all of these things were irrelevant if the man turned out to be a cad, like Erik. The same went for education or even ability to use apostrophes. As obvious at it seemed, she was realising that it was personality that counted, not looks or education. And Jim was doing well so far, as he'd made her laugh about fifteen times since they'd left the hotel steps.

'So, where do you come from then, Grace? Your voice has that unplaceable accent of boarding school, so you could be from the wilds of Scotland or the moors of Cornwall, for all I know.'

'From round here, actually. Ravenscar, just a few miles up the coast.'

'Chuffin' eck, t'lass is from Yarkshar,' he said.

'That's it! But how do you know Yorkshire dialect?'

'I had a grandmother from Filey. She spoke like that and we teased her mercilessly.'

'Ah, that's not far away. Where are you from then? I can't place your accent either.'

'I'm from middle England, that's why. We have no idea who we are in the Midlands. We're influenced by the West Country, the north, the east and the south. We're a mishmash of all of them, entirely devoid of personality.'

'Where exactly, though?'

'Oxfordshire,' he said, with the thick burr of a local.

'Oh, I studied at Oxford so I know the county well! Whereabouts?'

'A few places. Witney for a few years, Banbury, Bicester, Henley-on-Thames. My father was a shopkeeper and got bored easily. He kept finding new shops he liked better so we moved about a lot.'

'You don't sound like a local, to be honest.'

'No, my mother thought it would be a good idea to pay for her only child to have elocution lessons, to make me eligible for a life other than that of a village idiot. All it served at the time was to get me beaten up in the playground. But I suppose it's useful now.'

The sound of trickling water accompanied them as they reached the end of the steep path. There was a running brook, banked by slates and rock gardens, which led down to a pond in which had been built a little red and yellow Chinese pagoda of sorts, beside a wooden bridge. They walked across the bridge and stopped for a moment to watch the various water birds – several moorhens and a couple of querulous ducks – floating about on the pond.

'Did you come straight here from Oxfordshire?'

'Oh no, I left school at sixteen and started an apprenticeship as an electrician, but I soon got bored with that, so I switched to training specifically in telephones; then I got bored with that too so I switched to radios for a while and then I got bored with *that* and I ran away from home at the ripe old age of seventeen.'

'Really? How thrilling! I always wanted to do that. Where did you go?'

'My cousin was an actor so I joined his troupe and travelled around with them for a few years, performed in theatres all over the country and abroad, in America and Canada. I wasn't an actor, alas, though I'm sure you'll agree I have the dashing looks and gravitas for it. I was on the electrical side of it, lighting and sound and so forth. I did that for four years but when I knew war was coming, I came home and joined the Navy straight away. They saw I'd had a bit of training in electrics and telephones but decided my forte was in wireless, as I'd been a keen radio ham for years. And that's how I ended up at Scarborough on the wirelesses.'

'Really? Gosh, what a life! What things you must have seen!'

'Yes, you might say that. A graduate of the university of

life rather than the University of Oxford.'

He winked at her and smiled. She knew he was having a little dig at her credentials and even a year ago she would have been a bit offended that somehow he was suggesting she was naïve and unworldly, for all her learning. But in recent months she had come to the conclusion that this was precisely what she had been since leaving school. The books she had read would pile up to the sky, but her knowledge of the real world had been severely lacking until now.

'You're right,' she said, simply.

'Oh, I doubt that very much.'

She looked at him. 'Why do you say that?'

'Well, I joke around a lot to cover up the fact that I know very little.'

'I don't think that's true,' she said, seriously. 'I've realised that book learning is one type of knowledge and truly living is another kind and that neither is better than the other. And I know for a fact that I've been replete in the former at the expense of the latter. For example, there are different kinds of reading. I can read a whole library of books but I can't read a motorcycle engine like Audrey or read the components of a radio like Muriel, two of my Wren friends. It's just another type of reading, just as skilful – and some might say far more useful.'

'You know, that's very true. I've never really thought of those skills as reading before. But they are.'

'Absolutely. That's just one of many realisations I've had this year. Joining the Wrens has taught me that and so much more. It's opened my eyes to the world. And I needed that. I spent my childhood and student days wrapped in cotton wool, to an extent. Now I'm mixing with people from all sorts of backgrounds and I really feel that it's taught me to be a better person. And I'm so grateful for that. One could never be grateful for a war, of course, but one can value the good qualities that we've been forced to develop because of it.'

'You're rather wonderful, aren't you?' he said, looking at her intensely, all hint of mischief gone from his brown eyes.

'I'm really very ordinary,' she said and looked away, watching the ducks tip up and waggle their backsides. 'I've not done anything interesting with my life. Not like you.'

'Ah, it's all relative. I've not read a book since I was at school, so we both have gaps in our repertoire. Everyone does. But isn't it nice when you meet someone who's so different from yourself? You can start filling in those gaps, talk a lot, learn a lot from each other. It's like jigsaw pieces coming together. How dull it would be if we were all facsimiles of each other. And it would make a rotten jigsaw. Difference is the stuff of life.'

'I like that,' she said and she linked arms with him.

'Ah, so that's all I need to do to get close to a smasher like you? Spout some pseudo-philosophical nonsense, pretending to sound profound?'

'Stop putting yourself down, Jim. That's my job.'

He laughed with a look of delighted surprise in his eyes.

'I see you're going to keep me on my toes, Gracie.'

She grinned and said, 'Oh, I do hope so.'

They walked on, following the meandering paths through the trees to a wide opening where a large lake was graced with a huge pagoda, about five times the size of the previous one, sitting atop a waterfall which tumbled down over stone steps to the lake below where couples and families pedalled and rowed about in boats. They talked easily together for over two hours, strolling about and sometimes sitting on benches here and there. Grace noticed that once he relaxed, the constant jokes subsided and so she saw more of the real Jim beneath the humour. He was thoughtful, not a reader but definitely a thinker – and a deep one at that. He might mock himself, but she could see that a lively and pensive mind was at work there and it attracted her deeply, just as much as his liquid brown eyes did.

Suddenly they realised they'd been gone so long that if they didn't make haste they'd be late for their next shift, so they rushed back up the steep hill to the top, both dreadfully out of breath from the climb but also from the laughter, as Jim complained all the way he was made for sitting on his backside listening to radios, not running up hills. They only had time for a fleeting goodbye before she had to hurry into her own hotel to get ready. Nancy wanted to hear all the gossip but there was simply no time because the truck arrived minutes after, Jim jumping on it too, so they couldn't talk about it. But Grace did tell Nancy one thing before they left.

'He didn't even try to kiss me once, even though I could tell he wanted to.'

'What a gent!' said Nancy.

'Yes, yes he is,' said Grace. 'And I love that about him.'

It was such a relief to talk to a man and not be either fending him off or wanting him to shut up and kiss her. She realised that she truly desired to hear everything that Jim had to say, that his mind was far more interesting to her than any other quality of his. She'd had a taste of it in their couple of hours round the park and now she was hungry for more. And that felt marvellous.

Chapter 15

July 1940

Dear Harry,

Thank you so much for your kind letter from Burniston. I'm glad to hear you've settled in well at Burniston Farm and that the owners are treating you well. You are such a polite person and so easy to talk to that I can't imagine anyone treating you otherwise. I hope your work goes well there. You are only about seven miles away, as the crow flies. I thought you would be sent far away, so it's quite something to think you're only down the road. Of course you must come to visit us, when you can. We all agree what super company you are. The girls will be home for the summer holidays soon and I know they'd be delighted to see you. I will keep a glass of whisky here for you, as requested. And yes – in answer to your other question – we should go on a walk a bit further afield. There's a lovely walk down to the beach where a colony of seals tends to bask in the sunshine at this time of year. It is peaceful there, despite the crashing of the waves, so I think you will appreciate it.

Thank you for telling me that you find me a peaceful kind of a person. It may well be one of the nicest things anyone has ever said to me! You strike me as a peaceful kind of a person too. As life unfurls, I feel these days that peace and also kindness are what I seek most in the world.

Life goes on the same here, with our petty little dramas, I suppose! Today it is the Ravenscar Agricultural Show in the village hall, which I have helped to organise. Jessop is exhibiting some prize produce, whilst Mrs B and I have cooked up some delicacies in the kitchen, using the best ideas to get around rationing. It is awfully muggy here today, so I hope our efforts won't melt in the heat of the village hall before they get judged! Anyway, I'm sure all of that is exceedingly tedious to you, so I won't go on.

Very best regards to you and do let us know when you'd like to come for that walk.

Rosina

She wondered if she'd been too effusive in her letter. He had suggested they call each other by their first names and he had said some lovely things about her in his letter, as well as clearly wanting to come and see her again as soon as possible. She assumed this must be because he was bored in his new posting and she was a friendly face. She thought often about the day they'd stood beside the ruined cattle and he called her beautiful and said that he did not think of her as a mother. Well, that was nice of him. No more than that. He was just being intense, as some young people are. And now he was probably lonely. They could help him with that, the girls and her and Mrs Bairstow. Sometimes, she thought quite differently about him, particularly late at night, alone in bed. She put that out of her mind and sealed up the envelope. But whether or not she really wanted to consider what his feelings might be for her, and however much she tried to deny that it was any more than his boredom and isolation, she was excited at the thought of seeing him again.

She put the letter for him into her handbag, then glanced at the one she'd received from him. On first opening it, she'd noticed that he'd listed his name on the back as Henry Woodvine. So, Harry must be a nickname. Henry made him sound older, somehow. Looking again at the letter, after a quick consideration, she picked it up and folded it carefully, then put it in her handbag too. She didn't want the maid or anyone else to see he'd written to her, wanted to keep it safe from prying eyes. The maid might dust her desk or the girls might go into a drawer to look for something. So her handbag was the best place for it, she decided. She also tried to push down the thought that his letter was also a very precious thing to her and she liked to keep it close.

Before she turned to leave the room and head for the kitchen, she saw from her window that Ronnie, the evacuee, and Throp, the under-gardener, were carrying boxes of prize vegetables from the greenhouse. She smiled to think of how both of them, the boy and the man, had come on in leaps and bounds since they'd been under Jessop. They had purpose in life now and it suited them. She smiled as she left the room and felt how oppressive the house was on this warm, close July morning. In the kitchen, she found Mrs Bairstow putting the finishing touches to their ration-book cooking display. They had spent hours choosing the right recipes, assembling the ingredients and cooking the two dishes together and Rosina had enjoyed every second. She found Bairstow's company very easy and comforting, something akin to time spent with her mother so long ago. She wasn't a maternal woman, Bairstow, but she had that kind of smooth, mid-toned voice that put you in a bit of a trance when you were with her for long periods. Together they had made a type of meatless sausage and a savoury roll with rabbit meat. The 'sausages' were made of onion, stock and oatmeal, mixed up with suet and Worcestershire sauce, then coated with batter and fried. They did not taste as awful as they looked and were actually quite adequate for a meal, considering the ingredients – especially if drowned in gravy. The savoury roll consisted of potato suet paste, mixed with rabbit meat, parsley and breadcrumbs and a few other herbs, tied in a cloth and steamed.

As she entered the kitchen, it was as hot as hell, with the steaming having begun very early that morning and only just finished. The roll had a lovely meaty smell and really did not look too bad so Rosina was proud of their accomplishments. Bairstow was looking at them set out on the table and next to her, saying encouraging things, was their daily maid, Mary. Rosina was glad they'd been able to hire a local woman to be their daily and Mary seemed a cheerful character, no nonsense and efficient.

At Rosina's entrance, Mary looked up and said, 'Morning, ma'am. I'll be off to do laundry with Sheila now.'

'Oh, didn't I tell you?' said Rosina. 'You and Sheila must have the day off for the show. I'm so sorry, I thought I'd said. I don't know where my mind is lately.'

With Harry over in Burniston, she thought. *My mind is always with Harry and it's making me forgetful. Silly woman.*

Sheila came in and Rosina repeated it to her and Sheila looked delighted, then Mary and Sheila went off, Mary saying that she'd pop home to fetch her children and take them to the show.

'Oh yes, please do. There will be plenty for them to do and it will be good to get them out and in the sunshine.'

Once alone, Bairstow looked at Rosina and said, 'These

sausages would be best tasted when freshly fried. They've gone soggy now.'

'Oh dear,' said Rosina. 'Nothing we can do about that, I'm afraid. And we did our best. Don't lose heart. I still think we might win, as we've been inventive with very simple ingredients and that's the main thing, eh?'

The cook nodded, but looked unconvinced.

'Bairstow, I must quickly just pop off to the post office. I won't be long.'

'Oh, I'll send Sheila with it, as we're due at t'village hall any minute.'

'Erm, no, don't bother Sheila. She'll be getting into her glad rags for the show. I'll do it.'

Rosina knew her cheeks had gone red. She could feel them burning. Mrs Bairstow raised an eyebrow at her before she hurried off, her face hotter than ever. She hated subterfuge, but she didn't want anyone posting Harry's letter but herself. She felt strongly that Mrs Bairstow couldn't possibly approve of, or understand, her friendship with Harry, so she'd much rather keep it to herself. And Sheila would only gossip about it and that would be even worse. The thought of the villagers and her tenants thinking of her preying on a nice, young officer, the older widow . . . it didn't bear thinking about. Such a horrid image. No, it was best all round that she posted the letter. She walked quickly up to Station Square and the postmistress did not bat an eyelid, so Rosina hoped she wouldn't gossip about it either and, if she thought of it at all, she would think it was some sort of official business with the RAF. Once the letter was gone she felt happy that it was on its way to Harry and, as she walked swiftly back home she patted her handbag a couple of times, happy too that his letter was in there. How she loved his handwriting: not too swirly but quite curvy and rounded for a masculine hand. It had been fascinating to see it for the first time and to think of his hand as he wrote it. What a cherished thing a letter could be.

Once at the village hall, with Bairstow beside her and their offerings on the table, Rosina was pleased to see how the event she'd helped to organise was unfolding. First were the displays and judging and a few fun stalls, then later there would be tea and a dance. As the people began to arrive, they soon filled up the hall with their bodies and accompanying heat. Rosina could feel that her armpits were wet with sweat but she was glad there were so many attending and paying the small entrance fee, as all the proceeds were going to good causes. She saw people admiring Jessop's vegetables, as he chatted away with old friends, Mrs Jessop beside him, along with Throp and Ronnie, all beaming and proud of their hard work. There were turnips, beetroot, carrots, runner and broad beans, peas and radishes, all plump and well shaped. She saw

Sheila come in with a local boy, the maid looking very grown-up wearing red lipstick and a pretty frock. Mary, the daily, arrived too with her four children, who all ran to the tombola and begged their mother for tickets. Rosina felt inordinately pleased that her staff were happy, that the village folk seemed content – and now Harry had written and she would see him soon, all felt right with the world. But then she had a twinge of anxiety; she had felt like this in the past, before her mother got ill and the Great War came and she had lost the three she'd loved best. Ever since, she had believed that whenever she felt happy, something would come along to ruin it. She must try to grow out of that, she thought. She was a girl then, a woman now and such superstition was silly.

She saw the farmer Popplewell come in and felt she ought to talk to him so excused herself to Bairstow and made her way through the crowd to have a word. Again, she thought of Harry, of how the day with the cows was the last time she'd seen him. Again she pushed down thoughts of him and scolded herself inwardly.

'How are your remaining cattle?' she asked Popplewell.

'Well enough, ma'am. But they've been skittish ever since and don't like t'new bull we got for 'em.'

'Oh dear,' said Rosina.

'But we mustn't grumble, as some have it much worse. Like Mrs Precious.'

Rosina was hoping she'd see Phyllis Precious and Elsie there today, as she felt it would be good for them. She still hadn't given birth and Rosina had sent a note to her suggesting she come, but had had no reply. 'Still no word from her husband then?'

'Tha didn't hear then? It were yesterday t'news came. Postmistress told me yesterday afternoon. She likes a good gossip about t'telegrams, does t'postmistress.'

Rosina felt alarmed at the thought of the postmistress being loose-lipped but far more important information was missing. 'What news? What's happened?'

'Wilf Precious is dead. Lost at sea.'

'Oh, no! Oh, how terrible.'

'Aye. Young and with bairns on t'way. Rotten, it is.'

'Thank you for telling me. I'll see to it that Mrs Precious is taken care of.'

'Kind of thee, ma'am.'

Rosina shook her head but had no more words. Popplewell made his excuses and moved on and Rosina felt sweat trickling down her inner thighs. The heat was stifling now. How she wanted to run out of there! At the moment he'd told her that Wilf Precious was dead, an image of Harry, dead and gone, assaulted her mind. She hated herself for that, for the selfishness, of thinking of that young man when Phyllis had lost her husband. She resolved to suspend Phyllis's rent for a time to help.

Yes, that would be a good start. And she would pay for someone to look after the children so Phyllis could have a bit of a break from them from time to time. God, it was too awful, that haunted young mother, alone with three children. How sickening war was, how pointless and bloody awful.

Then a ripple of alarmed chatter came bubbling through the crowd from the door of the hall. People were shaking their heads, eyes wide, mouths open. Something bad had happened. Rosina saw Sheila and edged through the crowd and touched her arm.

'What's happened, Sheila? Do you know?'

'Village of Burniston been bombed, ma'am! Last night! Who'd a thought it? Little village like that.'

Burniston! The village of Burniston . . .

Rosina hurried back to the table where Bairstow was standing, arms folded, frowning, trying to discern the news.

'Burniston's been bombed!' said Rosina. 'Harry Woodvine is staying there.'

Without pause, Mrs Bairstow said, 'Go. Go and see if he's all right.'

Rosina was surprised but so glad to hear it. 'We've hardly got any petrol left in the car.'

'This is important. Go now.' Bairstow leant down and grabbed Rosina's handbag and thrust it at her.

Rosina shared a glance with Bairstow, the like of which they'd never had before. There was an urgency in it, of the situation, but also an acknowledgement, somehow, of Harry's importance. Rosina nodded at her and Bairstow nodded back then Rosina pushed her way as politely as she could through the crowd and out into the hot day. A bit of a breeze had struck up and it hit her face and turned the sweat on it cold. Rosina broke into a run up Raven Hall Road and along the tree-lined avenue to the house; and as her feet pelted along the hot road, she felt terribly alive and truly nauseous at the very same time.

Chapter 16

The drive to Burniston was only around fifteen minutes along the road towards Scarborough and her mind was filled with the very real possibility that Harry could be hurt. Or even dead. She still felt sick and focused on the twisting road ahead to calm herself. There were lots of houses in Burniston and lots of people. And the bombing might have only destroyed farm outhouses, not homes. Nothing was clear, only rumours that had flown around the village hall. As she drove, she actually crossed her fingers, her hands clamped on to the steering wheel. She saw a singular magpie and saluted it. She didn't want any sorrow today. She knew she ought to have grown out of such silly superstitions by now, but they comforted her – any hope that one could affect the blind forces of fate was comforting.

Coming into the village of Burniston, past the baptist chapel and the post office, she saw there were lots of people on the streets, standing on corners talking and walking along the pavements, all stern-faced. Then she saw the first of the bomb damage. There were several houses that had suffered and she pulled up at the side of the road and got out. She stopped a woman in the street and asked where Burniston Farm was, and she was directed up the street and down a lane. She saw, on her way, that there was actually a Scarborough coach pulled up and people were getting off and pointing at the rubble. It seemed they had come up specially from Scarborough to see the bombing. She heard one of them say, 'It's a nice day to see t' Burniston Ruins, I must say!'

It all seemed very ghoulish and she did not want anyone to think she was one of them, a disaster tourist. She approached the farm to find the main building destroyed. What if Harry had been in it? Surely he would have been there, asleep, at night? Her chest felt tight and her eyes strained as she scanned the ruin, which looked as if a giant had stepped on it carelessly. The whole roof had caved in and great splinters of wood stuck out at all angles, with bricks and stone lying in haphazard piles, a random window frame perched there, its broken glass left in jagged shapes clinging to the wood. There was no sign of the owners or any inhabitants standing anywhere near the buildings.

On the road, quite a few people were milling around and two children were trying to climb over the low picket fence. They were stopped by a woman who gave them both a quick clip round the ear. There was a fire engine of sorts parked up there: it was a motor car with a trailer attached, a large tank in the midst of it painted red and the rest of the trailer painted battleship grey. She saw two men who looked like firemen drinking cups of tea by the entrance to the farm and people were coming up to them and thanking them and they were nodding and sipping their tea. As she walked over to them, she heard a woman say, 'They'll pull 'em down, all t'bombed ones. They say they rose up off t'ground and crashed back down again. Not safe to live in now.'

Rosina swallowed down her nausea and fear and approached one of the tea-drinking firemen.

'Excuse me, I'm looking for someone who was staying at the farm.' She couldn't bear to say the next sentence, but in the absence of anything forthcoming from the taciturn firemen, she went on. 'Was there anyone injured here last night? Or . . . worse?'

One of them said, 'We pulled a young fella out of t'rubble. Unconscious but breathing. He's gone off to Scarborough Hospital.'

'Do you happen to know his name?'

'No, duck,' said the other man, 'but someone said he were a sergeant in the Raff.'

'That's him!' said Rosina. 'Harry Woodvine?'

'Aye,' said the other fireman. 'The owner said his name were Harry.'

Oh, the relief that Harry was alive! 'How badly injured was he?'

The other firemen took a sharp intake of breath. 'Well, as I say, unconscious. His arm looked broke and he didn't wake up before t'ambulance came. I wun't like to say, duck.'

'Thank you, thank you,' said Rosina, acutely aware that her voice was trembling and her eyes filling with tears. The two firemen eyed her curiously.

Rosina felt their scrutiny and said, 'We hosted him and his men when they were working near our house.'

Both men looked away, seeming unconvinced. After all, tears were rolling down her cheeks now. 'It's so good to know our boys survived this cowardly attack.'

'That is true, ma'am,' said one fireman.

'Thank you again for your help.'

She turned away and hurried up the road, stumbling a little before she made it to her car and threw herself inside and slammed the door. Fear swelled up in her and broke like a wave. She sobbed over the steering wheel, searched desperately in her handbag for a hankie and dried her eyes, trying to pull herself together because a couple of passers-by were staring at her. She started the car and left quickly, driving without thinking along the road towards

Scarborough. She looked at the petrol gauge and saw that there was very little left; it would probably get her to the hospital but not home again. She didn't care. She simply had to get there. If the car didn't make it, she'd get out, abandon it and walk.

The traffic in Scarborough was busy, army trucks everywhere and dozens of folk on bicycles weaving in and out. When she finally reached the hospital, the petrol gauge was below zero and she patted the wheel to thank the car for getting her there, especially since the last bit must have been on fumes. She checked her face in her hand mirror, saw her eyes were puffy and she looked pale. Well, nothing to be done about that. She half walked, half ran to the hospital entrance and went inside, going straight to a woman who was sitting at a table greeting visitors and pointing them in the right direction.

When it was her turn, she said to the smiling woman, 'I'm looking for Sergeant Henry Woodvine, brought in here either late last night or early this morning from a house bombed in Burniston.'

'Let me see . . . ' said the woman and checked a list. 'Yes, I can see where they took him, though I've no idea if he's still there. Are you family?'

'Yes,' said Rosina, as she suddenly thought they wouldn't let her in if not.

'Fine,' said the woman and directed her to the correct ward. Rosina again crossed her fingers as she climbed the stairs and headed for the men's ward. At the door, she stepped inside to be immediately met by a brisk nurse who blocked her way and said, 'Visiting time has just finished. Or it will in about two minutes.'

'I'll take the two minutes then,' said Rosina, her fingers still crossed.

The nurse looked annoyed and asked, 'Name of patient?'

'Harry. Sergeant Harry Woodvine or Henry Woodvine. Is he here? Is he all right?'

'Woodvine,' the nurse said, momentarily considering the name.

But even a moment was too long for Rosina and she blurted out, 'Let me in. I'll look for him.'

'No, you won't,' said the nurse sharply. 'Woodvine, yes. Over there, at the far end.'

Over there, she'd said. He must be alive at least!

As the nurse stepped aside at last, Rosina hurried into the ward, the beds all filled, men coughing and sleeping and saying goodbye to visitors. And there he was, at the far end as the nurse had said. She hurried towards his bed and saw he was asleep. She only had two minutes, but at least she could see him. His face was battered, one eye swollen shut and a split lip. His left arm was splinted and raised up on a pillow. She could see it was horribly bruised and puffy but the other arm looked normal although he looked very small, lying there. His hair was sticking up as if with fright and she reached over and smoothed it down, the feel of it soft yet gritty with brick dust. Then he opened his eyes.

At the sight of his, her eyes blurred with tears and she let them fall. She didn't care any more about looking like a fool. He was alive! Harry was alive and that was all that mattered.

'Hello, you,' he said. That use of the word 'you' felt so intimate, it made her gasp.

'Hello, you,' she said back. 'Please – don't speak if it's tiring.'

'I'm all right. Dislocated shoulder and a bit knocked about. But I'll be proper jam again soon.'

'I'm so glad. I heard at the village hall about the bombing and I drove straight over there. Th-they told me you were here.'

'I'm so glad,' he said, very sleepily.

'I'll leave you,' she said and stood up. Other visitors were moving towards the door now.

'No,' he said firmly. 'You've only just got here.'

'Do your parents know you're here?' she said.

'I think they're telling Mother. My dad died a long time ago.'

'Oh, I'm so sorry. I didn't realise that.' She sat down again. She hoped the officious nurse wouldn't notice her.

'He died in the Great War. I was only three. I never knew him.'

'I'm so dreadfully sorry.'

'It's all right. Remember my grandfather with the chickens? He became a second father to me. And I think I helped him too, after losing his son.'

'I'm sure it did. You didn't mention it when we spoke about your grandfather and the chickens.'

'It didn't seem the right time. Too much comedy value in chickens to talk about death.'

He smiled wanly and she smiled back at him.

He added, 'And anyway, I didn't know you well enough then to share maudlin personal stuff. I feel I know you better now.'

'I'm glad you feel you can tell me things.'

'I honestly feel I could tell you anything and you'd never judge me.'

'Yes, as a mother wouldn't. Perhaps you miss your mother.'

His face darkened. 'No, I don't see you as a mother. I've told you that before. I have a mother, a perfectly good one. I see you as a woman.'

'All right, keep your hair on,' she said, lightening the mood. His face altered and he smiled again. 'It's funny though, isn't it, that we're so different in age and yet we get on so well.'

'Age makes no difference at all,' he said. 'Two souls come

together and connect. Who cares how long their feet have trodden the earth?'

'That's very true,' she said.

'Do you miss your husband?' he said suddenly and she was taken aback. It shocked her momentarily. But then, without hesitation, she looked at him squarely and said, 'No. Not at all.'

They looked at each other and a long moment passed without speech. Then the nurse was behind her, telling her to leave in a scolding tone. Rosina apologised and Harry looked annoyed.

'Before you go,' he said, 'they might send me somewhere to recuperate. I'm not sure where. But . . . if they let me . . . could I—?'

'Yes,' she broke in. 'Yes, you can come and stay at the Hall. You must.'

'Thank you,' he said and smiled a broad and beautiful smile, despite his closed-up eye and his crazy hair.

She bade him goodbye and walked away with the nurse, who saw her off like an interloper. But she didn't care, for she was walking on air as she left the ward and floated down the stairs. And she still had not a trouble in the world when she remembered that the car was out of petrol and she'd have to get the train home and leave the car here. She would have to collect it when they had another petrol coupon next month and she wondered how she would look when she told Mrs Bairstow that Harry was all right and that he was coming to stay. But something in the way Bairstow had looked at her when she had said to go, that certainty, made her feel that she wouldn't be judged, even if she cried tears of relief when she told her. For everyone was fond of Harry Woodvine. She was sure Bairstow felt motherly towards him, as Rosina herself ought to, with eighteen years between them. And, strangely, she realised that there *was* something akin to a maternal fondness for him, especially seeing him lying there in that hospital bed, seeming smaller and broken. But when their eyes met and he smiled at her, her feelings were a world away from a mother's and all she wanted to do at those moments was kiss him on the mouth, feel his arms surround her and never let her go.

Chapter 17

August 1940

As the summer went on, Grace settled in to Scarborough well, spending the little free time she had with Jim or Nancy and the girls. Wartime Scarborough was a bustling service community, with plenty of pongos (Navy slang for soldiers) and RAF training wings staying in the hotels and guest houses all over town. There were even Polish airmen and soldiers stationed near to the Hotel Cecil, so the Wrens threw a party for them in a dance floor that the hotel owners opened up in the cellar of the hotel itself.

Jim and Grace had their first dance there. And their first kiss. And it was smashing, both romantic and sensual, and followed by a nice cuddle and no hint of expectation. Grace was in no hurry to rush into sex again. This time she wanted it to feel totally right and Jim seemed to have the same feeling. Any spare hours they had off work together – when they weren't trying to catch up on sleep – they would spend cycling or walking in the Yorkshire countryside, riding horses one afternoon in her bell-bottoms, feasting on double egg, bacon and chips at the Falcon Inn at Cloughton, watching open-air theatre doing Shakespeare at Northstead Manor. In the evenings, there were dances at the Olympia Ballroom or the Grand Hotel and other venues and sometimes they just stayed in, sitting in the lounge of one of their hotels or on a bench in Peasholm Park, his arm around her shoulder, talking or reading.

It was so easy with Jim, such fun one minute and the next relaxed. She had never realised that a man could make her feel peaceful and it was lovely. Nancy was seeing a Polish airman who was very handsome and she was enjoying herself immensely too, in a different, far more risky way, but Grace trusted her to keep her head screwed on. Nancy had the ability to keep her men in check and never let them get the upper hand. She had them calling at all hours, desperate to see her, and she always made them wait. She had no intention of choosing one. She enjoyed the thrills of dating all sorts and anyway, as she said, 'They might be sent away any minute, so what's t'point of settling?'

Grace understood the logic of that and loved hearing Nancy's stories of her sexual adventures, but she herself wasn't built that way. She was an all-or-nothing girl, she had decided. She either wanted someone she felt a full

270

connection with, in her heart and mind, or no one at all.

Work went on the same, yet busier than ever. The U-boat transmissions increased quite a lot, which they were pleased about on the one hand as it relieved the monotony of the long shifts, yet of course it was also a sign that the manoeuvres were increasing and that brought with it a sense of stark foreboding. At the end of particularly busy shifts, Grace felt as if her very brain itself was crackling with Morse. Some Wrens were finding the stress of the job was really getting to them and the phrase 'going off my nut' was thrown around quite a lot. The intensity and tension of listening out for the elusive U-boats was, in one Wren's words 'quite deadly'. Grace found that too, but she also delighted in finding that she had gradually improved in her work. At times she began to feel a sensation she could only describe as a sixth sense, a kind of premonition that things might be about to happen and often they did. Other telegraphists reported the same phenomenon and it was strange how it happened that way, like a vibration in the air that they sensed. Grace and the others also found that they were now starting to recognise particular subs. Each operator had a way of sending Morse that was individual, a kind of signature. Some were more confident than others, for example. Some seemed to stutter in their Morse sending – perhaps they were newer recruits – while others sent beautiful, rhythmic Morse which was a pleasure to listen to. Very rarely, a surface boat would be heard and Grace wished there were more of these, to break the monotony of waiting for the subs.

Her wish was to be granted when First Officer Ludlow informed her and five other Wrens, including Nancy, that they were to be sent down south for ten days to another station to get some practice listening to surface vessels. So, off they went on the train to Winchester, to then be taken by bus to Flowerdown, an RN station on the outskirts of the cathedral city. Grace was delighted to be in a new place and such a city with the rich, historical heritage of Winchester, once the capital of England. She'd never got round to visiting Winchester and was thrilled when the bus passed by the imposing cathedral with its majestic spires. They'd been told before they left that they'd have seven days on and three days off, so Grace made a pact with Nancy that they'd use their days off wisely and travel about a bit. The station at Flowerdown had quite a different atmosphere from Scarborough, less intense and stressful than the U-boat listening, though just as much on the job. The staff was made up of quite a few Wrens and also ex-Naval signalmen, many of whom lived on site with their wives in quite rudimentary huts, in two of which Grace, Nancy and the other Wrens from Scarborough also stayed. Grace heard one fellow complaining that it took his wife all day to cook the Sunday roast. Another was saying at least they could use the grounds at Flowerdown to snare plenty of rabbits for the meat and pick blackberries in the summer. Despite the simplicity of the accommodation, it all sounded rather idyllic to Grace, who began to feel their somewhat bleak situation on the moor by Scarborough was not half as nice.

There was a long building with telegraphists in the first section, and teleprinters in another. Beyond that was a 'top secret' area and nobody knew what was going on down there and nobody asked. There were also lots of dispatch riders – a mixture of male and female – coming and going at all hours, as the station wasn't too far from Station X at Bletchley Park, just a couple of hours on a good day, one rider said. Grace thought how Audrey would love it down here. Maybe the roads would be better for her motorcycle than the crazy twists and turns and ups and downs of the North Yorkshire moors.

One evening Grace, Nancy and the others went for drinks and a dance with some of the dispatch riders who were all a bit wild and a jolly good time was had by all. Grace became the favourite of a dashing dispatch rider everyone called Bunny (as his surname was Warren, as in rabbit). He was a tall, ginger-haired Adonis but her heart belonged to Jim, so she spurned his advances good-naturedly. Bunny was rather insistent though, so she kept having to dodge him round the dance floor. In the end, he gave up and told her, 'I'm really jolly envious of your feller but I respect your loyalty. It's hard to find these days in chaps or girls. Good on you, Grace.'

After that, they chatted amicably, joined by Nancy and a very young sailor with whom she'd danced away the evening. Once Bunny backed off and treated her as a friend the night improved and they all had rather too much of a jolly good time, as they all felt rotten on the next shift. Grace cursed herself as she wanted to crawl back into bed and sleep instead of listening out for surface ships for hours.

On their first day off, Grace and Nancy went into Winchester and explored the cathedral and other historic parts of the city. They had their second day off soon after and decided it might be fun to get the bus up to Aylesbury and see if they could visit Grace's old friend from university, Patricia, the one who'd given her the orange dress. Pat was married now, with little ones, and still living in the town. The first two buses that arrived were both packed full, so they decided to hitch up the A34 and at least they'd get some time in Oxford, if they couldn't get as far as Aylesbury.

Their first ride was an RAF lorry which wasn't going far, so they were off that soon enough and thumbing another ride. Next came a stinky fish van, which they instantly regretted and got off swiftly. After that, a truck carrying logs in the back, which had a much more pleasant odour. They'd gone past Newbury and got stuck in a traffic jam for a while, then things moved on. And they'd been barrelling along at a fair old place for a while, when the truck driver muttered, 'What's all this then?' and began to slow right down as they approached several cars pulled up by the side of the road. Grace looked ahead and saw a motorcycle on its side on the verge and, beyond it, a figure lying on its side.

'Stop the truck!' cried Grace, feeling suddenly queasy.

'What is it, Grace?' asked Nancy, but there was no time to answer and Grace opened the door while the truck was still moving and jumped out on to the road, Nancy behind her. They ran over to the scene where a little group of onlookers were standing, as well as a policeman who had seemingly just arrived. As he bent down to inspect the motorcyclist, Grace said, 'Excuse me, 'scuse me,' and pushed her way through to look down at the driver and find that her first and sickening thought, that the man on the ground off his bike was Bunny Warren, had been correct. She'd caught a glimpse of orange hair beneath the helmet from the truck . . . He was coming round, moving his limbs and muttering, so it looked as if no serious damage had been done, thank heavens. But he might be concussed or worse and his bike was a wreck, dented, the lights smashed, with the front wheel bent to one side. There was no way it could be ridden without major repairs. Beside Bunny, on the road, was his canvas dispatch bag.

Grace knew instantly that it would be full of urgent dispatches of the most secret nature. If they fell into the wrong hands, who knew what might be done with the information. It was far too dangerous to leave it there or even to trust the policeman with it in case it got left lying around in the station or wherever. No, Grace thought, it was too important to leave to chance, and though she wanted to stay and see if Bunny was going to be all right, she knew that the most crucial need was to secure those dispatches immediately and get them to safety. There was no time to think about it, so she simply stepped over to the bag, picked it up and slung it over her shoulder. The policeman glanced up at her, distracted by tending to the groaning Bunny.

She said, 'I am Chief Petty Officer Calvert-Lazenby of RN stations Flowerdown and Scarborough and these are our dispatches which we will deliver for the driver . . . Warren.' She nearly said Bunny, but realised it wouldn't sound right and she didn't know his real Christian name. She didn't wait for the policeman to reply and turned tail, hoping Nancy would get the gist of things and follow. Grace marched off at a quick pace along the road, hoping the truck with the logs might still be there, but the blighter had driven off, so she just kept going. Nancy fell in step beside her and once they were far enough away, Grace turned to Nancy and said, 'I've no idea what I'm doing!'

'Yes, tha do, Chief Petty Officer Calvert-Lazenby. Me and thee are going to get those dispatches safe to where they should be.'

'I can't believe the policeman didn't even ask us any questions or try to stop us!'

'I couldn't either! I think thi tone of voice was so bossy, and he was a bit flustered dealing with Bunny, he didn't have time to think, let alone stop thee!'

'Well, I'm glad, because we couldn't trust this lot to him or anyone.'

'Tha's right. So, what's t'plan?'

They were walking along the grass verge of the A34 carrying their tin hats and gas masks, as well as the dispatch bag. It was past lunchtime now – inwardly Grace cursed herself for not making an earlier start that morning – and they had miles to go and no signposts to show the way. It would take too long to get back to Winchester – the dispatches were needed as quickly as possible. Grace racked her brain to recall the roads around this area and the rough mileage between them, trying to estimate how much further it would be to Oxford, then to Aylesbury and, beyond that, the certain destination of the dispatches, Station X at Bletchley Park. But whether they managed to cadge lifts or even had to walk all night, Grace and Nancy would get them there, safe and sound. On that, she was utterly determined.

Chapter 18

'First, we need to work out a route,' said Grace as they carried on walking, a little out of breath as this stretch of the A34 was a long, shallow hill that slowly exhausted them by degrees.

'Does tha know it well round these parts?' said Nancy. 'Tha lived here for three year.'

'Reasonably well, I'd say. I mean, I'd never been down to Winchester or Newbury, but I went to Aylesbury several times. There's probably a more direct route to Bletchley than via Oxford, as the crow flies, but the trouble is that with no signposts it's hard to know where we are. I remember that Bicester is sort of on the way to Bletchley from Oxford, so if we could head to there and then veer north-easterly, we should make it. But anyway, let's hope we get a few lifts.'

'I say we ask each one for t'next main town and stagger it that way. It dun't feel right asking anyone to take us to Bletchley,' said Nancy.

'Yes, I'm sure you're right about that.'

'It feels like giving away too much information.'

'It does. And I can't hide this dispatch bag under my jacket or stuff it into the gas mask box, more's the pity. So I don't want some random driver eyeing it up and connecting it with Bletchley.'

'Here, let me have thi box to make things easier.'

'Thank you, dear.'

On they went, thumbs out, ignored by the few passing cars. The day was cloudy, not hot, but a bit muggy and Grace felt damp in her uniform, thirsty and ravenously hungry. They had apples in their gas mask boxes but had planned to eat lunch in Oxford or Aylesbury, whichever one they got to first. Now they retrieved their apples and ate them, the juice delicious and thirst-quenching on their tongues. After an hour and a half of slog, it was by then two in the afternoon and a vehicle finally slowed down. It was a van with rolled-up carpets tied to the roof. There was just room for both of them to squeeze in beside the driver, an older man with a shock of white hair and large moustache, looking exactly like the Geppetto character in Disney's *Pinocchio* which she'd seen on a poster the week before. He was talkative and friendly and far too nosey, asking them questions about where they'd been and where they were going and what they were doing, all of which they wriggled out of with vague replies. Grace was pretty sure the man was no German spy, but she felt uncomfortable with his curiosity, as most people didn't ask you much at all, following the well-known maxim that 'careless talk costs lives'.

Nancy had clearly had enough of him as she said, quite sharply, 'That's enough chit-chat. Keep thi mind on t'road.' It must have given him the hump, because only a few miles further on up the road, he said he wasn't going to Oxford and dropped them off grumpily.

Another hour of walking and the afternoon was waning, Grace's feet were beginning to rub in her shoes and the thought of a beetroot sandwich – something she was sick of back in Scarborough – seemed like paradise and yet utterly out of reach. They each had a few shillings in their pockets, not much to play with, even if they did find somewhere to buy something to eat. Grace had counted on some afternoon tea at Pat's house, but that wasn't going to happen now. Nancy suggested they sing a few songs to cheer themselves up, so they did and it worked for a while. At least it took Grace's mind off her sore feet as she tried to keep her singing in time with her steps and keep her thumb up every time something went by. Eventually an army truck pulled up, with a bunch of pongos in the back, all cheering at the sight of two Jenny Wrens. The driver, seeing how bedraggled they were, told his passenger to get in the back and let Grace and Nancy sit up front with him, thankfully.

'Where yer heading?' he said.

'North,' said Grace. 'Oxford, or beyond.'

'We're going up to Coventry.'

'Too far. But we'll get out at Oxford, please.'

'Won't ask yer what yer doing,' he said.

'Good,' said Nancy. 'Any food?'

'Yer forward, I'll give yer that.'

'We've had an apple since breakfast,' said Grace. 'If you have anything, we'd be so grateful.'

'If we see a tea van in Oxford, we'll drop yer there. How's that?'

'Marvellous, thank you.'

'Yer welcome,' he said.

After that, much to their relief, the driver didn't speak any more and just drove silently on, while they sat exhausted, letting the motion of the truck jog them nearly to sleep. Grace felt it was important that at least one of them stayed wide awake though, in order to keep a close eye on the dispatches bag at all times. She nearly nodded off at one point and woke with a start, looking round at Nancy, who was watching her.

'Have a little snooze,' Nancy said. 'I'll keep my eyes peeled.'

Grace smiled at her friend and patted her hand. She closed her eyes and sleep took her instantly. But it seemed only a blink before the truck was slowing and she was opening her eyes again, seeing her university city outskirts unravel around her.

'There's one,' said the driver and pulled over beside a Women's Voluntary Service – or WVS – tea van. Grace and Nancy thanked the driver several times and he said, 'Be careful, Jenny Wrens. And good luck to yer.' Then off they went, the pongos in the back jeering and whistling at them as they trundled away.

The tea van was closing up but agreed to serve them. They couldn't afford much but the lady was kind and gave them a sticky bun each and some old cheese sandwiches they were going to throw away. Grace could have kissed her, but she was too busy shoving the bun in her mouth, with no decorum whatsoever. They sat down on a low wall outside St Aldate's Church, the railings having been taken away. The food and the tea went down a treat and they both cheered up and felt human again. It was early evening by now and they still had miles to go. But with their stomachs fuller, Grace felt more optimistic than they had all day.

'Funny how a bit of grub can make you feel like you can do anything,' she said.

'We *can* do anything,' Nancy said. 'We're Jenny Wrens.'

'Absolutely,' said Grace. 'Right. Come on, then. We need to get out of Oxford and on to the road towards Bicester. It's the A34 to begin with, then I think it changes. So let's see if we can find someone heading north, towards Banbury, I suppose.'

As Grace led Nancy through the city, it was so tempting to give her a running commentary of all her favourite city haunts – the Radcliffe Camera, Christ Church Cathedral, Magdalen College, the Sheldonian Theatre, the Ashmolean Museum, the Bodleian Library. How one city could house so many wonders had never ceased to amaze her when she was a resident, but, of course, there was no time for all that.

'Look at everyone going home for tea,' said Nancy, with longing.

'Keep your pecker up,' said Grace, though she too felt incredibly jealous of the office workers hurrying home on the pavements and in the buses, while they tramped on, with no idea when or how they would reach their destination. What she did know was that this war was testing her harder than anything in her life to this point and as she went on through the city she'd lived in for three years, she felt that the person she'd been when she'd last walked these streets was a total stranger to her: shy, awkward, clumsy, nervous and never been kissed. Her mother had said she walked taller now and it was true, in every way. She was resolute that she would rise to this latest challenge. The papers she carried in that bag were far too important to fail now (even though her feet were rubbing like billy-o).

She knew they needed to head north, so she led them towards Summertown, with the Banbury Road leading in the right direction right through the midst of it. Once they began to leave Summertown behind, they put out their thumbs again, as vehicles were likely to be leaving Oxford rather than merely driving around it to get home and it was gone six in the evening when they finally got a lift from an RAF flight lieutenant in a nice blue Hillman Minx staff car. He was business-like but pleasant, in his forties with a bristly moustache. He didn't ask them a word about what they were doing but only where he could take them.

'We're heading for Bicester,' said Grace, as she shut the rear door. She and Nancy sat in the back together.

'Is that your final destination?' he said, looking at her in his mirror.

She wanted to trust him. If you couldn't trust the RAF, who could you trust? But they'd been so careful thus far and it felt right to keep their movements as shadowy as possible, from everyone, just in case.

'We'll get out there, thanks very much, if that's where tha's going,' said Nancy.

Grace glanced at her and Nancy nodded. She clearly felt the same.

'Fine,' he said. 'I can take you to Bicester. I'm going up to Banbury, but it's only a short detour.'

'Thank you,' said Grace.

The flight lieutenant clearly did not want to make small talk, which was a great relief to Grace. She spoke in a low voice to Nancy, saying, 'Your turn for a nap.'

'Oh, I'm grand, duck. If tha needs a sleep, have one.'

'No, it's your turn. Fair's fair.'

'All right then, I will,' said Nancy and within seconds was nodding off, her head bumping against the window but nothing would wake her up. She was far gone. Grace forced herself to stay awake by counting trees outside. Occasionally she'd glance at the mirror and see the flight lieutenant staring at her. She looked away, beginning to feel uncomfortable. There was an atmosphere in the car, but she couldn't pin it down. If she hadn't been so shattered, she would have asked him to pull over and let them out. Besides, she wanted Nancy to sleep. Then, the flight lieutenant spoke.

'Are you Wrens on leave? Going home?'

'Something like that,' said Grace, hoping he wouldn't ask anything else. He was quiet for a time, driving onwards, glancing in the mirror from time to time. Then he spoke again.

'Silky nightdresses in that bag then?'

Grace clutched the dispatches bag closer to her. She

didn't like what he'd said. It felt personal. Salacious. Unsettling.

'None of your beeswax,' she said, trying to maintain a friendly tone.

She could see he was smiling.

'What if I suggested you were adrift?'

Grace knew what that meant. It was absent without permission.

'Then you would be wrong,' she said.

'I'm not sure about that,' he said. 'I think I'm right.'

Another silence. Grace thought she should wake Nancy, but she was sleeping so peacefully. What was this fellow's game?

'If I find a defaulter in my car, I don't treat that lightly. I report them.'

'Look, we're not defaulters. We're on official business.'

'Says who? For whom?'

It was unnerving having a conversation with a man's back, only seeing the odd glimpse of his eyes when he chose to look at hers in the mirror.

'You know better than to ask us that, sir.'

He drove on a while longer and Grace willed Bicester to come into view. She did not know the villages in these parts that well, so she needed Bicester to ground them. But she was now beginning to feel that staying in this car was folly, yet also she did not want to be stuck in the middle of nowhere with night approaching, with this man and no houses nearby.

'I have a little house in Banbury,' he said and just let that fact float there, in the close air of the car.

'I think it's time you concentrated on driving and stopped insinuating things,' she said, her head buzzing with the stress of keeping her nerve.

More silence. Then she started to wonder if they were on the right road, heading for Bicester and not Banbury. But she was pretty sure the road to Banbury was smaller than this one.

'What have you really got in that bag?' he said. His voice was infuriatingly calm, a little snide.

'You know better than to ask that.'

'I want to know. But if you don't want to tell me, you can show me what you've got up your skirt instead.'

Grace reached over and shoved Nancy, who awoke with a start. 'We here?' she mumbled, her eyelids still drooping.

'It's time to let us out now,' Grace said loudly.

'But we're not at Bicester yet,' he said.

'We want to get out. Stop the car please.'

But he just kept on driving.

'What's going on?' said Nancy, much more awake now.

Grace looked at Nancy intensely and shook her head, a warning in her eyes.

'Pull over. Now,' said Grace loudly.

'Do as she says,' said Nancy, cottoning on that something was wrong, very wrong.

'Whatever next?' he said. 'A couple of Jenny Wrens giving me orders. I'm a hero, a pilot, shot down Germans and saved lives. What have you ever done?'

'What's he talking about?' said Nancy. 'What're tha talking about? If we tell thee to pull over, tha do it, man. Or I'll report thee when we get out of here for harassing two Wrens on official duties.'

'Don't be ridiculous,' he said, still with that maddening coolness. 'Who would believe you over me? A couple of defaulters like you? Look at you both. Shabby and dishevelled. You're a disgrace to your uniform.'

'How dare you!' said Grace in a low voice, filled with her anger from all the times a man had made her feel small these past months. Erik, Vic, the officers who looked through her as if she were transparent, the chargehands at work who rolled their eyes when she came into the room. All those men who made her feel like so much less than them, like nothing. Well, not any more.

'STOP THIS CAR!' she shouted as loudly as she could and actually saw him flinch. 'STOP THIS BLOODY CAR NOW, YOU INSUFFERABLE BASTARD!'

It had worked with Vic in the army truck near home. But not this time. The man had ice in his veins.

Grace and Nancy stared at each other. They had to get out of this car, get away from this man. Their voices had been ignored, as so often had happened to her as a woman. Well, it would have to be a physical intervention then. She shifted forward in her seat, put her thumb and forefinger together and flicked the man on the back of his neck really hard.

'Ow!' he cried. 'What the bloody hell?'

Nancy caught on and she leant round the other side and did the same thing, flicking him really hard in the back of the neck.

'Get off, you harpy!'

Grace leant forward again and did it three times in quick succession, Nancy joining in the other side. They were laughing now, the ridiculousness of the situation coming home to them, overtaking their fear. The car swerved as he tried to bat them away, Nancy and Grace thrown to the side.

'You're insane! Bloody mad bitches, the two of you!'

'That's what they've always said about women who dare to stand up to men,' said Grace. 'They call them mad. Then they burn them at the stake or slap a scold's bridle on them or drown them or do anything they can to shut them up. Not this time though, matey. You're not shutting us up. Now pull this car over before I spit in your ear!'

Then the man drove to the side of the road and applied

his brakes savagely, throwing everyone forward. He turned round in his seat and Grace could see his face for the first time. He was red with rage.

'Get out. GET OUT!'

'With pleasure,' said Grace, smiling sweetly and throwing open the door, ensuring she had the documents bag safely over her shoulder before she got out.

'Do us all a favour and drive thissen off a cliff,' said Nancy, before hopping out after Grace.

She slammed the door behind her and the man screeched off, wavering erratically before disappearing round a bend.

Grace and Nancy collapsed in laughter and shock.

'Tha were bloody brilliant!' said Nancy. 'What were he saying before I woke up?'

'Just being disgusting. Abusing his power. He had other things in mind. Well, I wasn't having it and I'm sick of it. These bloody men, thinking they can do what they like.'

'Damn, I were going to look at his registration plate before he drove off. So we could report him.'

'Well, it's probably just as well you didn't. He was right. Who would believe us over him?'

'They might do.'

'You have more faith in the system than I do. Let's face it, we're the lowest of the low.'

'Nay, we're Chief Petty Officers. That's not nowt, Grace.'

'But don't you see, with these men, it means nothing?

We're just females to them. We're either a nuisance or invisible or something to be used. Men are hateful.'

'Not all men are like that, flower,' said Nancy softly. 'My dad for one. And thi Jim.'

Grace realised she was panting and sweaty from fear and anger. Her head felt swimmy and she put her hand to her head.

'Gosh . . . ' she muttered and closed her eyes.

'It's all right, pet. Tha's going to be all right.' Nancy was putting her arm around her. 'Tha's just knackered and upset.'

Grace opened her eyes and breathed deeply. It was evening and she was grateful it was summer because the sky was still light enough to see their way, though it was overcast and deep grey.

'Come on,' she said, gathering herself. 'We've got a mission to complete.'

So they walked on, along the long road towards Bicester. They reached it after about half an hour of walking, then Grace decided to take the initiative and try a different tack. She saw a car outside someone's house and knocked on the door. A woman in her forties, smartly dressed, opened it and stared agog at them. *What a sight we must look*, thought Grace. But she soldiered on with her plan.

'Good evening. We are Chief Petty Officers Calvert-Lazenby and Bird. We need transport. Does your car have petrol?'

'Why, yes it does,' said the woman. 'I'm a driver for the WVS. Where do you need to go?' she asked, leaning over to a hat stand and grabbing her coat and hat.

'The village of Bletchley.'

'Right you are,' said the woman.

They all piled into the car and she didn't ask them a thing about their business. She asked if they'd like to nap on the way but they both said thank you, but no. Half an hour later the woman said, 'Here we are. This is Bletchley. Anywhere in particular you'd like to go? Bletchley Park, is it?'

Grace was sick of subterfuge by now. And after all, quite a few people knew that lots of Wrens worked at Bletchley Park but they wouldn't know what was going on there behind closed doors – even most Wrens knew nothing about that – so, surely it would be all right to have this last little bit of the journey made slightly easier by telling the woman where they were going.

'Just pull over here, please,' said Grace, changing her mind. If you were going to do something, then see it through to the end and do it properly.

'Right you are,' said the woman and dropped them off. They thanked her and she nodded, smiled and drove away.

'Last stretch!' said Nancy and grinned. 'Shall we carry on along this road? I think she were taking us there anyway, so we're probably in t'right direction.'

'Good plan,' said Grace, too exhausted to think about

much. So they tramped on. Grace knew her feet were raw with blisters now, but just focused on putting one foot in front of the other. Nancy's reasoning proved right and, before long, the large Victorian house with guards at the entrance announced itself as Bletchley Park. To see it materialise before them, after the most hideously shattering day, was akin to seeing heaven. Grace could have cried with relief. But it wasn't over yet. She knew it wouldn't be easy to explain themselves. More bureaucracy to get through. She steeled herself as they approached the guard at the gate.

She explained that they had urgent dispatches to give in and the guard said he'd take them; Nancy said no, they must be delivered by hand to an officer. Grace was glad she said that – the thought of giving the precious documents to some minion seemed ridiculous after everything they'd been through and she trusted nobody by this point, especially after their run-in with the corrupt RAF officer. The guard demanded their paybooks which they handed over and he sent another guard off inside with them. Eventually, he came back out with a man in civilian clothes who invited the Wrens in. He said nothing to them as he led them to a large, empty dining room and told them to sit down, eyeing them curiously as they did so.

'What have you got for us, then?' he said.

'Urgent dispatches from Flowerdown,' said Grace. 'The dispatch rider came off his motorcycle on the way so we retrieved his dispatches bag and decided to deliver it for him.'

'How on earth did you get here?' said the man.

'Shanks's pony,' said Nancy.

'You *walked*? All the way from Winchester?'

'We hitched some lifts along the way, here and there. Did a lot of walking too, though,' said Grace.

'Extraordinary,' said the man and stared at them, a wry smile on his face, shaking his head. 'Listen, I'm Mr Brown of the German Naval section. I'll take your dispatches and get them to the right place.'

Grace found she was still clutching on to the dispatches bag protectively, as she had been all day. Finally, she was going to be able to give them up, hand them over to the right person. She hesitated and Mr Brown said, 'You've done your duty brilliantly but you may relinquish your charge now. And then I'll get you both a cup of tea.'

Grace glanced at Nancy who nodded. She took off the bag and handed it over to Mr Brown. She felt lighter without it and also, truth be told, light-headed after all the drama.

'Can we have a breadcake or a sarnie too?' said Nancy. 'We're famished.'

'I'm not entirely sure what either of those are,' said Mr Brown. 'But I'll get you something to eat.'

And off he went.

Grace and Nancy held their breath until he'd left the

room, then let out a relieved laugh and sighed a lot and patted each other on the back.

A short time later back came Mr Brown with a tea tray replete with a pot of tea, a milk jug and two rounds of hot bacon sandwiches. Grace had never tasted anything so marvellous in all her life as that crispy bacon in the soft bread, the fat greasing her hands and lips as she shoved it in. Mr Brown had left them to eat, then he came back.

'You know, everyone's talking about you,' said Mr Brown, that wry smile back again. 'There was a general alert put out this afternoon throughout the whole country for two ladies dressed up as Wrens who had pinched crucial papers from an injured dispatch rider!'

'Chuffin' 'eck!' said Nancy.

'Indeed,' said Mr Brown.

'Is the dispatch rider all right?' said Grace. 'We knew him.'

'I've not heard any bad reports, so hopefully, yes. But anyway, what you've done is extraordinary. Don't be surprised if you receive letters of commendation from your Commanding Officer. You're down from Scarborough, I understand?'

'Yes, we are,' said Grace. 'Both of us, born and bred in North Yorkshire.'

'They build them well up there, clearly,' said Mr Brown and smiled. 'Your actions today may well have saved lives. You should both be inordinately proud of yourselves.'

He then explained that they should take the next day off. He'd give them travel vouchers to get back to Flowerdown and would arrange for them to stay at a local YWCA hostel that night.

'But we can't take t'day off tomorrow – we're back on duty first thing in t'morning,' said Nancy.

'Oh, I'll see to that,' said Mr Brown.

Once they were at the hostel, they washed themselves, paying particular attention to their poor, blistered feet and crawled into a bunk bed. Thankfully, the other two bunks in the room were unoccupied, as neither felt like socialising that night.

Laying her head down on that hard YWCA pillow was blissful. Grace predicted she'd be asleep in minutes. But actually she lay awake for a while, going over the events of the most bizarre day of her life.

She let out a long sigh and Nancy, who Grace thought might be asleep by now, said, 'You all right, love?'

'Yes. Yes, I'm all right. Are you?'

'Aye. I'm all right.'

'We bloody did it,' said Grace.

'Aye, we bloody did,' said Nancy.

'Bloody mad bitches, we are,' said Grace.

'Aye, we are,' said Nancy and they both chuckled. Then, within moments, they were snoring.

Chapter 19

August 1940

When Harry came to stay, he had his left arm in a sling but his face looked much better, almost back to normal. He was grinning from ear to ear and, apart from his arm, he looked quite all right. Rosina had lovingly prepared a guest room for him, with fresh flowers in a vase and a small table set up with his favourite whisky in a decanter with one of her finest glasses beside it. She'd also put a small selection of reading material she thought he might like beside his bed: some John Buchan books and a new one by Graham Greene called *The Power and the Glory* which she hadn't read yet. She loved Greene's writing and though she found him a bit depressing at times, she thought that Harry would appreciate Buchan and Greene as they both seemed manly. Standing in the room and looking around it, Harry was so appreciative, told her she shouldn't have gone to so much trouble, especially with the books.

'I wanted to,' she said, simply. 'I love to read. I used to write short stories, once upon a time. But it's been years.'

'I think you should rectify that. Just think of the opportunities war presents for interesting new material.'

'Most of the war so far has been simply a grind and deadly dull,' she said wryly.

'Not all of it,' he replied and smiled knowingly, perhaps referring to her, to them. She smiled in return. 'And anyway,' he went on, 'it wouldn't be dull to those reading in the future. Times like these need to be documented. I think you should start writing again. And I'd love to read whatever you write, if you'd let me.'

Rosina looked away and murmured, 'We'll see.' She had lost confidence in her ability to write anything that anyone would want to read over the years. Her husband had read a story of hers once and said it was 'tedious'. That was the word he used. So cruel. She'd written a bit after that, but lost heart. But Harry was right: now was an excellent time to start again. The thought of Harry reading what she wrote made her prickle with anxiety, but this was also tinged with an exciting edge of possibility. Why not write again? Why not let him see it? Rosina felt that her future was beginning to open up, its door edging outwards, revealing an as-yet unknown view of what might be.

They went for gentle strolls around the grounds at first, or stayed in and played cards or chess. They read the newspapers together and discussed the progress of the war and the politics of the day. He became tired quickly, so she left him to rest often, and, after all, she still had her household duties to attend to, though Mrs Bairstow took up the slack willingly. She seemed genuinely delighted that the RAF had allowed Harry to recuperate with them. It would be around three to four weeks until he could use his arm again and he explained that his work was technical and mostly required two hands, so he was not to return until he was in 'full working order', as Harry put it.

As the days went on, the ease between them grew and they talked about more personal subjects, from their childhoods to past relationships. Harry had had none of note, he said, just passing fancies. He asked Rosina lots of questions about her husband and she was quite candid with him about the fact that she had grown to dislike George, but held back the truth that she had mostly despised him after the infatuation had worn off. She felt somehow ashamed, that she had made such a bad choice of husband, that she had had five daughters with a man she hated. She didn't know quite how to explain to a young man like Harry that life is often about making hard decisions when you have so little choice. Continuing to have children despite her loathing of her husband was one of those kind of decisions, making the best of a bad thing. She might have felt cold towards George, but at least she'd got her five daughters from him and that had kept her sane and happy enough over the years. But she wasn't ready to share all of that with Harry, not yet. It was too intimate somehow.

Then, one evening they turned to the subject of Harry's recent past. He had been explaining about his Cambridge days and his BBC training in London. 'And then I went to fight in Spain for a while, before it all kicked off here and I came back and joined up.'

'I've been dying to ask you about your experiences there and why you went. Do tell me everything. I'm agog. I read all about it at the time and was appalled by it, such a tragedy. That awful man Franco and the poor Spanish people fighting so valiantly and losing.'

He looked down at his arm in the sling and sighed heavily.

'I'm sorry,' she said. 'That was a stupid, insensitive thing to say.'

'Not at all. It's all true. They did fight valiantly. And they did lose.'

His face looked so different, his usual wry smile gone, his eyes distracted, looking just past her, seeing memories that must have been painful.

'W-we don't have to talk about it,' she said.

'No, I'd like to. Nobody really asks about it any more.

Now we have our own war, Spain has been forgotten by many.'

'Start at the beginning, if you like. And here . . . ' She poured him another measure of whisky. She felt he might need it.

'In some ways, I think I was probably destined to fight against the Fascists one day. I grew up in a political household, you see. My mother and grandfather were always talking about current affairs and the rights of workers, despite the fact that they sent me away to school. They wanted to give me the best chance in life, even though morally they didn't really agree with private education. As a young boy in Shropshire, the parents of many of my local friends worked in industry. When I was sent away to boarding school, I came across a different breed, of course. I didn't fit in very well there – I had a scholarship that paid for most of it – so I strove to fit in, not always successfully. But I hated blind authority. Even there, several of my teachers leant towards the left. The General Strike of '26 was discussed fiercely at school and home. And then, as a young man, I joined the Officer Training Corps. I wanted to learn how to use a gun, you see, and I was always interested in armies from history books, not the generals but the ordinary soldiers. They were my heroes. I wanted to understand the army from the inside out. I was sure war was coming in the thirties and I wanted to be ready for it.'

'I always hated guns. My father wanted me to be a hunter, but I never took to it.'

'I didn't dote on them, like some fellows do. But I could see the value in being able to defend yourself. I quite enjoyed the OTC but mostly I was just fascinated by the mindset of military people. I knew it wasn't for me, but I was glad I knew how to use a weapon, just in case. Anyway, by '36, I was working for the BBC, as you know, and I'd been hearing so much bad news about what was going on in Spain. As I saw it, the Republican government was being trampled on by fascists under Franco, it was as simple as that. And in my own country, the Fascists – Mosley and his hideous Blackshirts – were marching in the streets of Britain and beating up Jews. I talked about it constantly with my old Cambridge friends and my BBC colleagues and some fellows were going off to Spain to join others of different nationalities to help the Republicans. One day I decided that at some point one had to stand up and do something about what one believed in, not just jaw about it. I didn't tell many people, just my boss at the BBC and some lads from Cambridge. My boss said he'd be happy to have me back when it was all over. He applauded me going, actually! I didn't tell anyone else I was going, just sent my family a letter from London before I went.'

'How did they react?' She thought of how she would feel as his mother, having this golden boy going off willingly to fight in a war that had nothing to do with him. Well, all wars required a humanitarian response to the suffering, but she felt she would have fought to hold him back from putting his life in danger. She wouldn't want her boy caught up in it.

'My grandfather wrote to me once I had an address to give them. He said my mother was too angry to write to me, which I quite understood, and while he said he was proud of me, he advised me to help for a while and then come home, knowing I'd done my duty, that I didn't need to give everything to it. I know why he felt that way, but I didn't. I simply wanted to fight against this lethal bully, Franco, to show the world that you can't just let men like that stomp all over democracy.'

'It's tremendously impressive,' she said, shaking her head.

'Not at all,' he said, firmly. 'It was just the right thing to do. And I'll admit that there was a sense of adventure about it. Going off to Spain felt to me like the way I imagined it must've felt for the Pals regiments going off in the Great War. I heard a lot about it as a boy growing up. Oh, but I've said something wrong. What is it?'

Rosina had turned her face away at the mention of the Pals. It brought back such painful memories, memories that could still instantly elicit an overwhelming sadness in her. She never really spoke of it. But of all people, though Harry had been a baby when it all started, she felt able to speak of it with him.

'I had two brothers who joined the local Pals regiment and they were both killed.'

'I'm truly sorry to hear that.'

'Thank you. My mother died around that time, too and it was the end of everything. The Pals idea, of sending lads from the same village in the same regiments, was a dreadful mistake. All the lads from round here were killed, as in so many villages across the country. They changed the policy, of course, but it was too late for many families and places.'

'Would you like to talk about your brothers?' he asked and she was touched; it was a question that showed his sensitivity.

'Another time,' she said. 'Please, tell me what happened next. How did you get to Spain?'

'The Communist Party paid my ticket to Paris and my travel onwards into Spain by train and bus. There were all sorts of nationalities there: lots of French and Belgians; Scottish and Welsh lads and plenty of Irish; Germans who'd escaped Hitler and some Austrians; Italians who were anti-Mussolini; there was a Polish battalion, even some Canadians, Australians and Americans. Fighting alongside Germans and Italians has made me feel quite differently going into this war, knowing that so many in those countries didn't agree with their leaders.'

'I know what you mean,' she said. 'When I'm reading about the war in the newspapers or listening to the news on the wireless, I often think of the German mothers doing the same, sitting beside German wirelesses. There's that poem by Siegfried Sassoon, written during the last war, where he talks about German mothers knitting socks for their sons while their faces are trodden deeper in the mud. I never liked the poem much; it was rather too damning of women, I thought, but the image stuck with me, of German mothers feeling just like English ones did.'

'I'm glad you think that way,' he said. 'So many people are gung-ho about war and I'm not at all. I just feel you have to fight it, because you must. It's not a game, or an adventure, as I learnt to my cost.'

'Tell me, what was it like in Spain?'

'Spain was beautiful in some ways, a bit of a mess in others. I have a vivid memory of the fields of crocuses, grown for saffron, and the women who would gather the flowers and sit and pick out the stamens. But the people were very poor in the rural areas. They were always generous, though, would bring supplies to the hospitals for soldiers and offer food to us, even though they had so little. Most of the Spanish lads we fought beside were illiterate and I decided that once we won the war – I mean, there was no doubt in our minds that we would win – I'd come back to Spain and work as a teacher, teaching these rural children to read and write, that this was probably the most politically useful thing they needed. In the meantime, we had to win their country back for them, so that they had a chance of a better future. And for that, you need guns and ammo and planes and so forth, not just ideals. We had very few weapons. There were some old rifles from the last century and rotten ammo – I mean that literally: some ammo had rotted and weapons were dangerous to use.'

'How dreadful. They couldn't afford to buy more guns in?'

'Oh, it wasn't that. I'll never forgive the British government for not getting involved. They claimed neutrality but they weren't neutral. Their policy of non-intervention meant that the Republicans couldn't buy arms. They knew Germany and Italy were marching in men from Africa and flying in planes. But the British did nothing to stop it.'

'I knew nothing about this,' said Rosina, genuinely horrified. She'd always felt that her government had done the right thing, not getting involved. Now her beliefs were shaken. It was amazing how little you knew about the truth, just from reading newspapers.

'Well, we did our best with the weaponry we had. Many of the other nationalities had conscription in their own countries, so they were better trained for fighting than the English lads, but my OTC training helped a bit. We began by fighting house-to-house in Madrid and many Brits were killed then – the losses were terrible – and our side really suffered from basically having no proper air force. That's partly why I wanted to join the RAF for this war. Some help came from the Russians but it was too little, too late and there was so much in-fighting on the Left. The whole thing was a bloody mess, to be honest, and so the ordinary people of Spain never stood a chance. The forces of history were trampling inexorably over them.'

He looked down grimly into his whisky glass then and took a long swig, draining it.

'We can talk about something else, if you like,' she said softly.

'No, it's all right. I may as well finish the tale. I just get a bit angry about it all sometimes.'

'Of course you do. But only go on if you want to.'

'Well, it came to an end when I was injured near Madrid. Many of my friends were killed in the same battle. We were under heavy fire and I was hit in the leg and fell down. I couldn't move and I lay there all day and night because there was no medical help in that area. Thankfully, a friend came back to find me. He dragged me out of there and so saved my life. Sadly, he died later in the war. He was twenty-one years old . . .'

So much tragedy in one short speech. She didn't want to interrupt him again, but she wished she could have touched his hand at that moment, to show him she understood something of death, of grief, though she had never been at war like that. But she could not find the courage to touch him and she instead she waited quietly. All words seemed trite in the face of his stark honesty.

'My wounds took a while to heal and they sent me back to London to get better medical treatment. I saw my mother and grandfather there and they were so desperately upset, but I felt very strongly I wanted to go back. Instead I was sent to Paris as my French was good. My leg healed up perfectly, but they felt I was best serving the cause by helping volunteers in Paris. I followed events closely and could see it was getting worse and worse and it started to dawn on me that we weren't going to win, that the Fascists were going to beat democracy and that was appalling. And sad. So dreadfully sad. The dream of democracy in Spain was lost. Then the League of Nations said that all foreigners should leave Spain. That was in late '38. So I returned to London and my BBC boss came good and gave me my old job back. We knew then that war was likely and I signed up for the RAF on the day they announced it. The truth is that it's all one war, just a continuation of it. The fight against fascism.'

He sat and stared at the bottom of his whisky glass. She was so grateful he'd shared it all with her, yet hated to see his face so forlorn, his body seeming rigid with anger. She had no idea what to say.

'Another whisky?'

'Better not!' he said. 'I'm already a bit squiffy. And as you can see, I do get a bit maudlin when I've had one too many.'

'If you didn't get maudlin about something so devastating, you wouldn't be human.'

He looked round at her and his face was difficult to read. He was frowning but didn't look annoyed, just curious, as if he were trying to understand her through gazing.

He said quietly, 'Nobody wanted to talk about it. The war came here and so then Spain quickly became a footnote and I realised how fickle the world is. One of the hardest lessons I've ever learnt. It. . . changed me.'

There was so much to say to that but all she could think of was how grateful she was for this time they shared together, for the hours and days and evenings they had in which he could open up to her, slowly, gradually, peeling off each layer of his introvert nature and revealing more of his true self. And every time he did so, she loved each uncovering more and more. She realised at that moment that he was so much more than the phrase 'young man' could ever sum up. It was actually a bit insulting, as if he had not lived and was somehow green. She saw that this man was full of experience and emotion, and he had an understanding of some of the deep truths of the world.

And just because he was eighteen years younger than her, it meant nothing. He was her equal and she actually felt wanting in the face of his quiet heroism. Yet, she also considered that she herself had experienced sorrow and loss and he responded to that in her, to her experience of the world and her serious nature. Perhaps an older woman like herself was more appealing to an old soul like him, someone who could meet him at the same level and not find him too pensive or dull, but instead revel in it and match it gratefully.

'What an extraordinary person you are,' she said and thought he'd laugh it off.

But he just looked at her very carefully and said, 'It's you who is the revelation.'

'But I'm so . . . commonplace,' she said, truly believing that, never having thought of herself as possessing any special qualities whatsoever.

'How can you say that? How can you even think it?'

He was staring at her intensely, then the clock struck ten and broke the tension in the room. They both commented on the lateness of hour and she got up to clear away their things, before wishing him goodnight. Walking slowly up the stairs afterwards, she felt that if the clock hadn't chimed at that moment, she might have stood up, walked over to him and leant down and kissed him. She was glad that she hadn't. For this intimacy between them, of talking and sharing their memories, their thoughts and feelings, was more valuable to her then any passing physical fancy. It was, she realised, the most precious time she'd ever spent with a man in her life.

Chapter 20

The girls returned from school for the summer holidays and the quiet times with Harry were over, but as much as she missed their privacy, it was such a joy to see three of her girls back home again and hear their laughter and bickering fill the house. The girls were delighted to find Harry there and bombarded him with requests to entertain them in various ways, so thrilled were they to have a male audience for their girlish exploits. He was endlessly patient with them, responding to each, carefully calibrating his reaction based on their character.

To Constance, he talked of the cricket he'd played at school and at Cambridge and, with his good arm, he showed her how to bowl. He spoke of radio waves and gravity and the stars with Dora, making her marvel at the wonders of the physical universe. With Daisy, it was obvious he knew very little about classical music, but he asked to listen to her play and he told her about his favourite big bands and even showed her a couple of dance steps, which her mother was amazed to see her enjoying and even practising when he wasn't around. He really brought out the best in all of her girls, without even trying somehow. He was just a natural with them and they adored him.

It was not only her own children he charmed. The twins had made friends with Ronnie Holt, the evacuee, had more or less adopted him in their first couple of weeks of the holidays. They came back to tell Rosina and Harry one dinnertime about Ronnie's sad story, that his parents in Hull would beat him and not leave any food for his dinner, that he would sometimes come home from school to find only a bag of elderly oats in the cupboard and how he'd eaten them, dry and hard in handfuls from the packet. (This detail in particular broke their hearts in several places, Connie had explained.) Rosina had asked them if Ronnie really told them all that as, in her experience, the boy mostly nodded or shook his head and she had never heard him utter a full sentence, let alone such glorious details as 'elderly oats'. But Constance grew furious at the implication that she had been elaborating on the story. Harry stepped in and defused the situation by suggesting they should bring the boy in sometime and he'd teach him to play chess. They all thought that was a capital idea and so Ronnie was summoned the next day, his fingernails black from gardening.

Harry told the boy how bored he was of having his arm out of action and Ronnie would be doing him a great favour if he would concede to play a game with him. Ronnie looked alarmed but interested and, as usual, said little. Harry started him off with a game of draughts, then graduated to backgammon and finally started to teach him the rudiments of chess. Days were filled with the girls playing games, or the piano, or chasing the chickens about, whilst the quiet tap tap of chess pieces and Harry's quiet, encouraging words of direction drifted from the games room where he and Ronnie played peacefully, sometimes all afternoon. These sounds were a balm to Rosina and, if only Grace and Evelyn were here too, she honestly felt she could not have been happier.

The time came, of course, when Harry was fully recovered. He was told that he was going to be sent down south to an RAF station in the forefront of the aerial attacks that had been taking place during most of July from the German Luftwaffe. Rosina had known the time would come when he'd have to go, but she'd assumed he'd go back to somewhere quiet and carry on his secretive radio work. But no, the war had decided to use him elsewhere and in a place of danger. She had to get used to it, as did so many other households all over Europe. However, she hated the thought of him being in the line of fire. But there was never any point in harping on about such things, especially since they'd been lucky enough to have this hiatus of a few weeks together. She was ashamed to admit to herself that she even inwardly thanked the German bomber who'd dislocated his shoulder, which had meant she'd got to have him to herself for a while. He promised Rosina he'd write to her and to the girls and even send sketches of chess openings for Ronnie. He was going to be picked up by an RAF truck and taken to Scarborough, to report to his commander there. Everyone stood in the drive, Mrs Bairstow too, to wave him goodbye. Constance had given everyone hankies to wave because, she said, 'That's the proper way with soldiers' farewells.'

'Farewell then, all you lovely people,' said Harry and grinned at the girls. Dora and Constance held hands, waving the handkerchiefs furiously, while Daisy had tears running down her cheeks and used her hankie to blow her nose noisily. Then, Harry glanced up at Rosina and gave her an awkward smile.

It was torture, saying goodbye in front of company. Of course, the girls had to be there; they were all desperately fond of Harry. And Bairstow seemed sorry to see him go too. But as Rosina smiled back, she ached to be alone with him. There was so much she wanted to say, so much she could have said when he was there but had never summoned up the nerve to do it. They had skirted around each other with great care. And now part of her regretted it. He was leaving and she might never see him again. In wartime, one had to face that as a very real possibility. So, what harm would it have done to tell him how she felt? But she had shied away from it and here they were, standing stiffly in front of four others, saying goodbye, with everything left unsaid and no more chance to say it.

'Good luck then, Harry,' she said briefly and, after a pause, held out her hand to him.

He took it and held it softly, his thumb briefly and gently rubbing against her skin as they stood there, arms outstretched. Then his grip firmed up and she felt as if, in another place, another time, he might have pulled her into his arms. His gaze was almost fierce, his eyes an intense blue. He was speaking to her with them, she knew that. But the moment was over and they had to release each other.

'Thank you,' he said. 'I believe I might need it, where I'm going.'

She wanted to cry out, *Don't say that! You must stay alive and well!* She hadn't spent these weeks nursing him back to full strength to see him put in danger's way again so soon. But that was war and that was now.

'Keep in touch,' she said brightly and heard her voice crack. She mustn't speak another word or she'd cry. He sensed it and turned away, his feet crunching up the drive to the waiting truck. They all watched the truck turn around and leave, the girls still waving their hankies.

Even though she'd known it was coming and had prepared

herself mentally for his departure, Rosina was shocked by the strength of depression that settled on her the moment Harry was gone. Everything felt drab and tiresome again and she moped around when alone and though she put on a forced jollity for the girls, they could see she wasn't happy and neither were they. Everyone missed Harry. One afternoon, three days after he'd left, she was sitting at the kitchen table, peeling potatoes with Mrs Bairstow and she felt so dejected, as if a great weight was on her shoulders and would never lift. Her ability to reason herself out of sadness, as she had often done in the past, seemed beyond her at that moment. Somehow, the absence of Harry became synonymous with the emptiness she'd felt all those years ago when her brothers hadn't come home. It felt the same and it felt awful. She knew a tear was leaking down her face and saw it splash on to the potato peelings. She didn't even have the mental energy to wipe her eyes or try to stop it. She sniffed – and Bairstow put down her peeler and reached out to touch her hand. Oh, how soothing it was to feel a human touch at that moment.

'Oh, don't be nice to me. I'll just cry and cry if you are!' said Rosina and tried to laugh it off.

''Course tha's emotional,' said Bairstow. 'Tha miss him.'

Rosina shot a glance at her and one look told her that Bairstow knew more than she let on about the workings of

Rosina's heart.

'We all do,' said Rosina cheerily. 'He's such a nice chap.'

Bairstow carried on peeling. 'But it's more than that for thee.'

There was a heavy silence. Rosina went to say something, but stopped. She didn't have the energy to pretend. 'Yes,' she said quietly. 'It's much more than that for me.'

'I know,' said Bairstow. 'Tha love him.'

Rosina immediately countered. 'Oh no, that's silly. It's not love. I'm fond of him, in a motherly way.'

'We both know that's nonsense. I can see t'way you two look at each other. There's nowt motherly about it.'

Rosina stared at the potato she was peeling and smiled ruefully. 'You see straight through me.'

Bairstow smiled too and said, 'Nay, I wun't claim that. Tha's a mystery most of t'time, keep thi cards close to thi chest. But I know love when I see it. I know I never married and tha may think I'm just an old spinster who could never understand—'

'I would never think that!' said Rosina, although she had thought that very thing. But now it seemed uncharitable and crass to have done so.

'I wun't blame thee. Most people would look at a woman like me that way. But I loved a man once. He was much older than me. And married. So we saw each other in secret. It was wrong to deceive his wife like that, but he didn't love

321

her. He loved me. And I loved him. But he died in t'Great War and, after that, I knew that I'd never love like that again. So I didn't.'

'I had no idea. I'm so sorry.'

'It's all right. Some people go through their lives without ever knowing a love like that. And I've had it. And I'm grateful to him for that. I still have his picture upstairs, of him in his uniform, and I take it out and look at him sometimes. And it brings me joy to know that he was in the world once and made it better just by being in it.'

'Thank you for telling me that. It's a very precious thing,' Rosina said quietly.

'Tha's welcome. I just wanted thee to know that I understand something of what tha might be feeling, with him being sent away like that. One thing I've learnt about love is that, when it's true and solid and real, love knows no boundary, no age.'

'Well, yes, I do love him,' said Rosina, and it was such a relief to say it out loud. She had never said the words aloud, even to herself, and it sounded so simple when she said it that way that she felt amazed she'd never realised the simple truth of it. She *loved* Harry. But she couldn't help but bring herself down a peg or two. 'I know it's ridiculous.'

'How is it ridiculous?' asked Bairstow.

'Well, it's obvious, isn't it? The age difference. And I'm

not sure he feels the same way. I mean, why would he? I'm old and . . . wizened. Even if he is attracted to me, it's probably just for a conquest, an older woman to add to his young man's list of amorous adventures.'

Bairstow squinted at her, as if she was telling a far-fetched story like one of Constance's. 'He strikes me as being a very serious and mature young man, not prone to silliness. He's really lived, tha can tell it, in his maturity. Does tha really think that's true of him? Thee, just another adventure?'

Rosina was quiet for a moment, but she knew the answer. 'No. No, I don't.'

Bairstow nodded. 'Good. And as for being old and wizened, tha look ten years younger at least and tha know it. Also, so what? If he loves thee, he loves thee. Thi wrinkles won't put him off. And he's a shy man, for all his wit. He's about actions, not talk. Look at what he does, not what he says. Look at how he keeps coming back to thee.'

And for the first time, Rosina suddenly had a vision of a world in which Harry loved her. It was such a revelation, it suffused her with joy. She had agonised over her feelings and doubts that he felt the same way as she did. Now Bairstow, with her wisdom and keen observation, had offered her the idea that Harry loved her back. It was a beautiful thought.

Before she had time to respond, a light knocking was heard on the kitchen door.

'Who the devil's knocking?' said Bairstow. 'If it's that

Ronnie playing Knock a door run, I'll box his ears.'

Rosina smiled; she knew Bairstow would never raise a hand to the boy. She was just as fond of him as everyone else and gave him special treats whenever she could. She'd shared with Rosina that her cousins, his parents, were not good folk and she was glad he was here instead of there, had resolved to keep a close eye on him and give him as nice an experience as he could have being away from home, in the countryside, free of the unhappy home he'd come from.

Bairstow opened the door and there stood Harry, his kitbag slung over his shoulder. Both women stared at him, as if their conversation had summoned him, as if their words were akin to the rubbing of the genie's lamp.

'Afternoon all,' he said and grinned. 'I knocked on the front door but nobody heard. I thought I'd find you hard-working people down here, preparing victuals for the troops.'

'What on earth . . .?' said Rosina and stood up.

'Apologies for the impromptu nature of my sudden appearance. But I've got to get the train to London tonight and I had a few hours free and I tried to get a train up here from Scarborough but it was cancelled. So I thumbed a lift. I've come to say au revoir. But I'll only be able to stay a few minutes as it took me so damnably long to get here that I'll have to head back on the road straight away so I don't miss my train tonight.'

'Come on, lad,' said Bairstow. 'Let's get a cuppa for a start.'

Rosina was incredulous to see him there in her kitchen once more when she'd feared she would never see him again. The ordinariness of it – her hands starchy with potato juice, Bairstow filling the kettle with water – made it all the more beautiful, like an interior by Vermeer, the everyday details shining and comforting.

'I can't believe it!' she said and laughed, and Harry was laughing too. 'But surely you can stay longer than a few minutes.'

'Not really. The whole endeavour was daft, but I thought, why not? I didn't think it would take me so long to get here, though. There's so few cars around these days and I couldn't get a lift for ages. I walked for miles!'

'If only I had some petrol. I could take you to the station, but the car is still sitting outside the hospital where I left it, until we get our petrol ration card next month!'

'I know that. It doesn't matter.'

Then Bairstow said, 'What about Loftus? Remember he was just here yesterday, thanking you for sorting his compensation from t'army for his ruined fields. Harry helped with that and I told him so and he were grateful. I'll pop up there and ask if he can return t'favour and let us borrow his truck. I'm sure he'll say aye.'

'Oh, Bairstow, that's a marvellous idea.'

'I'll go now. Why don't tha two go for a walk and I'll have it sorted for when tha get back? It's a lovely day. Off tha go.'

Harry said he wouldn't mind, that he had walked for miles that day, so perhaps a gentle stroll would be good. Off Bairstow went and Rosina led the way outside. She took him through the grounds to an old wooden gate that led on to the moors and along to a path that led to steps down to the beach. Just as she'd mentioned to him before, this was the place where a seal colony loved to bask in the sun. And as they wended their way down the twists and turns of the steps towards the beach, Harry pointed one out, sitting up on a rock, curved like a grey banana.

'Looks like there's only one,' he said.

'Look again,' she said. She knew from a lifetime of experience how well camouflaged the seals were against the backdrop of rock, shingle and sea. You'd think at first glance there was only one or two, then as you looked more closely, their forms would begin to isolate themselves against the background and there would be another on that rock, and another one here and another one there, and some little heads bobbing in the water and as you got closer you could see there were dozens of them in the water, surfacing and diving down again, or popping up on to a rock to enjoy the afternoon sunshine. Harry was delighted with them and Rosina loved to watch his face as he watched them.

They chatted happily all the way back. There was no uneasiness between them and no unsettling intensity, just a pure kind of joy that they had this gift of time together, when it had seemed they would perhaps never see each other again. As they walked, she thought of Bairstow's wise advice, to watch his actions, not his words. And now his actions had been to walk from Scarborough to see her one last time before he left. He had gone above and beyond, had acted as if he could not bear to waste even a minute without her when he could be with her. Even then, with this clear evidence before her, she still found herself dismissing it; she could not believe that such a beautiful young man could be in love with her. As they came up through the grounds to the lawn, she hesitated a moment, then decided that she did not want to dither about any longer when it came to Harry Woodvine.

'Shall we quickly pop up to the king and queen's seats? One last look at the view before you go?'

'Yes, let's. I'd love to see that again.'

Rosina led the way, taking the time-worn steps upwards with deliberate, slow care. She wanted time to stretch out, each step seeming like an age as she ascended. At the top, she moved over to the wall at the edge of the viewing platform and, without looking back at him, she leant her elbows on it and looked out to sea. It was a clear, blue-sky day, the gulls wheeling about the heavens, the foliage below thick and lush in its summer dress, the scent of roses and the taste of salt on the breeze. She felt him beside her, his hip grazing hers, as he too leant his arms on the wall, nestling in beside her, their upper arms now pushed up against each other, warm and electric with the touch. She closed her eyes a moment, to preserve it. Then she turned to him.

'Darling,' he murmured and reached his hand up to her hair.

She let herself fall into the kiss, as if she were falling off that wall, the way she'd often wondered how it would feel to launch yourself off there and just freefall to your doom below. Her eyes closed, her hands reached around him and one of his hands caressed her hair, the other in the small of her back, urging her nearer. His closeness absorbed her completely, so that everything was him and everything was her and everything was them. Time truly had slowed to almost nothing as they kissed . . .

But time could not stop. And truly, time was against them as usual. She heard Loftus's van coming up the drive. This reminder of the real world broke the spell and she stopped, partly fearful that someone might be sent to find them, and partly terrified that if she kissed him again she would never want to stop. She stepped back but he wasn't ready to let go and he reached out and grasped both her hands firmly and pulled her in again.

'Someone might see!' she gasped.

'Let them see,' he whispered and kissed her again, this time even sweeter than the last, for it had not the surprise of it, had only the brand-new knowledge that he wanted her just as she wanted him. They kissed and kissed again, Rosina realising that they were secluded from view, unless someone purposefully climbed the steps to find them. They stopped a moment to simply hold on to each other and she revelled in the feel of his arms about her, her head on his shoulder, her hand on his chest, the blue roughness of his jacket under her fingertips. She drank it all in as if watching a film at the picture house, wanting to savour every frame. They stood like that for what seemed a long while.

Then she pulled away from him, because she missed looking at his face. She'd loved to do it before, but now it was all new, all different, because his face was hers now; it belonged to her and to look upon it was a thrill like no other, to gaze at him that way and let him gaze at her, a kind of proprietary delight that they belonged to each other.

'This is pure madness,' she heard herself say, though she hadn't meant to let her doubts creep in.

'Then take me to the asylum because I'm all in,' he said and smiled at her, reaching out and touching her cheek tenderly.

'What will happen to us?'

'Whatever we want to happen.'

'But what will people say?'

'Who cares?' he said and brought her to him again and held her close. He nuzzled her ear and kissed it, then whispered, 'We'll work it out together.'

She pulled back and looked into his cornflower eyes, so clear and direct. She believed him.

'I'd like to keep it quiet about us though, just for now. I think it would confuse the girls.' But it was more than that. It was the most precious secret she'd ever had and she wanted to keep it to herself, safe, away from the harsh light of day and the gaze of others.

'I agree. Let's keep it to ourselves, for now. It's nobody's business but yours and mine.'

'Yes, exactly,' she said and smiled at him. It was so good to just smile at him and see him return it, no more hiding, no more doubt.

'And now it's time to face the music. If I don't go now, I'll be in a whole heap of trouble.'

'We can't have that,' she said and took his hand. She stared at it and stroked it, then kissed it lovingly. 'Come on then, Sergeant Woodvine. Let's get you to the station.'

They went down the stairs holding hands, then when they reached the last step, they stopped. Beyond the end of that wall, they would be visible to anyone coming across the lawn. Thus, it was time to begin their secret life together and keep up the pretence of friendship, just for the time being. She let his hand fall and stepped out on to the path, the heat between them palpable in the air. She walked forward and he fell into step beside her. They did not speak as they crossed the lawn in front of the house and she saw that Loftus's truck was there. Bairstow had brilliantly sorted it. Rosina could take Harry to the station and have a proper goodbye, alone, with nobody else to bother them. And now, at the thought of losing him again, she felt an emptiness open up inside her, so in the midst of her happiness was the sadness of loss. Both made each other the sweeter.

Bairstow came out and handed them the key to the truck and Harry's kitbag, then said her goodbyes to Harry. Rosina felt she could not look Bairstow in the eye and wondered if it was obvious what had just occurred. But she didn't really care, knowing Bairstow would most likely approve. It was so good to have a confidante who understood her and did not judge.

Rosina wondered for a moment if they would be awkward with each other on the journey to Scarborough, now they had transformed into something new, but once they started talking about the girls and Ronnie's latest deeds, they just laughed about them and it was lovely. It was so nice to talk to a man about her children, not an opportunity she'd had in years. And not just any man, but a man who knew them and was fond of them. Rosina had female friends, not many, but two in particular she had confided to in the past but they had moved away from Yorkshire and though they wrote to each other regularly, it wasn't the same. She realised how isolated she'd been these past few years and how war had highlighted this further. Speaking to Harry reminded her, that even though she had the soul of a loner, she revelled in the close, meaningful company of one other person, a special person. What a treat it was to have had this last couple of hours with him. Whatever happened between them after today, she knew she'd always be grateful that he'd walked much of the way from Scarborough to Ravenscar, just to see her.

At the railway station, they went to the platform for the London train and continued chatting comfortably on a bench. As the time approached for the train's arrival, their talk petered out to nothing, the fact of his imminent departure looming large. The guard appeared on the platform and nodded to them as he walked by, ready to take up his position to greet the train as it arrived. Rosina stood and peered down the railway line, as if the train would suddenly materialise. Harry came to stand beside her and she smiled clumsily at him and he responded in kind. Now the moment had come, neither seemed to have any clue of what to say.

'Thank you,' she said. They were the words uppermost in her mind, so she wanted to say them.

'For what?'

'Coming all this way, today.'

'I wanted to,' he said, in an echo of what she'd said to him when he thanked her for arranging his room so nicely.

'I'm so glad you did. It . . . meant a lot to me, Harry.'

'Will you write short stories and send them to me? I want to read your thoughts.'

'Yes, all right. I'll do it. For you.' She saw in this how clearly he encouraged her to be her true self, more than anyone she knew, apart perhaps from Evelyn. She loved that about him.

'Listen,' he said, a sudden urgency in his tone. He stepped closer to her and took her arm. His touch was marvellous, the pressure and warmth of his hand through her sleeve glorious. 'I won't get maudlin, I promise. But one never knows in war what tomorrow will bring.'

'Don't!' she said, more loudly than she meant to. She lowered her voice, aware of the guard nearby and other people milling about on the platform. 'Don't say goodbye. Don't think like that.'

'I'm not. I'm not going to say goodbye. I'm going to say, "See you on Sunday". Because it's what I want, rather than what it is.'

Their faces were very close and she looked down at his lips and felt utterly drawn to them. She reached down and took his hand and they grasped each other's so tightly, it almost pained her. How desperately she wanted to kiss him! But the guard was very near them now and the sound of an approaching train made her look up. She caught the guard's eye by mistake and he smiled at her and nodded.

'Nice of you to come and see yer son off,' he said, then turned and announced the London train's arrival.

'Oh God,' murmured Rosina. The moment was shattered, everything broken by those few, careless words. Was it all a joke? A foolish middle-aged woman creating a ridiculous fantasy in her head? How despicable she was. How stupid . . .

Harry put his head very close to her ear and whispered urgently, 'Don't listen to that bloody fool, darling!'

People were gathering all around them now and the train was trundling past them, a cacophony of noise surrounding them as it clattered and puffed its way onwards until the screech of its brakes pulled it to a stop. Rosina turned away from him in shame as he picked up his kitbag and slung it over his shoulder.

'You will write, won't you?' he said, loudly, so that she would look up at him. His face was yearning, baffled and infuriated, all at once.

As shameful as the guard's comment had made her feel, she mustn't take it out on Harry, on this kind and sensitive young man who was going off to an uncertain and dangerous future alone, for the second time in his life. He needed her now and she wasn't going to let him down.

'Of course I will. See you Sunday.'

'Yes,' he said and beamed at her. 'See you Sunday.'

And with that, he turned, climbed up the step on to the train and was gone from view for a moment. She searched through the window, to see him appear in the next carriage, watched him shove his kitbag on the rack above and turn to the window. Other people were coming into the carriage behind him, so he sat down by the window and she saw him answering a query from another passenger, watching their lips moving and him nodding his head, all in silence to her, peering through the glass, feeling like an urchin outside a sweet shop at Christmas. The urge to jump on the train and sit beside him was immense. He turned back to the window, momentarily looking lost until he saw her face and gave her that broad grin of his she loved so much to see. They just smiled and smiled at each other, not moving their eyes from the other's gaze as all around them the business of the railway station was bustling on, doors slamming, the train itself creaking as if it were girding its loins to start the long journey south. All of a sudden the guard blew on his shrill whistle and the train jolted and it was time. His face glided away from her as she raised her hand and waved and waved frenetically and she could just make out his ghost of a hand wave back, obscured by the reflection of the platform that filled his window and looked as if it were sliding away from the train and not the other way round. And then Harry Woodvine was gone.

Epilogue

August 1940

Dearest Mummy,

Sorry it's been a while since you've received an epistle from yours truly. Work and life in general have been absolute, pure madness. I can't give you details, of course BUT I can tell you that myself and Nancy recently received letters of commendation from our Commanding Officer for going above and beyond the call of duty! We're absolutely thrilled and very proud. I think you'd be proud of me too, Mummy, especially if you knew all the details. Perhaps I'll be able to tell you one day, when you're a little old lady in a rocking chair and I'm a mother with grown-up children of my own, who knows! Suffice to say, it was a great test of our mettle and I'm very glad to say we proved ourselves worthy.

Other news is that I'm still seeing that chap Jim I told you about. He's really such a nice sort, Mummy. I'm absolutely convinced you'd like him so much. I can't explain why I like him so much really. It's not that he's a very extraordinary person really. But I think that's what I like, that he has ordinary virtues. It makes one feel so comfortable in his company, the fact that he's not too much of anything. But now I'm worried that makes him sound boring, which he absolutely is not, in the slightest. Oh, I'm making a hash of this! I think what I'm trying to get at is that when I started going out for dances and so forth, I found myself swept away by the very handsome chaps or the very tall ones or the very good dancers or the very brave ones and so on. And now I find that anything that's 'very' is all a bit too much for the mind, you know? It all gets a bit exhausting. And what I love about Jim is that he makes me feel calm. Again, don't get me wrong – he's an absolute hoot and makes me laugh like a drain! And his mind is so interesting. But also, when we are just being together, just existing, I have this lovely feeling of harmony that is really wonderful. Oh, I hope I've explained it all right!

I should imagine you're thinking that the time has come when we should all meet for tea one day and I'd love him to meet you and the girls. But it'll have to be very soon, darling, because I have other news. I'm being transferred soon. I don't know where to but it may be abroad. It's all being talked about at the moment, so I don't have any firm news. But I'll let you know as soon as I do. Going abroad does sound very exciting and a bit nerve-wracking, I must admit. Who knows *where I might end up? It might even be somewhere terribly exotic and balmy, fringed with palm trees or wide expanses of dusty desert! Oh, but Mummy, please try not to worry about it though. I'm really not the same person I was going into this war. I have had to truly grow up and be stronger than I've ever been. I feel able to cope with anything these days, I really do. So if I am sent away, please know that all your love and support over the years has enabled me to grow up straight and tall and capable of looking after myself. I've learnt so much this year. The power of good friendship – with Nancy, who is the closest friend I've ever had. It's incredible really, when you think how different we are. But closeness is forged in adversity, I believe, and we've had a fair bit of that these past months. We are quite the sisters in arms now.*

What else have I learnt this year? Well, not only the value of friendship; I've learnt never to judge people by appearances, that men are not all bad, or all good – they're just a mixed bag, like women. I've learnt about the power of working with others towards a common goal. And about the importance of family and being grateful for those who love you and who you love. I really do think this war has changed me for the better.

So, I'll be in touch with you soon about bringing Jim over to Raven Hall for a cuppa, so long as we're not sent away without a moment's notice! Fingers crossed.

I do hope all is well with you at home and you're not

too bored of it all. I know nothing much is going on at Raven Hall and the days must be long. But you are doing your bit as surely as the rest of us, with all the produce you grow and making do around the house and the things you organise locally and the help you give to your tenants. You're an absolute brick, Mummy.

All my love to you. I'll write – and hopefully see you – soon.

Love,
Grace

* * *

Rosina picked up her cigarettes from her desk and went outside. It was late afternoon after a hot day and the view across to Robin Hood's Bay was stunningly clear. She lit up and took a deep, delicious drag. She walked pensively across the lawn, not really having a plan of where to walk, just letting her feet guide her. A couple of weeks back she'd met Grace's young man for the first time. He was a nice one and she approved. He made Grace laugh too, which was always a good thing, especially nowadays. They all needed a laugh. It had done her good to see her daughter so happy and so in love. If only she could tell Grace that she herself felt just the same way! But she couldn't, of course. Her love for Harry Woodvine was unconventional and some might even find it laughable or disgraceful. So she kept it secret, only Mrs Bairstow being in on it. Bairstow's heart was deep with secrets too, so Rosina knew she could trust her. Knowing that Harry was out there in the world gave her a sense of great peace, just as Grace had described in her letter. Rosina marvelled that she'd never felt that either, in her long life. Never felt that sense of calm at the knowledge that she loved someone so completely.

Or, at least, that sense of peace was what she had felt until just that morning when she had received word from Harry. It was a very brief letter, simply stating that he was being sent abroad and that he would write as soon as he could from wherever he was being posted. That was all there was, just a few words dashed off in a scrawl. He must have been in a dreadful rush and she was so grateful that he'd found the time to tell her, knowing she'd worry.

He'd written to her several times over the last couple of weeks, almost using his letters to her like a kind of journal and she was delighted he'd left no detail out, as she was thrilled to read every single one of them, however small. He couldn't tell her about his work, but did tell her stories about people he'd met, their jokes and quirks, a nice dog he'd made friends with at the RAF station, the vagaries of the weather and books he was reading. She wrote back to him in similar detail about the trivial little happenings at Raven Hall, at first concerned they would bore him, but as she received his letters she took courage and wrote everything she could think of. She'd have to start working on some short stories soon and send them to him. After all, she had promised she would. Maybe that would be more interesting to him than the minutiae of the daily life of Raven Hall.

There had actually been one important occurrence at home recently and that concerned Ronald Holt, the evacuee. Both of his parents and an uncle and aunt had been killed in a bombing in Hull, which had been truly shocking, horrible news. But some good had come of it. It had been decided that he should stay with the farming family he'd been with and there was talk that they'd adopt him, according to Bairstow. Rosina had taken even more interest in the boy after that, and the girls continued to dote on him, Daisy having taken on the chess playing with him since Harry's departure.

Other news was that Evelyn's work as an artist in London had dried up and Rosina was hoping she'd come home. But Evelyn had done her customary thing of doing the opposite of what everyone expected and instead had joined the firemen of London, joining the Auxiliary Fire Service, the AFS as it was known. Before this war Rosina would have been livid and written to her straight away, ordering her home, just as she'd done when Evelyn wrote to her before the war to say she was staying on with artist friends in France and not coming home. But it hadn't done any good then and she knew it would do no good now.

Working with the fire service anywhere carried its dangers, but surely London must be the absolute worst for that? At least the German bombers were not targeting London yet in any sort of wholesale manner, focusing instead on RAF stations on the south and east coasts, where Rosina daily feared for Harry's life. But she did wonder if it was only a matter of time before the Luftwaffe turned its attention to the capital. Either way, she knew nothing she could say would persuade her second daughter to change her mind, so stubborn was she. And despite her fear for Evelyn's safety, she was also immensely proud of her. And of Grace and the younger girls too, particularly for their care for Ronnie and their stoicism in the face of shortages, hardly ever complaining and just getting on with it. She wrote about all this and more to Harry, comforted by the knowledge that he cared about her girls seemingly as much as he cared for her, as he always asked after them with genuine affection.

She had reached the steps up to the battlements now and took them steadily, noticing as she always did the way each step was worn down in the middle from years of passage over them by Lazenby feet. As she reached the top, she walked to the king and queen's seat and leant on the wall as she'd done with Harry not so long ago.

It had a new meaning now, this place. It was now *their* place, hers and Harry's. The weather was stunning, just as it had been that day they'd kissed there in the sunlight. She looked out across the sea, patchy and mysterious, green here, grey there, bluish towards the horizon. To her left, Robin Hood's Bay twinkled in the sun. A breeze made the trees in the grounds wave lazily at her while swallows dipped over the grass and seagulls fought graceful battles with the wind above. It was idyllic here at Raven Hall, her ancestral home. How lucky she was to have been born here, raised here, to still be here. But for how long? Would the Government come for it soon, turn it into a hospital or a training establishment? She had read this was happening all over the country and she guessed they might be next. Then she recalled that she'd stood smoking a cigarette and looking out to sea just like this almost a year ago, full of similar fears that were shadowy and frightening.

The war then had seemed like a dark behemoth coming for her across the sea. But for weeks nothing seemed to really happen in Britain, nothing much to change their lives. So people had said it would all be over by Christmas. But it wasn't and it dragged on. Then there was Dunkirk. And now the RAF was fighting for all their lives in the blue skies over the English channel. A year in and the future was just as uncertain, but she knew now she would rise to it. Not merely a feeling that she would, but a knowledge. She would and her daughters would. The war would go on. When would it all end? And how many would be lost before it did?

Standing there, looking out over the ever-changing sea

she said a quiet prayer for her girls, for her staff, for her tenants, for her friends, for all the sons and brothers and fathers of everyone she knew who were far away and in danger. And lastly, she said a prayer for Harry Woodvine, hoping that her small entreaty would drift across the sea and find him in whatever foreign field he'd been sent to and protect him from harm.

The war had brought them many things – shortages, challenges, danger and even death – but it had also brought them all closer. It had brought them friendship. And love.

Glossary of Yorkshire Dialect

In this series of books set in North Yorkshire, when rendering the speech of local people, I have attempted to give a flavour of the regional dialect and accent, rather than a fully phonetic representation. This is to prevent general readers from finding the phonetic spelling of too many words a distraction when reading.

'appen = maybe, perhaps (short for happen – expressing
    doubt)
Bairns = children
Breadcake = bread roll
Chuffin' 'eck = an expression of surprise or dismay
Dun't = doesn't
Early doors = earlier than usual
Grand = very good, excellent
I'n't = isn't

Missen = myself

Nithering = freezing cold

Nobbut = only

Nobbut middling = said in response to 'How are you?', meaning not too bad, just all right.

Nowt = nothing

'Ow do = hello (shortened form of 'How do you do?')

Owt = anything

Sarnie = sandwich

Summat = something

T' – used for *the*, shortened to a half-pronounced *t* sound or a glottal stop

Tha/thee = you

Tha's = you are

Thi = your

Thissen = yourself

Wun't = wouldn't

Author's Note

Some extra information on the historical context of this work of fiction:

- The history of Raven Hall, as presented in this novel, does take some information from its actual history, such as the details of its construction and loss through gambling, as well as the metal trees. The hall in reality became a hotel in the late nineteenth century. Obviously, I have changed this aspect of its history to keep it as a home for the fictional Lazenby family. The descriptions of the grounds and the outside of the building are all from my own observations having visited on a number of occasions. Details of the inside of the house have been fictionalised, based on accounts of country houses at the time. You can visit the wonderful Raven Hall Hotel yourself if you wish and walk in the footsteps of the Calvert-Lazenby women. The photograph of Raven Hall on this book cover was taken by me on one of my visits.

- Details from the newspaper coverage of Dunkirk were quoted from *The Courier*, 31st May 1940 on the following site:

https://www.thecourier.co.uk/fp/news/scotland/474479/immortal-story-courage-sacrifice-endurance-faith-heres-courier-covered-battle-dunkirk-articleisfree/

- The Prime Minister's radio address in the Prologue is quoted verbatim from the original BBC sound recording.

- The Y Station at Scarborough actually changed from Sandybed Lane to Irton Moor in 1943. The former premises were much simpler and more rudimentary, whilst the latter was a major operation. In research, there was far more information available on the latter. I've taken artistic licence and amalgamated the two in my descriptions, to make the representation of the Y Station simpler.

- The Hotel Cecil in Scarborough was named by two Wrens in their memoirs as having been the place they stayed while working at the Scarborough Y station. One of these Wrens was Muriel Davison, author of *A Wren's Tale*, who I've paid homage to by inventing an incidental Wren character called Muriel who worked on the radios, just as her namesake did. However, it may be the case that the hotel was a convalescent home for servicemen at the time when Grace and Nancy would have been there in 1940, perhaps only later becoming accommodation for Wrens. However, for the purposes of fiction, I kept the Hotel Cecil despite the earlier date, as I wanted to keep as close as possible to the Wrens' experiences. Also, there is no evidence that the Outlook Hotel housed the naval ratings who were also working at the Y, so again I've used artistic licence here. I visited Ryndleside, the road on which both hotels are situated and strolled around Peasholm Park, just as Grace does. I'd just like to add here that I read a wide variety of books about or by Wrens and one of my favourites was *Do March in Step Girls* by Audrey Johnson, which was not only beautifully written but searingly honest about both the wonderful and the awful experiences of being a Wren in World War Two.

- The Open Air Theatre in Northstead Manor Gardens was in fact closed 1940-43, though the gardens themselves remained open; thus, I've taken a little licence here to have them being visited by the Wrens in 1940. (Thanks to Stewart MacDonald for this fact).

- The bombing of Burniston really happened, slightly earlier than my chapter – on the night of June 26th 1940. Five cottages were damaged badly by nine bombs, some of these cottages being demolished afterwards. No deaths luckily. A man was injured and I've replaced him with Harry Woodvine. Firemen from Burniston did indeed attend the scene.

- Despite the secrecy surrounding what went on at Bletchley Park, Wrens did know it as Station X and some certainly knew where this was situated.

- The motorcycle accident and walk to Bletchley was partly based on a real life incident involving two Wrens, Mary Earl and Rosemary Vaughan, recounted in the fascinating book by Christian Lamb, *I Only Joined for the Hat*.

- I have been fascinated by the Spanish Civil War since studying it at university, as well as watching a range of documentaries and movies about this tragic conflict, all of which influenced the details of Harry's experiences. Also helpful here was the recent documentary *Hemingway* by Ken Burns and Lynn Novick shown on BBC4 in 2021, as well as the moving collection of memories from British members of the international brigades in the excellent book *The Real Band of Brothers* by Max Arthur. One day I'd love to write a novel about that war using all the knowledge I've rather obsessively gathered about it over the years, as it truly does haunt me.

- Lastly, eagle-eyed readers of the Ironbridge Saga might have noticed that Harry's surname is the same as Anny's family introduced in *The Daughters of Ironbridge*. It is my belief that Harry is a distant relation of the Woodvines of Ironbridge and carries on their noble name and good character.

Acknowledgements

Huge and grateful thanks to all of the following:

Patricia Owtram, Simon Robinson and Peter Hore – Patricia, a Wren in her nineties, whose book *Codebreaking Sisters* was extremely useful yet Pat also kindly agreed to let me interview her one summer afternoon. She was incredibly helpful, as well as having perfect recall of events from eighty years ago of her work as a wireless telegraphist. Talking to Pat was the most valuable research I carried out for this novel and I'm so grateful to her for sharing her experiences with me and answering my many questions. It was an absolute honour also to meet her in London, where she signed my copy of her excellent book. Thank you also to Peter Hore for welcoming me and my daughter to his book launch for *Bletchley Park's Secret Source: Churchill's Wrens and the Y Service in World War II*. His book was another very helpful addition to the research. Thanks to agent Simon Robinson for the introductions and other help with research; to Tara Loder for the initial introduction; lastly, Jon Elek and Ajda Vucicevic for their part in tracking down Simon Robinson!

Stewart MacDonald – author of *Scarborough at War*, who sent me an excellent bibliography and many links to other sources, plus read the first draft and made such useful suggestions. Stewart has really been so generous with his knowledge and time.

Jon Elek, my publisher and Rachel Hart, my editor at Welbeck for their wonderful work on this series and their faith in me as a writer. Huge thanks also to the Welbeck team for supporting this saga in such a professional and enthusiastic manner, including Maddie Dunne Kirby, James Horobin, Nico Poilblanc and Annabel Robinson. Also particular thanks to Alexandra Allden, for superlative book design and a delightful long conversation about books, war and Cotehele.

Eternal gratitude to my awesome agenting team from United Agents: my incredible agent Laura Macdougall and brilliant assistant Olivia Davies. Thanks also to agent Millie Hoskins, Laura's maternity cover, for help when we needed it.

Nina Hughes – an artist based in Scarborough who also happens to work at the Raven Hall Hotel, who I started chatting to at the hotel by chance and she gave me stacks of information on the house and local contacts for historians, both while I was staying there and later on an epic phone call!

The two ladies I met summer 2020 at the Ravenscar Tourist Information, who helped so much with books on Ravenscar and other resources.

Jim Middleton – from the Scarborough Museums Trust – who put me in touch with Val Russell, who very kindly sent me archive materials on Ravenscar. Thanks so much to you both.

John Grant – local historian of archives based at Gladstone School who was also very helpful with resources.

Eileen Beaumont – author of *Ravenscar Village Life*, an extremely helpful resource – particularly for her brilliant phone call where she answered my questions with great knowledge and humour.

Alison Cyster-White and her brother Alan Cyster – for their information on local families and their stories about farming in Ravenscar plus an article on a local plane crash.

Ravenscar Life Facebook group: Wendy Normington who put me in touch with Eileen Beaumont; Derek Baker who tagged David Russell and also gave me the video *The Town that Never Was*; Jeremy Thorn on the false town; Jim White on the radar station and search light locations; Deirdre Smith and Joan Baker on other local details; Julie Johnson about the Stoupe Brow plane crash; Will Warwick about the Junkers plane crash.

Angela Kale, Outreach Librarian for the Scarborough Library and Customer Services Centre – for sending me an excellent array of articles from local newspapers (during lockdown) and John Patrick, for very useful articles on Scarborough boats' involvement in Dunkirk.

Donna Hydes, for helping me choose a Hampshire village for Grace's telegraphy training.

Kathryn Hall, for information on farming in North Yorkshire in April.

Jean Fullerton, Lizzie Page, Elaine Roberts and members of the Facebook group *Second World War Authors*: Shanti Mercer, Anna Osborne, Paula Harmon, Fenella Miller, Rachel Zaouche, Paul Williams, Clare Flynn, Angela Petch, Kathryn Gauci, Ann Griffin, Janet Oakley and Shaun Loftus for information on contraception in the 1940s.

Michelle Robinson, owner of the Outlook Hotel, Scarborough and also a genealogist, who called me on the telephone, as well as allowing me to visit her at the hotel and so generously gave me a plethora of information about both the Outlook and the Cecil Hotel and much other local information. Michelle is a genealogist at Bloodlynz: https://bloodlynz.com/

Members of the *Scarborough History* Facebook group who helped with details surrounding the Hotel Cecil, in particular Andy Wood, Ben Vickers and Alison Hodgson.

Angela Caldin, who kindly gave me contact details for Sister Pamela Hussey, a World War Two Wren who worked at Scarborough.

Lou Crisp, for help with North Yorkshire dialect and Suzie Tullett for the introduction.

Mary Jayne Baker, for advice on North Yorkshire dialect and the suggestion to read James Herriot for help with period-specific dialect.

Kelly and Adrian Furniss, for advice on North Yorkshire dialect.

Stuart Nielsen, for a fascinating conversation on Norse languages and their influences on Yorkshire dialect.

Rosemary Saunders, my auntie – for reading the first draft to check accuracy of Navy and Wrens information, as well as my mum Liz Beeson for her recollections of training and Wren slang.

Pauline Lancaster, for reading the early draft so quickly and your wonderful support, as ever.

Thank you to book bloggers and readers who contact me via social media regularly with questions about the books and enthusiasm for this new saga series as well as the Ironbridge Trilogy – bless you for your support.

Tara Loder, for commissioning me to write this series and discussing the story and characters so brilliantly, as ever. Also, for not minding when I rang her without warning for a video call to show her Raven Hall!

My friends, family, writer pals and Facebook buddies who keep me grounded and put up with my nonsense and profanity, some even encouraging it, shamelessly . . .

Lastly, much love to the special trio in my life: Poppy, Clem and Tink. Here's to many more happy times consisting of eating pizza, baking French pastry delights, playing Overcooked and watching *Dexter* on the telly, with Tink providing random appearances while we whistle the *Jurassic Park* theme tune at her, her favourite thing.

About the Author

© Emma Shardlow Hudson

Mollie Walton is the saga pen-name for historical novelist Rebecca Mascull. She has always been fascinated by history and has worked in education, has a Masters in Writing and lives by the sea in the east of England. The inspiration for the Raven Hall trilogy came when she visited the stunning Raven Hall Hotel with her daughter and fell in love with the beautiful cliff-top view. Under Mollie Walton, Rebecca is also the author of the historical fiction trilogy, the Ironbridge Saga.

Coming Spring 2023

Book Two of the Raven Hall Saga

A Daughter's Gift

*As the Blitz begins, Rosina must rise to the challenge when
Raven Hall is requisitioned, whilst Evvy decides to put her
life at risk by joining the Auxiliary Fire Service.*

*But who will be safe? How can Rosina protect all those
she loves? And is love even possible with such high stakes?*

WELBECK

PUBLISHING GROUP

Love books? Join the club.

Sign up and choose your preferred genres to receive tailored news, deals, extracts, author interviews and more about your next favourite read.

From heart-racing thrillers to award-winning historical fiction, through to must-read music tomes, beautiful picture books and delightful gift ideas, Welbeck is proud to publish titles that suit every taste.

bit.ly/welbeckpublishing

WELBECK

ANDRE
DEUTSCH

MORTIMER

MORTIMER

WELBECK